LIGHT OF THE SKY

OF THE GODS - BOOK TWO

GINA STURINO

Editor: Finishing by Fraser

Proof Reader: Briggs Consulting LLC

Cover designer: Magnetra's Design

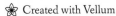 Created with Vellum

For my family and friends. From Milwaukee to Monterey,
you've helped create memories I will always treasure.

PROLOGUE

Sprawled on the grass, I looked up to pillowy clouds floating on a canvas of pastel pinks and blues. Wisps of sunshine leaked through, warming my bare arms. Over my shoulder, white butterflies and vibrant wildflowers danced in the wind.

Fifteen years had passed since I'd laid eyes on the surreal beauty of the Hark. It still took my breath away.

Lucille's lithe footsteps tapped against the stone path, and I reluctantly pushed to my feet. In the few days since my return, she'd allowed time for me to decompress and relax, which should have been easy when sleeping in a bed made—*literally*—of clouds, yet I'd tossed and turned the last several nights.

Slipping in alongside me, Lucille, my guardian, followed my gaze to the majestic mountains towering above a crystal-clear lake. My twin brother, Neal, preferred the energy of ocean waves to the stillness of the pond. As kids, we'd take turns altering the terrain in the back of our cottage. Only in the Hark could a tract of land change as easily as our moods.

Lucille softly spoke, breaking the serene silence. "I had hoped your homecoming would bring you peace, Novalee. It brought Arthur and Anya peace. They found redemption." She paused. "They found *you*."

Tears immediately sprouted in my eyes. "I didn't even get to say goodbye," I replied in a shaky whisper.

"They understand, and Mira does too. You have earned the ultimate reward, a home in the Kingdom. They are happy for you."

Hearing Mira's name only made my heart sink further. My dearest friend, I'd discovered, was my sister. The revelation came minutes before my mortal time ended. Our parents, Arthur and Anya, never knew I existed. Hunters first took Arthur, then returned for Anya during childbirth, just as Neal and I were born.

I brushed the wetness from my cheeks and eyed Lucille. With a porcelain-perfect complexion, delicate nose, cherry lips, and glassy blue eyes, she reminded me of the dolls I used to buy for my niece. She looked young enough to be my kid sister, though I knew she was at least several centuries old.

Questions swam in my head. When I was a child, innocent and pure, distrust and doubt didn't exist between me and my guardian.

But I was tainted now, soiled by humanity.

"Did you know Arthur and Anya? You've never talked about my parents."

Lucille sucked in her bottom lip, then released it along with a soft sigh. "Your mother was *the* mother. I met her long before your time, before she was reborn as Anya. She went by Anna then."

"Hunters took her before she even got to hold us." I

shook my head and wrapped my arms around my chest. "She was stripped of her station... Arthur too."

Arthur, a scribe of the Sky, had fallen in love with Anna, mother to the Land. They didn't recognize each other as gods from different realms when they first met, but soon realized their fatal mistake when hunters—the militia of the divine—brought them to the superiors. My parents' transgressions and their forbidden love warranted harsh punishment, resulting in them both being stripped and reborn. Neal and I were taken to be raised in the Hark, home to the walking gods.

"When you and Neal came to me as newborns, I knew you were unique. Being born of both the Land and Sky, of course you would have an unusual energy, walking gods usually do. But you are fated for greater things. I always believed you would earn your wings. It is your destiny."

I stared at my feet, toeing a patch of emerald-green grass. "A destiny that comes at the expense of my family. I'll have to leave them." I'd never again see Mira's surreal gardens, share a glass of wine with her or hear my niece Calla's sweet giggles. And, more pressing, there was my twin brother to consider. "I'll also have to leave Neal."

Lucille's small, soft fingers gently grasped my arm. Her touch sucked away the pain threatening to shatter my fragile composure. She understood my misgivings. She recognized the pain of humanity. She was tainted too.

"Oh, Novalee. I wish you did not feel this way, but I suppose the child I knew is gone. You are a woman now." Lucille released her hold on my arm. Strawberry-blond strands of hair blew across her cheek. She tucked them behind her ear. Along with everything else in the Hark, Lucille was breathtakingly beautiful. "You have learned the truth, and now you have a choice; claim your wings, or buck your destiny."

She made it sound so simple, but the consequences of my decision would last for eternity. Accepting my fate meant the ache of my humanity would cease, but so would my time among the mortals. I'd no longer be able to transcend the realms. I'd never see my family again.

I could claim my destiny, my rightful place among the divine in the realm known as the Kingdom. A place of perfection. *The heaven of heavens*. I'd be whole again, cleansed of humanity, purely divine. An angel.

Or I could refute my fate and remain a god, part divine and part human. I could choose to remain tainted.

Lucille interrupted my thoughts by clearing her throat. "Cami will be waiting for you, to get you settled. Novalee, I know you will not remember this, but you must allow others to fight their own battles. We know Cami's heart, and her intentions are good, but I worry her desire to save Celia will be her downfall. And Neal... I fear far greater for him."

My stomach twisted at her warning. Once as close as siblings, Neal, Cami, Celia and I were raised under Lucille's firm but loving guidance. Cami, an orphaned demigod, assumed the role of surrogate older sister, while Celia, a walking god like Neal and me, was the doted-upon darling of our group.

In the mortal realm, we had divine assignments that lead us along different paths. Cami became my confidant. Her station as a lumineer, a patron of light and hope, made her an invaluable ally in completing my mission. Neal and Celia, on the other hand, strayed from their calling, disappearing without a trace.

I hadn't heard from Neal in years. At one time, my estranged twin and I shared a connection that went beyond blood; we were two halves of a whole. Our journey to the mortal realm severed that bond. Neal discarded his divine duties and left me to deal with the repercussions. I'd spent years angry with him, resenting him for deserting me. Now I feared I'd never see him again.

"You warned us, Lucille. Human emotion, temptation— we fell into its trap. There were times I put my wants and needs ahead of the mission, ahead of Neal and Mira." Guilt gnawed at my conscience. "And Neal, well, I think he just gave up."

My twin's actions led him so far from the divine, I wasn't sure he'd ever find his way back.

How can I leave him while he struggles?

"You have always been logical, Novalee," Lucille said. "That is why among the mortals you became a lawyer, a bargainer of right and wrong. You are questioning your destiny, conflicted as to whether you should accept your station as an angel, whether you are worthy of perfection, but you are neither judge nor jury. Mortals revere faulty courts of law that dictate good and bad, guilt and innocence, but sin and temptation are a part of humanity. They are inevitable. As I have always said, you will be tempted, Novalee, but profit and gain are not worth the forfeit of the soul."

Sighing, I shook my head. "Right now, I don't feel so logical. I don't know what to do. I need to see Neal. Before I make this decision, I have to see my brother." I pinched the bridge of my nose, a trick I knew Mira used to ward off tears. She was the emotional one while I was always the logical one. "Arthur, Anya, and Mira may have found peace, but I haven't."

Mira, my sweet friend—my sister—found more than

peace. She found her lost love, Nicholas, and finally, after many years of heartache, her family was reunited.

Closing my eyes, I envisioned Mira. *Flowers and giggles. Mother and child. Husband and wife.* She had everything I'd ever want for her, and I knew in my heart I'd fulfilled my duty as her protector—and as her big sister.

But I also knew I had a duty to my other sibling.

I opened my eyes and repeated, now with conviction, "I have to see my brother."

Lucille gave a firm nod and looked up to the sky. Her lips moved, but no sound came out. The plump, marshmallow clouds thinned into wavy, white wisps, and the fresh, earthy scent of an incoming rainstorm permeated the air.

"How does this work?" I asked with a trembly voice.

"Like a bolt of lightning, a falling star—"

"A fallen god," I sadly interrupted.

"I hope not. The destiny you deserve—the destiny you *earned*—is a home in the Kingdom, a life among the saints and angels." She nodded toward the swirling clouds. Rays of sunshine danced through gaps, illuminating the strawberry streaks in her blond hair. Her cobalt-blue eyes blazed, and for a quick second, I thought they'd turned into gemstones. Shifting her stare from the sky back to me, her eyes dulled out and rounded with worry. "Novalee, I hope you find the answers and closure you need before *they* find you."

My jaw dropped as I realized who Lucille referred to. *Hunters.* The same militant gods who had ripped Neal and me from our mother during childbirth would eventually catch wind of a fallen god. With their mysterious messengers—the divine creatures who acted as their eyes and ears—my time was certainly limited.

"Are you *sure* you want to do this? It is going to hurt. On this journey, you will not have the powers of the gods, nor knowledge of the divine. You will wake with some memories of your mortal past, bits and pieces that may confuse you. Ultimately, your soul shall decide what memories are revealed to help you choose your fate."

I understood, because everything she said rang familiar. My memories had been masked, my powers stripped, when I was first sent to live among the mortals fifteen years ago. Upon waking in a strange, new world without the security of the divine, a barrage of emotions nearly crippled me. Lucille, my mother figure, provided me with a fake history, a pretend past to assimilate with the mortals, and then she was gone, no longer there to guide me. Her sudden loss was as immense as losing a parent.

To prove myself as Mira's protector, I had to overcome mortal challenges and obstacles, live life with human reasoning and emotions, and complete my mission in a harsh, new world filled with ambiguity.

Now, I'd chosen to return there and allow my soul to lead my heart. I would decide my fate without the security of the divine.

Uncertainty breeds unimaginable fear; I quickly realized that as my heart began to pound.

"I'm scared—" I started to speak, but my words were cut off by the crack of lightning, a sound so loud it nearly shattered my ear drums. Bright, vivid flashes blinded my retinas and burned my veins. I lifted my hands to shield myself, but the next bolt struck something so deep within, my body and the world around me shuddered, vibrating and blinking from the flash of a million lights.

Blindingly white... then blackness.

PART ONE

For I know the plans I have for you,
plans for welfare and not for evil,
to give you a future and a hope.
(Jeremiah 29:11)

ONE

Two Percocet contributed to the first eight uninterrupted hours of sleep I'd had in a week. I woke with a leg kicked over my suitcase and an arm draped across its side—the most intimacy I'd had in months.

Rolling onto my back, I stared blankly at the ceiling, consumed with nagging thoughts and a leftover headache. At least I didn't have that dream again, the one which had haunted me since the car accident. I could thank the Percocet for that.

On the nightstand, next to the prescription bottle, my cellphone ignited. It slid across the smooth surface, vibrating like a hissing jumping bean. I swatted it to the ground where the carpet cushioned its noise.

Not yet. My head felt the best it had in seven days.

Taking a moment to brace myself for the sharp jolt to my ribs, I swung my legs over the side of the bed while simultaneously hoisting myself to a sitting position. My body had always been agile and responsive, the result of ballet classes as a child and an affinity for yoga as an adult.

Now, my limbs seemed to require an extra push from my brain.

It'll pass. I'm okay. I'm alive.

I shuffled into the adjoining bathroom and leaned over the vanity to assess the garish bruise and gash above my left eyebrow. Skin glue held the thin, jagged edges of the cut together. Even with the guarantee of scarring, I counted myself lucky. Thirty-three years of life and I'd never had actual stitches.

Then again, I could hardly call the events of the last week lucky.

Sweeping a finger gingerly across the ghastly reminder, I squeezed my eyes shut and willed away the horrid memory of the accident.

My cell ignited once again, lighting up and vibrating with a muffled groan against the carpet. A throb at my temples pulsed along with it.

Time to face the day. Time to face the music. And time to face Darrell.

THE PRINTER next to my laptop roared to life, quickly spitting out a sheet of paper. Lifting the still-warm page from the tray, I waved it gently to allow the ink to dry, then folded and stuffed it into a legal-sized envelope pre-addressed to Darrell Loft, Senior Partner of Loft and Associates.

My office access fob and other work-related technology had been salvaged from last week's car wreck and returned to Loft. Now, the only thing separating me from a life free of Loft lay in my hand, tucked within the envelope.

Before I could lose my courage, I swiftly tapped the screen of my cell and held the phone to my ear.

"Thank you for calling Loft and Associates, how may I direct your call?" a familiar voice sounded through the earpiece.

"Ellis, hey, it's me, Nova," I replied.

"Novalee?" Ellis asked, surprise evident in her tone. "Is that you? I mean, how are you? I heard... obviously."

Yes, obviously. The crash made the paper and local news. Usually does when a lightning storm, three-block power outage, and Jaws of Life are involved.

I wasn't quite sure how to respond. How was I? *Terrible.* But when people ask that question, do they really want the truth? Would Ellis want to hear about the nightmares, the shock, the tears, the life-changing minute in which I witnessed what may have been an innocent person's final moments?

I still hadn't the heart to inquire about the driver or that woman's status.

So, instead of honesty, I gave Ellis what was expected, responding with a soft smile and an equally soft voice, "I'm okay, hanging in there."

"I'm glad. We're all so worried. I heard you may be out for another week?"

"Yes, well, I need a minute with Darrell. Is he free?"

"Darrell?" She paused before releasing a deep sigh. "Sure, Novalee, let me check."

Through the phone, I heard the heavy clink of Ellis's fingernails on her keyboard, pounding along with the throb in my temples. Darrell brought out aggression in everyone.

After a short wait, Darrell must have replied because Ellis muttered a faint "good luck" before transferring the call. She knew I'd need it.

As president of one of the region's leading corporate law firms, Darrell demanded the best of everything, and nothing but the best from everyone. Valet parking, top floor, corner unit. Top recruits, long hours... your soul.

Not mine, not anymore.

"Hang on, Nova," Darrell spat once the line connected. When he spoke next, I knew his words were directed at the unlucky associate in his office, but they still made me sit up straighter in my chair.

"No, unacceptable." Darrell's firm voice held its usual edge of annoyance. I'd been on the receiving end of it many times.

A smile tugged at my lips. This may be one of the last conversations I'd have with the senior partner and president of Loft and Associates.

"Tomorrow, nine sharp. We're done." Darrell dismissed whoever was in his office without a goodbye or thank you. No small talk or pleasantries when it came to my boss. His voice came full throttle through the line as he switched his focus to me. "Well, this is unexpected. Has Mackroy contacted you?"

Pete Mackroy, a litigation lawyer and family friend of Darrell's, had reached out several times over the last few days, but I'd sent each call to voicemail. "Yes, thanks again for passing my phone number to Pete."

"He's the cream of the crop, and I only want the best representing you."

Darrell's sudden concern threw me off. He only cared about one thing—himself. The female interns in the office may have the hots for him, coining him the "silver fox", but they rarely got a glimpse of the ruthless man behind closed doors. Sure, I could see his appeal from their naïve perspective. Darrell Loft was the epitome of money, power, and success.

But he was cold, ruthless. And he'd cheated on his wife.

"Nova?" he asked impatiently, snapping me back to the conversation.

I cleared my throat. "He's been quite responsive. I appreciate your concern."

"I understand you want more time off. I'll be frank, unless it's medically required, I need you back in the office next week." Arrogance tinged his voice, and it confirmed I was making the right decision.

When Darrell didn't respond to the text I'd sent the previous night requesting more time off, I knew what I had to do. I'd accumulated weeks—*months*—of vacation time over the course of my career with Loft, yet I had a hunch Darrell would not be open to an extended leave of absence.

"I'm leaving." The words fumbled from my lips, even though I'd prepared a long, eloquent speech, much like I would before an important meeting. I took a calming breath and squared my shoulders, personifying the lawyer that still lived somewhere in my broken mind, but Darrell interrupted before I could continue.

"*Where* are you going? I thought you wanted the extra time to recover?" *Recover* rolled off his tongue sarcastically.

"That's not what I mean. I mean, I'm leaving." *I should have just emailed him.* "I'm quitting, Darrell. I'm done." The neatly folded piece of paper that contained the words I wished to spit out burned under my fingertips.

The accident caused more damage than a concussion and bruised ribs. It knocked out an entire part of me—the part that held my fierceness, confidence, and poise—everything that allowed me to excel at my job. I felt different, indescribably so, as if parts of my mind and body were paralyzed.

"Well, this is a surprise. Explain," he commanded.

"No, there's no use. I'm sending written notice, but I wanted to talk to you before I slip it in the mail. I would have done this in person, but I'm not feeling quite up to it. I understand you've already reassigned my project, but I want to give you as much notice as I can, all things considered. I'm leaving," I repeated with finality.

"You have a non-compete agreement, you realize."

I nodded and muttered, "Yep." I didn't plan to practice, at least not for a long time.

Maybe never.

"*What* are you doing, Nova?" I didn't recognize Darrell's tone, but it sent a chill down my spine.

"I don't know, but I need to figure things out. Call it a near-death experience, but," I shrugged, "something's off."

AFTER DROPPING the letter in the outgoing mail bin in my apartment building's lobby, I waited impatiently for the snail-paced elevator to deposit me back on my floor.

The elevator door groaned open, and I stopped midstep. The noise and my movement sent a sharp jolt to my temple. The never-ending headache. Leaning into the wall, I waited for the pain to pass, then rounded the corner only to stop again.

An unfamiliar figure hovered outside of my neighbor's apartment door, crouched over a pile of crisp, unread newspapers. The man peered up, and his aqua-blue eyes met mine.

"Hey, you read this stuff?" he asked in a low voice. A

chunk of black hair flopped over his forehead, and he lifted a tanned hand to brush it off. His eyes didn't leave mine.

"Excuse me?" I blinked, momentarily caught off guard by the intensity of his gaze. My arms instinctively wrapped around my torso. "The newspaper?"

"Yeah, I try to avoid current events, the news... depressing shit. Ignorance is bliss, you know?" He cocked his head and grinned, flashing perfectly straight, white teeth. They popped against his dark summer tan.

Everything about him was dark. His tan, his hair, his clothes—everything except those aqua-blue eyes and flaw-less, white teeth. He had an edge, like he was dangerous.

But in a good way—an exciting way.

"Right." I blushed, realizing I'd been staring. Although, a guy like him was probably used to being ogled by the opposite sex. He was the perfect combination of rugged and handsome. Full lips, square jaw, striking eyes. His fitted T-shirt showed off biceps that could put Chris Hemsworth to shame.

"You live on this floor?" He stood up, towering over me, which wasn't hard considering I barely hit five-two when barefoot. The flip-flops I'd slipped on before heading to the lobby added nothing. "Oh, that probably sounds creepy." His smile widened, crinkling the edges of his eyes. Extending a hand, he jerked his chin toward the door. "I'm Dane Killbane. Just moved in."

"Oh." I looked from his eyes to his outstretched hand. A nervous flutter in my belly prevented me from taking it. The guy might be hot, but he might actually *be* dangerous. "What happened to the lady that lived here, with the little girl?"

Work kept me busy, leaving little time to socialize, but

thinking of that sweet kid brought a smile to my face. *Flowers and giggles.*

"No idea." Dane shoved his extended hand into his pocket and dug out keys. "If you have their number, let them know they need to forward their paper." He glanced back to me as he opened the door, pointedly allowing a glimpse into the cleared-out loft, which mirrored mine in layout. The strong scent of fresh carpeting wafted into the hall.

This guy would be my new neighbor.

My *gorgeous* new neighbor.

"Sorry, I'm Nova." Now it was me extending my hand. "Novalee Nixon. I didn't mean to be rude."

"No problem, I get it. Can't be too careful these days." Dane took my hand and gave a gentle shake. "Nice to meet you." His fingers seemed to linger, warming my skin before dropping down to his side.

"I live next door." I nodded toward my door.

"Cool. Now I know who to go to for a cup of sugar or some milk." His easy grin took the edge off the sharp angles and dark gruff of his jawline.

"Oh, that wouldn't be me. I don't bake. Or cook."

"Really? I find baking therapeutic, especially cookies." He chuckled and ran a hand over his flat abdomen. "Even if it means a few extra push-ups at the gym."

It appeared he spent *plenty* of time in the gym. The image popped in my head... him on all fours, fingers splayed, pushing up, his muscles taught as he lowered his body again, a droplet of sweat slowly trailing between his shoulder blades... *Get a grip, girl.* Waking up to that suitcase every morning was giving me a complex. I gave a shake of my head and took a step back, creating extra space between us.

"That's a nasty bruise on your forehead?" Dane's observation pitched from a statement into a question, and my fingers flew to the yellowish bruise that encircled the gash. It wasn't nearly as tender to the touch, but the headache beneath the blemish remained a constant reminder of the accident.

"Yeah. I was in a car wreck last week. Hit a pole," I whispered, the memory still too raw.

"You hit a pole?" Dane asked.

"Well, I was side-swiped, and then I hit a telephone pole. Corner of Clybourn and Lincoln Memorial Drive."

"Seriously?" Dane's eyes darted to my forehead. "I heard it. I mean, I *literally* heard it—I was staying at the Hilton on Clybourn. Bad lightning storm that night. Saw the fire trucks, police, everything. That was a nasty accident. You're okay?"

I nodded again and resisted the urge to shiver. "Yep, the doctor said I must have a guardian angel."

"Wow."

I gingerly traced a finger along the cut.

"Crazy." Dane eyed the bruise again, then his gaze lowered to meet mine. Thick black lashes contrasted with the striking blue of his eyes, and his pupils pulsed in and out as his focus intensified.

Strangers often stopped to comment on my eyes—also blue—and their compliments would throw me off guard. Now I understood. Sometimes you can't help yourself when it comes to pretty, shiny objects.

The corner of Dane's lip twitched up, dimpling his cheek. "So, have any of those ambulance-chasing lawyers found you yet?"

I laughed. "Hey watch it, Dane. I happen to be a

lawyer." *Former*. I internally corrected myself, although the signature on my resignation letter was barely dry.

"A lawyer, really?" His eyes rolled from the messy ponytail at the nape of my neck to the sleep shorts I'd worn the last several days. I'm sure I looked like I'd just rolled out of bed, which wasn't far from the truth.

"Well, a former lawyer, I guess." I tugged the hem of my wrinkled shirt. "That's a whole other story."

"I'd love to hear it sometime." Dane took the hint. He tipped his head toward me. "See you around, neighbor."

"Nice to meet you, Dane," I replied softly, giving a small wave as he stepped into his apartment.

It'd been a terrible morning, a terrible week, but something about Dane's voice, his smile, those eyes. The migraine was gone.

TWO

I shut the door behind me, and my hand lingered on the knob as I glimpsed around my sterile, gray loft. No pictures of family, no personal effects. Neat and tidy, without a chair or pillow out of place. A cleaning crew came once a week to dust and vacuum, even during the long stretches when I traveled for work.

I'd have to cancel their service. Being unemployed meant trimming the fat, although money wouldn't be an immediate concern. Loft and Associates paid generously, and I'd accumulated a solid nest egg over the last several years. I could thank Aunt Lu, who raised my twin brother and me, for that. She taught us from a young age to live without material things. Although, admittedly, my wardrobe now included ridiculously over-priced Christian Louboutin shoes and Louis Vuitton handbags.

You'll be tempted, Novalee, but profit and gain aren't worth the forfeit of the soul.

With my hand still grazing the knob, I sucked in a breath. I hadn't thought of Aunt Lu in a long time. Or Neal.

But since the accident, they seemed to be *all* I could think about.

Aunt Lu had been gone for well over a decade. So long, I could hardly envision her. And Neal, just as long.

With Lu I had warning, so I had made peace with her passing. Neal, however, slipped quickly and quietly out of my life. Last I knew, he was still strumming his guitar and riding the waves somewhere along the California coast. My blond-haired, blue-eyed, free-spirited twin wished for nothing more in life than to surf, sing, and sleep.

Twins, yet we couldn't be more different.

As children, Neal and I shared more than looks. Closer than brother and sister, we had our own special language, an impenetrable bond. A mental and physical connection. When Neal was learning to ride a bike and he fell, scraping his knee, I cried along with him for his pain and frustration.

Years later, I still remember the stinging sensation in my own knee as blood and dirt caked his.

Now, Neal was but a stranger.

If only he'd felt my pain, a fraction of my sorrow, when Aunt Lu died. If only he'd helped me sort through the grief and loneliness. Turning nineteen and being orphaned by the only family I'd ever known was a harsh reality.

I sighed, feeling almost as alone now as I had then.

When Neal fell off his bike, I thought I'd absorbed his pain, helped him cope. I figured he'd do the same for me, but either Neal didn't feel it, or he didn't care. The ease with which he'd discarded me from his life stung a million times more than any skinned knee.

I decided to forget about him just as he'd forgotten about me. For years, Neal rarely entered my thoughts. But now, he weighed heavy on my conscience. I could have *died* never having made amends with my twin.

Maybe it was my guilt playing tricks on me, because my distorted memory of the wreck starred Neal instead of the anonymous other driver.

The hours surrounding the collision were fuzzy—a symptom of the concussion—yet I had a clear picture of myself behind the wheel of my BMW X3, driving the short, familiar route from the airport to my studio. Rain clouds crowded the moon as I rolled toward the intersection of Clybourn and Lincoln Memorial Drive. Unusually rough waves had crashed against the rocky shoreline. Lightning bounced off the water, momentarily blinding me as I pushed against the accelerator and entered the intersection, just as a gray sedan snuck into my peripheral. My eyes had snapped left then right, catching a glimpse of a pedestrian—a young woman standing by a telephone pole—before shooting up to a crystal-clear windshield where I met the face of the driver.

In my warped nightmare of the accident, instead of a stranger behind the wheel, it was Neal. His eyes widened with horror as his car smashed into my driver's side.

In reality, I don't remember my car spinning out or colliding with the telephone pole—it'd happened in a blink. But I'd never forget the sound of screeching metal or the vivid cracks of lightning that seemed to shake me to my core.

After the vibrations settled, an eerie silence fell, and I distinctly remember the metallic taste of blood in my mouth and a unique, nauseating stench in my nostrils. It had taken a bit for me to place it... *singed skin.*

I still didn't know if it was mine, or *hers.*

I had tried to scream, but no noise came out. I had tried to move, but my limbs were trapped in a tangle of steel.

As lightning continued to crackle and thunder shook

the ground, my fear threatened to engulf me. But then I had the strangest feeling of comfort, as if I weren't alone. I'd thought *death* itself had come to relieve me.

But then I felt *it*—feather-soft touches stroking my cheeks, hushing my fears, sheltering me from the darkness. Blanketed in its warmth, my eyes had fluttered closed as I'd settled into the confines of unconsciousness. I'd been saved.

The doctors said I must have had a guardian angel to survive the wreck.

I may have been spared, but what about the woman by the telephone pole?

THREE

That evening, I crawled into bed with lingering thoughts of Neal and the accident on my mind. After tossing and turning, I gave up on my futile attempt to sleep and climbed out of bed to make a cup of chamomile tea.

While water warmed in the microwave, I went to the patio door. Another starless night. Even with the street lights, I could barely make out the park across the street.

Sliding the glass door open, I stepped onto the wet wooden planks. My bare feet cooled from the afternoon's leftover rain. I peeked over the balcony, and my eyes dropped to the fountain anchoring the park. Faint traces of water trickling into its basin sounded from below.

The flood light from a neighboring building blinked on, casting a yellowish, creepy spotlight over the fountain. Instant goosebumps rose along my arms. My eyes darted around the four corners of the park. An unsettling awareness spread through me, a feeling I wasn't alone. I was being watched. The wispy hairs on the back of my neck stood on end, and my heart began to pound, thumping so loud it drowned out the distant sound of splashing water. Fear fogged the air, thickening in my lungs and fuzzing my vision.

My eyes adjusted, zoning in on a blackbird that perched atop the stone figure of the fountain. As if sensing my stare, it took flight, bounding into the air and careening toward my patio. Its harsh, raspy *caw* echoed like a warning cry, and I stumbled back. My arms reached for the door behind me to steady my footing, but instead of finding the glass panel, I leaned into air, and slipped backward. A startled scream slipped from my lips as I landed on my butt.

Now my neighbor's patio light blinked on, followed by the swoosh of his door.

Dane stepped out and looked side to side, spotting me red-faced on my deck floor. He moved to the edge of his balcony and peered over. "You okay?"

I groaned, both from pain and embarrassment. Squeezing my eyes shut, I tried to calm my racing heart and steady my breathing before clamoring to my feet. "Yes, oh my gosh."

Dane eyed me, and then shifted his focus to the park, assessing it as if he also sensed something amiss. When his eyes returned to meet mine, concern softened his intense gaze.

"Sorry if I disturbed you," I offered, my face flaming.

"Not at all. I probably wouldn't have heard you, but I don't have cable yet. It's pretty quiet over here. You sure you're okay?"

Nodding, I flattened my palm against the left side of my ribcage. My breathing slowed, and the piercing pain faded to a dull ache. I looked down to my feet. "I am, thanks... just embarrassed. It's silly, really."

He tilted his head. "What is?"

"Nothing. I'm sorry. I'm tired. I should get back to bed."

Dane gave a firm nod, then spoke in a soothing tone that melted away any remaining anxiety and embarrassment. "Yeah, that's probably a good idea. You should get back to bed. Sweet dreams, Nova."

I nodded in response, then slipped back inside, up the stairs, and into my bed where I did just that. I had a sweet dream.

A *very* sweet dream that involved a *very* sexy, new neighbor.

~

JOLTING AWAKE THE NEXT MORNING, my arms rubbed against coarse, scratchy material. *Seriously? Am I really spooning a suitcase?* I pushed it away like a jilted lover, but it barely budged. My friend, Cami, had offered to unpack it during her stay with me, but I'd adamantly refused, already feeling bad for putting her out. As my emergency contact, she was first to be notified following the crash, and stayed with me the night after my release from the hospital.

With a hefty sigh, I slid from bed, gave the suitcase a final glare, then stalked to the bathroom.

After the accident, my morning routine included downing two Tylenol, but since the previous afternoon, the migraine had eased to a barely noticeable, dull ache. For the first time in days, I gave my reflection an assured smile and then padded downstairs, glancing at the patio door before moving to the small galley kitchen. My cheeks warmed. I wasn't usually so clumsy—or on edge.

The mug from the previous night still sat in the microwave. I pressed the screen to reheat the water. My fingers thumped against the counter as the seconds ticked down. With a work schedule that demanded late nights and early mornings, I usually drank coffee throughout the day. But Cami, who'd stocked my fridge, preferred chamomile tea and other crunchy health foods.

The microwave beeped. I added a teabag to the mug and moved to the living room. Sinking into the white leather couch that had cost a small fortune, I propped my feet on the freshly dusted coffee table.

Cami had done so much over the last week—cleaning, cooking, playing nurse. She wanted to stay longer, but I begged her off, arguing I'd get better rest alone. She relented after I promised to check in with her daily.

I took a sip of tea, then picked up my cell, and tapped the screen while leaning back into a buttery, soft cushion.

Cami answered on the first ring. "Nova! Sweetie!"

"Hey Cam, how are you?"

"Oh, fine, fine. How are *you*?" Her voice always percolated with happiness. It fit her—bubbly and sweet.

"Surprisingly good." I *did* sound good. "I did something crazy."

"Crazy?" she asked.

"I quit Loft."

"*What?*" Cami's shriek pierced my ear. "Because of London? Or San Francisco?"

She was the only person who knew about San Francisco. Well, besides Darrell, but I was certain I'd never hear a peep about it from him.

"Everything, really. I'll tell you about that later. Mind if I stop by sometime this weekend, maybe Saturday?" I replied, steering the conversation away from work. "I've been thinking about Neal."

"Oh. I wondered if you'd remember," she replied cautiously.

"What?"

"Well, his name came up a few times while you were out of it."

"I might try to find him," I said, my hand trailing over the expensive leather of my over-priced couch.

She sighed. "It's not as easy as it seems, finding someone who wants to be... lost." The hurt in Cami's voice made my stomach clench.

Years ago, Cami had a big blow-up with a friend, Celia, over a bad-news boyfriend. After their fight, Celia ran off with said guy, and they hadn't talked since. Years of friendship were destroyed over a man. Every so often, Cami would reignite her efforts to locate Celia to make amends, but each attempt came up short. I knew how much it hurt her to be cut from Celia's life.

I truly understood now, because I felt the same way about Neal.

"Yeah, but I need to at least try," I replied softly.

"I get it. I do. I just don't want you to get hurt, on top of everything else." I heard her sigh, an unusual sound from my spritely friend. Her tone quickly reverted to its typical cheeriness. "I'm running errands this afternoon. You need anything?"

"Thanks, Cam, but I think it's time for me to venture back into the land of the living. My head's been pretty clear. Fresh air and a walk to the Metro Mart might do me good." An idea formulated in my head, an idea I could credit to Dane. "So, I'll see you Saturday then? Maybe I'll drop off some homemade cookies?"

"Homemade cookies? Since when do you bake?"

Since today. "It's the least I can do to thank you for everything."

Cami knew I rarely cooked, not with my demanding

career. Take-out or delivery, working through lunch and dinner—I barely had time to eat, let alone cook. For years, my life ran on a tight schedule. A *very* tight schedule. Always in a rush, always worrying about work. Every day planned down to the minute. No time for myself.

Now I have time. A new beginning. A second chance.

Life could change in an instant. Maybe the accident was a blessing, a wake-up call. I'd take time for myself and do things that mattered to me. I'd not only find Neal, but more importantly, I'd find *myself*.

No more schedules, no more working through lunch and dinner. I'd learn to cook. I'd learn to bake. A batch of cookies for Cami... and maybe some for my new neighbor. Welcome to the neighborhood cookies for Dane, the mystery man whose seductive voice and smile sucked away a migraine.

I grinned, then frowned. Who was I kidding? I didn't even know how to turn on the oven.

Maybe I'd just buy them.

FOUR

I pulled a cart from the corral within the Metro Mart's entrance, jerking it back and forth until the gummed wheels straightened out. Wincing from the motion, I steadied my breath before continuing into the store. Thankfully my ribs were just bruised, not broken.

The store bustled from the lunch-hour rush. I navigated through a maze of people and produce bins, silently berating myself for not switching to a quieter cart. An old lady glared as I passed her, cart squealing, and I sheepishly backed away toward the bakery department.

A display piled high with boxes of cookies, brownies, pies, and scones stopped me in my tracks. I picked up a box of double chocolate chip cookies.

"Homemade are so much better," a familiar voice came from behind.

I twisted around, meeting sky-blue eyes.

"Dane." My cheeks instantly flushed as I remembered my spill on the patio.

"No-va," Dane said, annunciating the syllables in my name. "Do you know what that means in Spanish?"

"Huh?" I answered, blinking from confusion.

"Doesn't go. Your cart, No-va." Dane's eyes gleamed. "Your cart doesn't go. I heard it across the store."

I laughed. "Really?"

"Here, for the sake of everyone, please take this one." Dane pushed his empty cart beside mine and began transferring the contents.

"Thanks." My smiled widened.

"Hang on, I'll be right back," Dane called from over his shoulder as he pushed the squealing cart back to the corral. He returned to my side in seconds. "Shouldn't you be home resting?" He took reign of the cart, and I walked beside him.

"I need groceries. My fridge is literally empty."

"Did you walk here?" he asked, and I nodded in reply. The Metro Mart was only a three-block walk from our apartment complex, but I usually drove.

"Yep. My car's totaled." *The Bermer Beamer.* Totaled. I brushed away the guilty pang in my gut. I'd used my bonus money from the Bermer deal to buy a BMW X3. All that money wasted.

"Well, I figured." He tapped his forehead in the location of my bruise. "I have just a few things to pick up, but if you don't mind shopping along with me, I can be the gentleman my auntie always claimed me to be and will carry your packages back for you, madam." His bright eyes closed as he accented the word *madam.*

I hadn't thought about it, how I'd manage the bags with sore muscles and bruised ribs. *Cute and thoughtful, an uncommon combination in my dating experience.* "I don't want to keep you, but that'd be really nice."

We continued through the produce department. I added avocados, tomatoes, and lettuce to my other selection of vegetables in the cart.

"You eat like a rabbit." Dane pointed to the food. "Please tell me you also eat meat?"

"Of course," I replied, reaching for a cucumber.

"I make a mean cucumber salsa. So good over mahi-mahi." A grin flashed across his face, and my stomach reacted with a flutter. He grabbed one for himself.

"Oh, so you bake *and* cook?" I asked. "Impressive."

"Yep. Well, I can follow a recipe. Nothing gourmet or anything." He tilted his head, arched a brow, and said, as if offering clarification, "I'm a simple man with simple needs."

I blushed, unsure whether his proclamation had multiple meanings.

We pushed wordlessly to the deli. I picked at various artisan cheeses, and Dane appraised my selection.

"Nice, so you're a cheese eater. You kind of need to be here though, right?" A now familiar smile returned to his face. "The land of Cheeseheads."

"You're not from Wisconsin?"

"Just moved to the state. I've spent a lot of time in Chicago, but Milwaukee's new. Haven't even had time to check out any breweries, but that'll be changing soon."

"You'll love it here," I assured. Milwaukee, with its rich beer brewing history, had long been nicknamed Brew City. The area held all the culture, fun, and vibe of a big metropolis, but on a smaller, more accessible scale. With many quaint towns and the lake country surrounding the city, and Chicago less than ninety miles away, it was the best of both worlds.

"Yes, I think I will," Dane agreed, his playful eyes twinkling with what I thought could be another underlying message. Black hair fell over his forehead, and he raised a hand to haphazardly brush it back.

His hair was longer than the clean, classic cuts I'd

usually see around the office at Loft and Associates. His dark T-shirt and worn denim lent him an edgy appearance, like he rode a motorcycle.

"Did you move here for a job?" I asked, my curiosity piqued.

"Yep, a new gig. *Tequila* distribution." The word tequila rolled off his tongue with an authentic-sounding Spanish accent. "I love the stuff, and now I get it at a discount."

"So, beer *and* liquor?" I teased. A chilled glass of chardonnay was my drink of choice.

"As I said, I'm a simple man." Dane reached across to grab butter from the cooler, and his skin brushed against mine. It was just a gentle grazing, yet the tingle from his touch rendered me frozen. I stood in place, staring at the spot on my arm.

"Nova?" Dane called. He'd pushed ahead several feet. My eyes snapped to his bicep—where our skin had touched —and landed on the edge of a tattoo. It peeked from the corner of his T-shirt. I hadn't noticed it the day before.

I blinked, then met his eyes. "Think I'm set," I murmured, although I hadn't gotten the ingredients to bake cookies. Shopping with Dane had put that idea on hold.

"I need two more things—sugar and flour, since I now know my neighbor won't have any on hand." Dane glanced from over his shoulder, winking as he led us to the baking aisle. "You free tonight?"

I titled my head, nodding slightly.

"Want to make cookies?" He picked up a pack of chocolate chips, and then flipped it over to show me the recipe on the back of the packaging. "A lesson in baking."

I continued to nod, warmth filling my belly.

"Well, as a master chocolate chip cookie maker, it's kind of my duty to give you a lesson, since you don't bake. And, as your new neighbor, it's kind of your duty to bring the new guy cookies. So here we can kill two birds with one stone." He made an exaggerated tossing motion before dropping the package into his part of the cart.

Looks like I'll be learning to bake after all.

DANE CARRIED the bulk of the bags as we walked back to our complex, only allowing me to handle the lightest one which contained a loaf of bread. At the corner of Ogden and Van Buren, we waited for the traffic light to change. I glanced toward Winetopia, the lounge I frequented when I had a rare night out. Not only convenient, being just a block from home, it also carried the best wines and offered an extensive cocktail menu. The chic, modern ambiance attracted an older crowd, unlike the college scene at the bars and restaurants around Brady and Water Street.

"You should check out Winetopia." I pointed to their sign.

"That place?" Dane grimaced. "Looks snooty."

"I like it." I shrugged.

"Duly noted." A teasing smile lit his mischievous eyes.

"Dane!" I exclaimed, and he laughed. "I was just going to say how right your aunt is, thinking you're a gentleman, but never mind now."

A grin overtook his face. "I'm just joking, Nova. Well, not about that place, it does look snooty. But not you."

I blushed and self-consciously patted away loose strands of hair that had escaped my messy bun. I couldn't imagine *how* I looked at that moment—I'd made the quick trip to the grocery store in yoga pants and a tank top, not expecting to run into anyone, let alone my sexy as sin, new neighbor.

Dane used his fob to access the back door to our complex which opened to a rear stairwell. He held the door for me. I started toward the elevator, then looked back to offer an explanation since our units were only one floor up. Most days I'd skip the elevator and take the stairs. "I bruised some ribs in the wreck. Stairs aren't my thing right now."

Playful teasing gave way to a strange sense of intimacy in the elevator's small space. We ascended in silence. The door opened to our floor, and Dane waited for me to exit first.

"Here we are," he stated, handing over my bags. "Tonight, then?"

"Yes, tonight." I nodded my head.

"Come by at six." Dane slipped into his apartment.

FIVE

As I emptied the last grocery bag, my cell erupted. Pete Mackroy's number flashed on the screen. Silencing the phone, I let the call go to voicemail. By now, I assumed Darrell had notified him that I'd quit Loft and Associates.

Each time Pete had called the last several days, I'd replied with vague texts. I was not ready to discuss the accident, lawsuits, or insurance claims with anyone, let alone a stranger.

The phone buzzed, indicating the arrival of yet another voicemail from Pete. I sighed before snatching it from the counter and heading to the patio. Hitting the speaker, I listened half-heartedly to his message as I stepped outside.

Guilt gnawed at me. Returning Pete's call was the courteous thing to do, even if he was a friend of Darrell's. I tapped his name on my contact list. He picked up first ring.

"Hi Novalee, that was fast," Pete said.

"Hey Pete, I got your message. Sorry I missed your call," I replied, twisting a lock of hair between my fingers. My stomach twisted along with it. *Please don't ask how I'm doing. Please don't ask about the accident.*

"No problem. Figured I'd give it one more shot to see if we could connect while I'm in Milwaukee. Does tomorrow morning work—around ten?"

"Well," I hesitated, dropping the strands. "Ten works, but I... I don't want to discuss the accident. I just want to move on."

"Let's talk tomorrow. I'm in town regardless," Pete explained. His office was based out of Chicago, some big-name firm I should have been impressed with. "Is there somewhere near you where we could meet for coffee?"

"Dark Beans," I said, referring to the coffee shop located next to Winetopia. "It's on Ogden Street."

"I'll punch it into the GPS." Pete's voice soothed. He had an unusually calm tone, especially for an attorney. "See you tomorrow then?"

We said our goodbyes, and I clicked off the call.

I should have said no. I should have blown it off completely, but part of me felt I owed it to Darrell to at least meet with Pete. It was one of only a handful of times he'd gone out of his way to show concern.

However, a larger part of me knew exactly how much attorneys billed per hour, even over coffee. *Way to trim the excess.*

Leaning against the sliding glass door's frame, I glanced to the park before shifting my attention to Dane's patio.

Giggles and flowers. The muddied memory flashed in and out of my mind. I closed my eyes, wiping away any remnants of the strange images.

At least it wasn't a replay of me falling on my ass.

❧

AS EVENING APPROACHED, a mixture of excitement and nerves mingled in my belly. Getting involved with my neighbor, no matter how attractive and sweet he may be, was a complication I definitely did not need.

But I couldn't shake it. I hardly knew him, yet I liked him.

It's just cookies. A little baking. You wanted to bring some to Cami, right?

I nodded, agreeing with myself. Besides, having a friend next door offered a sense of security, someone besides Cami that I could count on in a crunch.

Before heading to Dane's, I raided the bottles of wine in my fridge, choosing a chardonnay from a local vineyard. Some of their grapes were shipped from California, but a majority were plucked off the vines in their own backyard. I grabbed the chilled bottle from the lower shelf, my fingers clenching nervously around the bottle's neck, then stepped into the hall.

The door to apartment 204 opened before I could knock.

"Right on time." Dane smiled, waving me in.

Boxes and sparse pieces of furniture, including an over-sized recliner, filled the small space that had been empty the day before.

"When did your stuff arrive?" I asked.

"This afternoon," Dane replied. "I don't have that much. One load, two guys. They finished a bit ago."

The walls between our units were paper-thin, and I recalled hearing the prior tenants daily. Little noises here and there, a bump on the wall or the high-pitched squeal of the sweet little girl who lived here. *Giggles and flowers.*

"The one benefit of moving often is you don't accumulate junk, and you know exactly what you need to live without the excess." Dane motioned me toward the sofa. "Would you like something to drink?"

I wiggled the bottle in my hand. "I know you like beer and tequila, but what about wine?"

"Ah, I spent a good chunk of time in wine country, yet never acquired the taste." He eyed the label. "A local winery, nice. I'll give it a try."

"Wine country? Napa?" I asked. I'd been there for business, which, when in wine country, mixes with pleasure. But too much wine at work events made for awkward morning meetings. I cringed at the memory of catching an inebriated Darrell with his assistant.

"Well, Monterey County, Napa's little sister to the south," Dane explained. He pulled several wrapped items from a cardboard box labeled "Kitchen" before locating a corkscrew.

"Do you need help? Looks like you're in the middle of unpacking?"

"Nah, this is it. I have one box of kitchen supplies." Proving his point, he dumped out the remaining contents of the box, swiftly unwrapping them from their brown packing paper. "The pots and pans have already been put away. I'm a plastic cup and paper plate kind of guy. That's it. This is my kitchen."

"Wow, sounds a lot like mine." Although I wasn't sure if I even owned a cookie sheet.

Dane pulled two red plastic SOLO cups from the cupboard. "Is it a sin to drink wine from these?"

"Well, you're not in wine country anymore." I leaned back on the sofa, feeling at home in Dane's man-cave of a living room. The blinds to his patio were shut, and the dim light from the kitchen spilled over Dane like a peek of sunshine, softening his dark edges.

"Those people would string us up by our toe-nails," Dane joked as he splashed wine into a cup.

"What did you do out there? Tequila distribution did you say?" I could not picture this man calling wine country home. He seemed rugged and tough, definitely more the whiskey or beer type than wine.

"I was an instructor at the Defense Language School in Monterey," Dane clarified. "The military drove me to drink, and now I'm working for tequila."

"Well, thank you for your service." I laughed, now understanding his rough undertones.

"My pleasure." Something flashed over Dane's face as if it weren't actually pleasurable. He poured a second glass of wine and handed it to me before taking a seat on the recliner. "To neighbors and bakers."

"To us." I tapped my red cup against his. "Not sure if I should be drinking."

"Still taking pain meds?" Dane asked. His eyes brushed over the cut at my forehead.

"I tried to stay away from them altogether, but I haven't taken anything the last two days. My head's feeling pretty good." My fingers absently grazed the edge of the gash. I cocked my head, realizing I hadn't had a single twinge all day.

Dane brought his cup to his nose and closed his eyes, swirling then sniffing the wine. "Hmm, delightful. Sun-soaked strawberries with a velvety finish."

I didn't swirl, but I sniffed, not noting any discerning scents. Scrunching my nose, I asked, "Sun-soaked strawberries, really?"

"Nah, I'm just playing." Now he slugged the wine, like one would beer, tipping the cup back. "But it is tasty."

I took a small sip, then a larger one, realizing I hadn't had wine in a good while. It went down too smoothly.

Dane stood up and returned to the kitchen to refill his cup. "Let's get this party started." He grinned and rubbed his palms together. I moved to the bar-height counter, sipping my wine while I watched him work.

Butter had already been set out. Dane pulled two eggs from the refrigerator, then unopened sacks of granulated sugar, brown sugar, and flour from the pantry. He laid the ingredients on the counter, setting them next to one of the bowls he'd just unpacked.

"Shoot, I forgot vanilla extract." He frowned and slapped his hand to his forehead. "I knew I'd forget something. If this batch turns out bad, blame it on the move. My mind's everywhere."

I took a long drink. The back of my neck warmed from alcohol. With a lacking appetite and an empty stomach, the wine hit quickly.

"Refill?" Dane asked, wiggling the bottle.

I held my cup up for him to top off. "I was laid up most of the week, but I'm feeling surprisingly good the last few days." I shrugged my shoulders. Not just the headache, I realized my bruised ribs seemed to feel better too.

"I have that effect on people." Dane chuckled. He had more than just that effect on people. My neck warmed again, this time not from the wine.

Light banter continued as we worked together in the close quarters of the kitchen. Dane instructed me to crack two eggs while he added softened butter to the bowl. He used a fork to cream them, then had me slowly add the flour, baking soda, sugar, and chocolate chips while he continued to mix by hand. I wasn't sure if I was thankful for the tiny galley kitchen, which offered minimal room to maneuver without bumping into one another. Each brushing pass of his forearm brought more heat to the back of my neck and another flutter to the pit of my stomach.

"Voila!" Dane exclaimed after he plopped the last heaping tablespoon of dough onto a greased cookie sheet. He pushed it into the oven and set the timer, then held up his hand for a high-five.

Our palms met. Our fingers lingered; his tips curled just over mine before he pulled away—but not quickly enough for the sudden jolt of electricity between us to go unnoticed.

I snatched my hand to my side, rubbed it against my pants and blinked at Dane who looked just as puzzled. His chin cocked, and he openly stared at me for what seemed like minutes. Giving a little shake of his head, as if brushing it off, he then reached for the wine bottle and split the remaining contents between our cups. I wordlessly followed him to the living room where he returned to the sofa. I perched at the edge of the recliner.

"I still don't have my TV or cable set up. Or internet. Not getting into the nitty-gritty until next week," he explained, easing into a cushion.

"How d'you go from the military to tequila?" *Did I just slur?*

"It's a distillery out of Carmel Valley. I got to know the owner during my contract with DLI."

"DLI?" I asked, straightening in my seat. "What d'you do there again?" *Definitely slurring.*

"Defense Language Institute." Dane eyed his cup. "Taught Arabic, but I also speak Spanish, French, Russian, and German. That gig was a contract job. I'm no longer active duty, but still trying to do my part."

"Wow." And here I had struggled to learn Spanish in high school. "That's impressive."

"Language is my thing." He smiled and leaned in. "So, what about you? A lawyer, huh?"

"Former. Gave my notice yesterday." I rubbed my temple. A light twinge started between my eyes, either from wine on an empty stomach or talk of work.

"Right. The other story."

"Yeah, I need a change, I guess. Near death experience, maybe? No more eighty-hour work weeks. No more jerk boss." I shrugged. Could it be that simple? Giving up seven years of college and almost ten years at a firm? I'd interned at Loft during school before being offered a position after graduation.

"Good for you. But are you a trust fund baby or something? Rent here isn't cheap." Dane again swirled his wine.

"I'll be okay, at least for a while, until I work something out for the long-term. I'm cutting back on some indulgences, like my cleaning lady. Cancel cable. Maybe have a garage sale. I'll figure it out."

"A garage sale? You're gonna sell your clothes?" Dane frowned.

"Purses. Lots of ridiculously over-priced purses." I laughed.

The timer buzzed, and Dane popped to his feet. He opened the oven door, releasing a mouth-watering aroma of freshly-baked cookies. Grinning, he pulled out the sheet and appraised our baking efforts.

I joined him in the kitchen and set my empty plastic cup next to the sink. Two glasses of wine were two too many.

"Perfect," Dane proclaimed. He used a towel as a pot holder, and set the sheet on the counter. "A few minutes to cool, and we can taste our creations."

We hovered around the kitchen, Dane opposite me with

the thick, quartz countertop separating us. Conversation had been easy the entire evening, but now, a strange shyness had me silent. My eyes moved from the cookie sheet to Dane. He unabashedly studied me. Something besides the sweet smell of cookies permeated the air.

I bit my lower lip as his gaze swept my face, settling to the spot near my collarbone where a trio of small freckles created a perfect triangle. My hands flew to cover it.

Dane's brow twitched, and his dark pupils overtook the blue of his eyes. His focus locked on me as he walked around the counter. With a gentle hand, he peeled my fingers away, leaning in to look at the three speckles.

Moving closer yet, his lips inched near mine, so close I could smell sweet wine on his breath. My skin tingled. My breath hitched. I looked up, tilting my chin. My lips parting...

"I think they're cool," he whispered, his warm breath brushing my cheek.

I took a step back, and my hands again flew to cover the freckles. I blinked. "Cool?"

Dane's eyes flashed to my hands. "The cookies."

A moment of sobriety zapped the wine buzz, and I reddened, groaning inside. Dane stepped away, wordlessly returning to the cookie sheet. He poked a finger at the golden cookies, then used a fork to lift each one off, setting them onto a paper plate.

When he again looked to me, I recognized his odd look.

Hunger. And not just for the cookies.

But the fleeting glint faded, and when he smiled again, it didn't quite reach his eyes. The benign atmosphere cooled along with the air-conditioning that kicked on.

He was going to kiss me. I was sure of it. Awkward

seconds passed. We stared at each other until I finally broke away, my eyes shifting to my feet.

"It's late. I should go," I mustered.

Dane nodded in reply, handing the heaping plate to me. "Enjoy," he murmured.

SIX

Since the accident, I'd traded designer power suits—a lawyer's uniform—for low-key cotton tank tops and stretchy yoga pants. Messy buns replaced my usual neat chignons.

As I dressed Friday morning for my appointment with Pete, I met in the middle between my old style and new, choosing a sleeveless cotton sundress and a low ponytail. Even if our meeting was informally held over coffee, and I no longer represented Loft and Associates, I supposed yoga pants weren't appropriate.

After containing my beach-blond curls with a hairband, I applied minimal makeup and gave a satisfied nod to my reflection. I looked good—*normal*. A new normal.

More importantly, minus the lingering embarrassment that flushed my cheeks each time I thought of Dane, I *felt* good. No persistent symptoms from the concussion, only the gash and bruise above my left eyebrow.

Preparing for a twinge to my ribs as I bent, I slipped a pedicured foot into a black leather sandal. Even that ache had dulled to nothing.

One week and two days post-accident, I felt *surprisingly* good.

I gave a once over in the full-length mirror beside my closet. The sleeveless dress hugged my curves, emphasizing my toned arms and legs. Hopefully I'd be able to return to yoga and spin classes soon. I may have a new normal, but they would stay a part of the new me's new norm.

Satisfied, I headed downstairs, first stopping at the kitchen counter to grab a cookie from the platter Dane had prepared before heading out. I stuffed it into my mouth as I locked my apartment door. Even without vanilla extract, the cookies tasted divine. I'd polished half of the plate before bedtime, pledging to leave the rest for Cami.

The old me avoided sweets; the new me devoured them. I was really beginning to like this girl.

EVER SINCE DARK BEANS' baked goods were featured on Sweet Kay's Cooking Show, finding an open table at the coffeeshop became nearly impossible. I pushed through their front door and scanned the crowded room before realizing I had no idea what Pete Mackroy looked like.

"Novalee? Novalee Nixon?" a familiar voice called from behind, and I spun to see a tall man with dirty blond hair and warm brown eyes extending his hand. Based on his casual polo, shorts, and flip-flops, the meeting would be informal—maybe even free of charge. "You must be Novalee. I'm Pete."

"Hi, yes, I am. Call me Nova, please." I smiled and shook his hand. "I was about to call you. I realized I didn't know how I might identify you." I waved toward the throng of people.

"Oh, right. I saw your picture on Loft's website," Pete explained, looking appraisingly at my face. "Have you ordered?"

"No, not yet. I just got here."

We joined the line, each ordering coffee and a bagel, and made small talk as we waited for a table to open.

Pete wasn't what I'd expected. Besides being much younger than I'd assumed, he had a classic handsomeness. Polished haircut, perfect teeth, toned body, healthy tan. Success and money, but not pretentious. Comfortable and confident in his own skin without seeming cocky.

A spot in the rear cleared, and Pete led the way. I sat with my back to the wall, having a view of the crowded café while Pete faced me.

As I waited for him to pitch his spiel, I pinched a piece of bagel and popped it into my mouth. Another first. The old Nova shied away from carbs, always ordering the egg white and spinach frittata at Dark Beans.

"So, I heard you left Loft," Pete said, his eyes carefully assessing my reaction.

I nodded, still chewing.

"Darrell was surprised."

"So was I." I laughed. "I don't really want to talk about it. In fact, I feel bad having made you take the time to come out here—"

"Oh, don't worry, I had extra time. I'm meeting clients at the ball game tonight. Cubs and Brewers series this weekend."

"Oh, good. Well, as I mentioned last night, I don't want to talk about the accident." Pete nodded as if agreeing. "I want to put it behind me. Focus on the future."

"The future." Pete's head continued to bob up and down. "Right, so what's going on—off the record. Nothing you say will go back to Darrell. I barely know the guy. He's an old pal of my dad's. Between you and me, I think he's kind of a dick." Pete stopped. "Sorry about the language."

"It's okay," I laughed. "I agree. You put it perfectly, though... he is a dick."

Pete's grin took years off his face, making him look young and sweet, like a high school quarterback.

The more we talked, the more I liked him. He seemed genuinely interested in me, asking how I was feeling, how I was coping, and listening intently to my replies, but not pressing as I glossed over the grisly details of the accident. As our conversation continued, I learned Pete had turned down a position with his father's firm, instead working his way up the ladder on his own. Chicago was his home, and baseball was his passion.

The conversation turned back to me and, inevitably, to what my future looked like now that I was unemployed and had a seemingly new outlook.

"Well, I always enjoyed writing," I offered. The thought had been there since my early college days when my freshman writing professor encouraged me to nurture my creative tendencies. "Maybe I'll look into writing classes or workshops. I haven't had time to think about hobbies or anything besides work for, like, the last decade."

"I'm in the same boat. I don't remember the last time I got out and it didn't somehow tie in to work—even the baseball game tonight, I'm meeting clients. Pretty sure they're Brewers fans, so I'll have to keep my mouth shut. My boss thinks this is a huge treat. The executive suite, catering, all that. At least it's not the opera." Pete shuddered.

"Seriously, you had to take clients to the opera?" I giggled, unable to picture him fitting in among the theater crowd. He definitely had a jock vibe.

"Yeah, I mean, I love live music. But opera? Nah. God, I haven't been to a concert in ages."

"Me either." I nodded my head. "Wow, now that I think about it, the last concert I saw was a group called Jarhead Junction. They're a local band, now turning mainstream. Have you heard of them?"

"Yes, I have, actually," Pete agreed emphatically. "I think they're cool."

I think they're cool.

I froze, Dane's words echoing in my head.

"Nova?" Pete asked.

"Sorry." I shook my head, waving off thoughts of Dane.

But a familiar figure at the far end of the café caught my attention, and I again found myself ignoring Pete.

Dane stood at the entryway, a leather cross-body briefcase slung over his broad shoulders. I watched as he proceeded to the counter to give his order. Pete turned, following my stare.

His head swiveled back to face me again. "You okay?"

I silently nodded, still watching Dane. The barista handed over a mug, and he turned, catching my gaze. His eyes darted to the back of Pete's head, then again to me as he took deliberate steps toward us, keeping his eyes locked on mine.

"Hello, neighbor." Dane's voice was low and gruff, sounding not so neighborly. He glanced at the table next to us—the man sitting there gathering his laptop, mumbling, "I'm just leaving," and quickly departing. Dane plopped down in the freshly vacated seat and proceeded to remove his laptop from his leather briefcase before looking expectantly at me again.

"Hi," I murmured back.

Pete either didn't notice the strange tension, or he chose

to ignore it. He looked at his watch. "I need to get to another appointment. It was really great meeting you." He hesitated, placing his palms flat on the table. "I'll be in Milwaukee a lot over the next few months. Since you fired me before I could start, I don't think there'd be an attorney-client conflict of interest if we grabbed dinner sometime?"

An image flashed—the luggage, my arms and leg wrapped around it, the empty side of the bed that greeted me every morning. I was due some fun, and Pete seemed sweet, our conversation easy.

And, unlike Dane, I hadn't made a complete fool of myself in front of Pete. *Twice.*

"Sure." I smiled.

Maybe it was my imagination, but Dane's fingers seemed to jab louder against his keyboard, punching keys deliberately.

"Great, I look forward to it." Pete stood up and pushed in his chair. "I have to run. I'll call you."

I sat still for a moment after he left, considering what to say to Dane.

"He seems nice." Dane broke the awkward silence.

"Yeah. You're working?"

"I don't have internet set up for my home office yet. Getting some things in order for next week." Dane eyed me. "You look nice."

I patted at my hair, instantly self-conscious by his sentiment. "Thanks."

"You must be feeling better?"

I nodded in response.

"How were the cookies?" His blue eyes and deep voice softened.

"Fantastic," I divulged, "even without the vanilla extract."

Dane nodded. "It's my magic mixing hands." He wiggled his fingers, then hovered them back over the keyboard. "Hey, I'm meeting a prospect tonight. I suggested Winetopia. Thanks for the recommendation."

"I thought you hadn't started with work yet?"

"The guy's here from Green Bay, owns a few sports bars up there and can meet tonight." Dane shrugged. "My new boss is itching to get stuff started around here, so I can't say no to a prospect. Or to a few drinks." He paused with thought. "Do you want to come with?"

"To your work meeting?"

"It'll be low key, just a few cocktails. He's here with some guys going to the baseball game tomorrow." Dane shrugged again.

My thoughts flashed to the black cocktail dress hanging in my closet, still baring its four-hundred-dollar price tag. I bought it when Beck and I were still a thing, saving it for a hot date. My ex-boyfriend, Beckman Allen Lindon IV, was the cocky, pompous lawyer-type I always seemed to attract.

But this isn't a date. And Beck is definitely not Dane.

From the look on Dane's face, I was certain the hesitation showed on mine.

"Being new to the area, it'll give me a little boost to have a local with me. Wisconsin and Illinois are my territory, but I hardly know my way from here to home. Be a friend?"

I found myself nodding. "Okay, what time?" Beck never deserved that dress anyway.

"I'll pick you up at seven."

"Pick me up? You plan to drive here?" I pointed to the wall Winetopia shared with Dark Beans. "It's less than a two block walk from home." The idea of getting into a car sent a shiver down my spine.

"Figure of speech, Nov." Dane laughed. I warmed by

his use of a nickname; it felt intimate, as if we'd been friends for longer than a few days. "I'll *knock* on your door at seven."

As I departed Dark Beans, crossing the city street on the short walk home, I mused at how quickly life changed in a week.

I'd nearly died, quit my job, and now had two hot dates lined up.

SEVEN

The time read 6:58 p.m. My foot impatiently tapped against the stool as I stared at the empty wineglass that sat on the kitchen countertop, waiting for Dane's knock at my door. I debated pouring more, just a half glass to calm my nerves, but then the expected rap came. Seven on the dot. I knew he'd be punctual.

"It's open," I called, sliding from the stool. The thin heels of my four-inch stilettos sank into the carpet.

"Hey, hi," Dane greeted. He stopped under the door-frame, filling it with his broad shoulders. His jaw twitched. "Wow."

I'd gone all out, summoning the old Nova and all her magic make-up and styling skills. Using a big-barreled curling iron to create smooth ringlets, my hair swept over my brow, hiding the gash. Smokey pencil lined my eyes, and two coats of mascara thickened my lashes. I looked nothing like the girl Dane had come to know over the last few days. I looked like the *old* me—sophisticated, smart, assured.

Dane continued to stare at me. Maybe I'd overdone it.

Maybe the red lipstick was a bit much. It was a work meet-up for Dane after all.

The appraising glint in his eyes said otherwise. His gaze traveled from my face to the sleeveless dress that high-lighted my toned arms. It had a scoop neck and flirty hem. I dressed it up with silver cuff bracelets and long earrings that almost brushed my shoulders. The bracelets clinked against one another when I reached for the shiny patent leather clutch on the counter.

"Hi to you too." I smiled, noting the dark trousers and black button-down shirt Dane wore. He looked professional while keeping his edge.

Dane remained at the door. The intensity of his stare brought heat to my cheeks. We stood silently assessing one another until I made the first move, walking the few steps to his side. I looked up.

"Ready?" My voice came out low, husky.

He gave a nod, then cocked his head to the side, continuing to study me as his hand lifted deliberately, brushing a blond lock over my shoulder. His jaw dropped, as if he were going to say something. Instead, he turned and led the way out.

THE TWO-BLOCK WALK to Winetopia was made in silence, except for the clink of my heels on the concrete. Dane walked beside me, glancing my way every so often but not speaking.

Loud music and an energetic vibe pulsed from the lounge as we entered. Winetopia attracted the young professionals in the area, the place to see and be seen. As we neared the bar, two patrons slid from their stools, offering us a place to sit. I glanced at Dane—seats at Winetopia on a Friday night were beyond impossible to secure—but he guided me to the bar without reservation or question, and then turned, asking what I'd like.

"Should we find your client first?" I asked.

"They'll be here at eight, I figured we'd come early to scope out a seat."

"Oh, okay. There's probably more space downstairs." Cushy booths and velvet sofas filled the lower level, along with a second bar that turned into a club after happy hour. I scanned the cocktail menu. "I'll have a gin and tonic."

Dane ordered my drink along with a beer for himself. As we waited for them to arrive, he twisted in his seat to face me.

"You're stunning," he said in a low voice.

"Thanks." I blushed, averting my eyes to the counter. I couldn't think of a time when a compliment had such a stomach-dropping effect. Certainly nothing like this from Beck.

After the bartender delivered our drinks, Dane closed our tab, then suggested we check out the lower level. He extended his hand, settling it under my elbow to help me from the stool, just as long, painted fingernails tapped his arm.

"Dane!" a whiney voice exclaimed. The garish nails now dug into his bicep.

Dane glanced to the hand, then to the face, his irritation obvious. "Hey, Lori."

"I wondered when I'd see you again—" She stopped, eyeing me. "Oh-kay." Lori shot accusatory dagger eyes, first to Dane, then to me. Her lip turned up as she squinted, looking squarely at me. "I see. Have *fun* with him. He's *great*." The voice was sugary, the implication was loud. She spun and pranced away on sky-high heels.

"Oh, she seems nice." Sarcasm danced in my voice as I slung the same line Dane had used about Pete. Maybe I sounded like a jealous teenager, but I couldn't help it.

Dane shook his head, brushing off the awkward moment. "She's in liquor distribution too. Well, shall we?" His hand returned to my elbow and firmly guided me from the stool.

We made our way to the wide staircase at the far end of the bar, and I caught Lori glaring at us. I resisted the urge to stick my tongue out at her, but did flash a snarky smile. So much for sophisticated, smart, and assured.

The lower level, known as Tangerine, was decorated in various shades of orange with splashes of white. Lounge music lulled in the background, and the bar bustled with the Friday night happy-hour crowd.

We claimed a vacant booth in the corner. I slipped in, careful to hold the hem of my short dress as I scooted over the white leather cushion. Dane finished shooting a text on his cell before joining me.

"Tom just cancelled," he explained, holding up the phone. "I appreciate you coming out tonight, but it looks like it was for nothing."

"No, it feels good getting dressed up. I feel... like my old self." I sipped my cocktail.

"Well, I don't know the old you, but I sure like the new you." He leaned in closer. I caught his scent—beer mixed with cologne, the sort of manly scent that makes a woman's heart race.

Everything about Dane screamed *man*. His large frame, strong muscles, broad shoulders. The dark lashes that lined bright, mischievous eyes. The thick crop of black hair that fell over his brow, and the haphazard way he always brushed it off.

The dark attire and salty attitude added an edge of danger. And the tattoo. I still didn't know what it was.

"What's your tattoo?" The words slipped out, and Dane looked at me with surprise. "I only saw the tip," I explained sheepishly.

"Oh." He glanced to his bicep. "I have a few. I can show you later."

"Or maybe I can ask Lori," I teased back, enjoying the shock in his eyes. When was the last time I'd flirted? I'd forgotten how much fun it was.

"What about you? Wait—I can answer that—you don't have any, do you?" Dane's eyes traveled along my bare arm.

"Actually, I do." I smiled sweetly. The wine from earlier, along with the added gin, emboldened me. "I'll show you mine, if you show me yours."

Dane's black pupils darkened, leaving only a small ring of blue.

The cocktail waitress took that inopportune moment to interrupt, asking if we'd like another round. I shook my empty glass, mumbling, "Yes, same please. Gin and tonic."

Dane relayed our order and as the girl walked away, he slowly exhaled, breathing out my name. "Nova." It rolled gently, almost regretfully, from his lips. He leaned back.

I leaned back too, biting my lower lip. The lounge had filled up. People now crowded around the booths, and the vibe changed. Club music replaced the chill tunes from earlier. Our second round arrived, along with shots of tequila.

"From the party over there." The waitress jerked her chin toward a group at the bar. "They bought a round."

"*Tequila*. Well, that's generous of them." Dane's eyebrows shot up. "I'll have to see if it's as good as my stuff."

I eyed the shot. Tequila was bad news.

"You ready for this?" Dane asked, lifting the shot glass.

I hesitated, then picked mine up, and tilted the glass toward Dane. "Cheers."

Lifting it to my lips, I tipped it back. The liquor flowed straight down my throat, and I shivered as it stung my nostrils.

"I was going to get us salt and lime, but that's impressive." Dane chuckled, then followed suit, emptying his glass in a fluid gulp. He shook his head. "Woo, that burns."

"Woo," I repeated, then laughed. "It's been a *long* time since I've had tequila." The liquor warmed everything, from my cheeks to my toes.

I had to slow down. I'd just gotten rid of the migraine; I didn't need a hangover.

Even with the warning ringing in my head, I downed my drink. Caught up in our conversation, I hadn't objected when Dane ordered yet another round.

"Think the tequila's gone right to my head," I stuttered, pushing away the cocktail that appeared before me.

"You okay? We shouldn't have had those shots." Concern flickered over his face.

"I'm fine." I smiled. "But I think I've had enough. Do you want this? I'd hate for it to go to waste."

"I'd hate that even more." He laughed, sliding the lowball glass in front of himself.

Maybe it was the alcohol or the pulsing vibe, but an energy flowed in my veins, humming along to the music. I felt more alive than ever.

Dane finished his drink just as the cocktail waitress

returned to our table. Without even asking for the tab, he handed over a wad of cash. "I think we're set, thanks."

Unpeeling the bills, her eyes lit up as she walked away. Whatever amount he'd given her must have included a hefty tip.

"Ready?" Extending his hand, Dane helped me to my feet. The crowd from the promotion party had moved to the dance floor, bumping and singing with the music. As we twisted through the throng, I tugged at Dane's hand.

"It's also been a *long* time since I've danced." I grinned, looking to him from under my eyelashes. And then I batted them, like a teenager.

"I'm not sure you can handle my moves." Dane laughed and pulled me into him. He gripped my hand, then spun me out and away before reeling me back into his hold. Taught arms held me for a second before casting me out again. He moved his right foot in a smooth motion, sliding toward the dance floor, sweeping me along with him.

His hold on my hand tightened as he drew me back in again, and I fell against him laughing. My flushed face turned toward his, and my giggles subsided as he leaned in. Soft, full lips brushed over mine.

The surrounding noises blurred to nothing, and it was just Dane and me under our own spotlight. The only two on the dance floor. His arms surrounded me, but I wanted more. The small space between us felt like an ocean instead of inches.

The warmth of his breath stroked my cheek as he whispered, "I know we shouldn't, but I can't help myself." His hand rolled from my lower back to the nape of my neck, and he pulled my face closer. Our mouths met again. His tongue slipped over my lower lip.

The tempo changed, and his mouth moved deliberately,

taking in my taste and exploring my lips. My body simmered from the little strokes of his tongue and the tug of his hands at my hair. I felt the heat and hardness of his body as he pulled me closer.

Another dancer knocked into me, hurling us back to reality.

Pop music percolated from the speakers, yet we remained slowly swaying. Amazed, surprised, shaken. A simple kiss that had taken us off the dance floor.

"Let's get out of here." Dane's voice was so low it sounded like a growl. He pulled me through the crowd and up the stairs. My heels clicked against the wooden steps as I struggled to keep up.

It wasn't until we were at the corner of Ogden and Van Buren that Dane stopped, and only because the pedestrian crosswalk signal wasn't in our favor. He looked down, pulling me again into his arms. This time there was no gentleness, no hovering or lingering, just pure desire as his mouth covered mine. His hands cupped each side of my face, and he held steady, drinking life from my lips until I was left breathless from his kiss.

A kiss I'd waited my entire life for.

When he pulled away, I took obvious breaths. My lungs heaved within my ribcage. He watched my chest rise and fall, then his blue eyes were back on mine. I blinked dazedly, drunk from the stormy look of desire that hardened his already sharp features.

Dane took my hand as we crossed the street, but he left a deliberate space, keeping a step ahead of me.

I didn't try to decipher the slight shaking of his head, as if he was saying no within the confines of his mind until we were under the security light at the back door of our complex. He slid his fob over the panel, ushered me in, then followed me past the rear stairwell. Instead of joining me in the intimate space of the elevator, he remained planted in the hall.

"I can't... I'm sorry, Nova. We shouldn't—" Dane's head continued to shake as the elevator door closed, cutting my view of his regretful eyes.

EIGHT

The next morning started with a blinding headache. I rolled from bed, pinching the bridge of my nose as I fumbled for the bottle of Tylenol on my nightstand. The child lock cap put up a good fight before twisting off. The last two pills fell into my clammy hands. I usually had a bottle of water next to my bed, but luck wasn't on my side that morning.

Dropping the pills onto the nightstand, I groaned. Sunlight from the arched window above the patio door amplified the pounding pain at my temples, and I resisted the urge to kick the stupid suitcase that continued to mock me. Mad at myself for drinking too much. And, mad at myself for *whatever* had happened with Dane.

I couldn't piece it together. What went wrong?

The chemistry. The kiss. That was right.

A kiss I'd waited my entire life for.

A buzzing noise erupted from my phone, which I had left on the kitchen counter the night before. After the disastrous ending to my evening with Dane, I'd crawled into bed still garbed in my cocktail dress.

Now, I peeled it off and kicked it to the floor, shaking my head as memories of Dane's remorseful eyes pounded at my temples. I slipped into shorts and a T-shirt, then headed into the bathroom to wash the smeared makeup from my face. A few splashes of cold water did nothing to calm my head, but at least I no longer looked like a deranged raccoon.

I grabbed the two pain killers on my way downstairs. Stopping at the kitchen faucet, I popped the horse pills into my mouth. A chalky taste bittered my tongue as I slurped tepid water directly from the stream. Droplets fell from my chin, and I didn't even bother to swipe them away.

My phone erupted again with the notification of a message. I saw Pete's name on the illuminated screen. My fingers flew back to the bridge of my nose, pinching away the pain.

I should just go back to bed.

Instead, I flopped onto the sofa and flipped on the television. I couldn't remember the last time I *had* time to get hooked on a series. Yet, I continued to pay the cable bill every month. Another expense I should eliminate.

A heavy, tingling feeling settled in my temples, then traveled to my eyes. I allowed the pain killers to lull me into a light catnap.

When I woke for the second time, the headache had diminished to a dull reminder. I peeled myself from the sofa and was resolved to get out of the house. Cami was not only expecting me, but she could cheer me. Perhaps she could help me make sense of the scene with Dane—his swift change from desire to regret, and the guilty, remorseful look on his face as the elevator door closed.

I climbed the stairs to my lofted bedroom and looked to the wall I shared with Dane, wondering if he was home. Wondering if he was as confused as I was.

I'd only known him a few days, but now I couldn't seem to get him off my mind.

～

I WASN'T much of an outdoorsy person, then again, I never had free time to spend outdoors. My twenties slipped by with studies and work. Now, I had nothing but time. Time to find my passion. Time to find my brother. Time to find my purpose.

Maybe the accident was the best thing to happen to me.

While a walk through the city of Milwaukee could hardly count as an expedition into the great outdoors, the parks along the route to Cami's yoga studio offered blooming bushes and vibrantly colored flowers.

The studio, much like Loft and Associates, was an easy walking distance from my apartment, yet I'd always driven. I wandered the city, feeling lost on streets I knew like the back of my hand. Before the accident, I could not remember walking *anywhere*.

Always rushing, always working, never a free moment for myself.

Cass Street hit Water Street, but instead of following the sidewalk, I gravitated toward the gravel path that led to a trail behind the abandoned Edson plant. The building, located in a prime area along the Milwaukee River, had been on the market for years, but asbestos deterred developers.

Urban dwellers seeking nature frequented the many footpaths behind the building and around the river. An occasional altercation, mugging, or drug bust made the news, but in general, the area was considered safe. Clusters of trees and shrubs, thick enough for privacy but too sparse to be considered a forest, offered seclusion.

The trail wound into the wooded area. I couldn't see the river, but the sound of its gentle flow was within earshot. Towering elms provided an umbrella from July's hot sun, cooling the air by several degrees and dampening the path. Goosebumps freckled my bare arms.

I stopped walking to rub at them. A rustle echoed in the distance.

Crunch, crunch. Frozen, I listened intently, unsure whether it was footsteps or an animal. *Swish, swish.* Fear caused the hairs on the back of my neck to rise along with the goosebumps on my arms. My head slowly twisted as I waited for further signs of movement. *Swoosh, swoosh.*

More alarming than the noise was the now familiar, unsettling awareness creeping over my skin. I was being watched.

Crunch, crunch. The logical part of my mind reasoned the sound could have been a bird or squirrel, yet I remained paralyzed, holding my breath, feeling more and more like prey. *Swish, swish.* The trees whispered with the wind, a warning making my hairline wet with sweat. *Swoosh, swoosh.*

The noises grew louder and closer, but I still was unable to place them. The leaves above swirled. I looked up and down, my eyes focusing on the overgrown bushes in front of me, darkened from the shadows of the towering trees above me.

My heart pounded, pumping my blood so hard I could almost taste metal in my mouth.

And then came a familiar sound, harsh and shrill. The guttural croak of a bird, followed by the rush of its flapping wings. Sounds bounced off the trees, creating an echoing roar that intensified with each slow second.

Terror paralyzed me before instinct kicked in, urging me to run. I spun and fled, my sandals slipping against the wet leaves that had fallen over loose gravel. I ran without seeing, without thinking. The sounds faded as I neared the sidewalk, but I didn't stop. No, my inner voice of caution catapulted me the eight blocks home.

It wasn't until I was outside of my building that my legs went still, and I bent, wheezing and clutching at my chest, desperate for air.

"Are you okay?" an all-too-familiar voice called.

I couldn't look up, partially from mortification but mostly from the stab to my lungs and ribs.

From my hunched position, I watched a set of legs bolt toward me.

"Nova, what's wrong?" Dane's palm flattened against my back, and his head bent toward mine.

"Nothing, I'm fine," I assured, but tears streaked my cheeks.

"What happened?" One hand stayed at my back while the other settled under my elbow, guiding me upright.

"I just…" I sniffed and swiped at my face. "I went for a walk and my ribs are still sore."

"You went for a walk?" Dane asked, unconvinced. "Are you okay?"

"I'm fine." The concern in his voice prompted fresh tears. I shrugged off his hold and repeated, my voice stronger, "I'm fine."

Dane followed me through the lobby and into the elevator.

"I saw you running like a bat out of hell." He placed both hands on my arms, turning me toward him.

"I'm *fine*, just drop it," I pleaded, meeting his eyes.

He gave a nod and let go.

We stepped off the elevator, each going to our respective doors. I jabbed my key into my doorknob when he called out again.

"Can we talk?"

I went still under the doorframe, and sighed. "Fine."

"Are you going to say anything besides *fine*?" Dane's tone softened.

"I don't know."

"See, that's better," he teased gently and trailed in behind me.

"Give me a minute." I didn't look back as I gingerly stepped up the stairs to my bedroom. In the confines of the bathroom, I pressed my fingers into my eyes, suppressing the tears, pushing them back down to my belly.

You're being silly. It was a bird—a harmless blackbird.

I splashed cold water over my face, not even caring as it hit the skin glue. It was barely hanging on anyway.

Returning downstairs, I stopped at the landing. Dane sat stiffly on the white leather sofa, staring absently at the abstract artwork that hung against a cream-colored wall.

Minimal décor in varying shades of grey and white adorned my lower level. Sterile, simple, sophisticated. I'd utilized the small space well, having had the help of an interior designer. I realized, glancing around, that she'd selected mostly everything in the apartment. *Nothing in here is me; nothing is mine.* I shivered, feeling foreign and alone in my own home.

I used to be a free spirit. I used to have passion. A lust for life.

"Sorry," I said, unsure whether I was apologizing to

Dane or myself. I sighed. Dane's head snapped to my direction. I dug a toe into the carpet.

"Are you okay?" he asked again.

"I am," I answered, nodding. "Really."

"Okay." He looked down to his hands. "I want to apologize for last night."

I moved to the accent chair across from him, settling myself onto a stiff cushion obviously chosen for aesthetics and not comfort.

"You're a beautiful woman, smart and kind. You deserve better than this. Me." His arm waved toward himself. "I don't know how long... I can't start something..."

"Okay. Is that it?" I stood up.

With the accident, quitting my job, and worrying about Neal, I hardly needed another obstacle. So why was his rejection prompting a fresh round of tears?

"Nova." His blue eyes pleaded.

"What?" Now I was angry and finding my backbone. "For someone who doesn't want to start something, you certainly extend a lot of invitations."

"You're right. And I'm sorry." His shoulders dropped, and he exhaled, sheepishly looking to his hands again.

"So, is *that* it?" I repeated, moving toward the stairs. "I need to lay down."

"Fine." Now it was Dane's turn to use the ambiguous *fine.*

I heard the door close behind him as I retreated to my room.

～

STARING AT MY BEDROOM CEILING, I wished for a complete redo of the day. A redo of the week—no, the month. The headache was gone, but a heavy weight sat on my chest. I returned downstairs, stopping to open the patio door before preparing dinner. My cell phone, which I'd abandoned on the kitchen counter since morning, reminded me of Pete's voicemail message from earlier.

I half-heartedly listened to his invitation to a cocktail reception and dinner. The excitement of his good looks and sweet personality had faded since the kiss with Dane, yet I shot a quick reply agreeing to accompany him, then drafted another message for Cami to check-in and reschedule my visit.

Even though I wasn't hungry, I fixed a salad. Carrying the bowl with one hand, I grabbed a pillow off the sofa, and slipped outside to the patio.

The sun still shone high in the sky. It illuminated the park below, casting a warm haze along the manicured bushes and flowerbeds. A humid breeze, thick with nature's scent, brushed against my cheeks. I inhaled deeply, desperate to find peace in the day.

I set the pillow against the brick wall to cushion my back and took a seat on the wooden planks of the patio floor. As I ate my salad, music from an outdoor concert flittered in the air. I glanced in the direction of Cathedral Park which hosted local bands on the weekend. My eyes caught Dane's empty patio before dropping down to the salad bowl.

Flowers and giggles. The little family next door. They are gone. I could hardly remember them—the woman and her young daughter—yet my heart seemed heavy at the thought that I'd never see them again. I wouldn't get the chance to say goodbye. Sighing, I dropped my fork into the bowl.

"Hey neighbor," Dane called from his balcony, which had been empty a minute ago.

"Hi," I mumbled.

"I knew it. You eat like a rabbit." Dane chuckled. He held a beer in one hand and a folding lawn chair in the other.

I rolled my eyes toward my bowl, not looking up.

Dane took a seat on his terrace. The metal poles of his patio fencing were a foot off from mine, offering a full view of his space, which meant he could just as easily see into mine.

"You're sitting on the floor?" he asked, pointing his beer toward my cushion.

"No, my chair is just really tiny. And invisible." Now I rolled my eyes at him.

The corner of Dane's mouth twitched up. "Fine. I was gonna offer you a seat, but enjoy your tiny, invisible chair."

I focused on my salad.

"Can we call a truce? Be friends again?" he asked.

But I hardly heard the words. A black flash from the park diverted my attention. I set the bowl down, and then pushed with the palms of my hands to leap to my feet. Goosebumps rose along my forearms, and I shivered, even though the outside temperature had to be over eighty degrees.

"Did you see that?" I whispered, leaning over the edge.

"What?" Dane looked from me to the park across the street.

"Over there." I pointed toward the northeast corner. My heart pounded. Tingles shot up my spine, and moisture dampened my neck. "What is that? A raven?"

"A bird?" Dane asked, cocking his head.

I turned on my heels, abandoning Dane and our conversation as I rushed out of my apartment and into the hallway. Flying down the stretch of doors to the exit, I took the stairs two at a time, nearly tripping as I jumped to the landing.

I pushed through the side door. The sun blinded brightly above—blinding like the lightning the night of the accident. I shielded my eyes, just as I did when I saw the driver and that woman.

Neal's face, his eyes widening before the darkness took over. The solemn, sad eyes of the woman by the telephone pole.

Dane called from above, but I ignored him.

An unnerving sensation. Feather-soft touches.

Memories of the accident rang in my head as I crossed the street and stopped under the arched wrought-iron gate. The sun's rays splattered the crisscrossing pathway that led from each corner of the park to the middle where the water fountain sat.

I drew in a gulp of air before moving from under the archway, a mix of anxiety and fear bubbling in my stomach. Bushes lined the fencing and flowers filled the space, making it hard to see the farthest corner from ground level.

But from my patio above, I saw *it*. I felt *it*, seemingly following me.

Hushing my fears, sheltering me as my eyes fluttered closed.

Something tugged at my hand, and I screamed.

"Nova!" Dane's hand wrapped around my bicep as concern creased his brow. "*What* are you doing?"

"A bird—" I stopped. "There was..."

I pressed at my temple with shaky fingers. My breath came out in heavy puffs as I shook my head.

"Please, tell me what's going on?" Dane asked softly. His concerned eyes shone as blue and wide as the sky.

I nodded but didn't speak. If I did, I knew the tears and

composure I desperately clung to would break free. Dane wrapped his arms around me, and I sunk against his chest. He pulled me closer, and I trembled from suppressed fear and confusion.

"You're okay," he murmured into my hair. His hands stroked my back until the shaking stopped. I pulled away, but Dane kept his arms around me. "Let's go upstairs."

I let him guide me across the street, up the elevator, and back into my apartment. Beelining to the patio door, my feet remained planted inside as I looked out to the park.

Dane gave me silence and space.

"You'll think I'm crazy," I whispered.

"No, I won't," he promised. "What happened?"

My hand curled around the edge of the door. I scanned the park. Dane came from behind. I not only heard his steps, but I felt him—the tingling sensation of his nearness.

"I think I'm going crazy," I whispered again. Dane's arms came from behind, and he gently spun me around.

He shook his head. "No. No, you're not. You're just shaken up. What happened? Just now—and earlier today?"

I traced the gash at my forehead, and then Dane's finger followed suit, gingerly trailing over it.

"The night of the accident..." I looked down to my hands. "The doctors said I must have had a guardian angel watching over me. But it wasn't an angel." I met his eyes. "It was death."

NINE

Dane took a step back, and I closed my eyes.

He thinks I'm nuts. I sound nuts.

"It's stupid. Just a silly feeling—"

"No, it's not," Dane insisted, reaching for my hands. "You had a close call, Nov. That was a nasty accident. Don't be so hard on yourself." His thumbs stroked over the fat part of my palm. "I know what near death feels like. When I was active duty, I was an infantry guy—a grunt. I've been there too."

I looked up at sincere eyes probing mine. Fresh tears sprouted.

"It wasn't just the night of the accident. I've had dreams, nightmares." I stopped, not wanting to even think about the horrid images and menacing sensations that had come alive in the last week. "A few nights ago, this morning, and now at the park... I can't shake this feeling that something's following me." Tears trickled down my face, and snot dripped over my lips. I used the edge of my tank top to swipe my nose.

Dane pulled me into his chest while his hand wove into

my hair. His gentleness only made me cry harder.

"I don't know what's going on," I choked the words into his shirt.

"You're safe now, Nova. It's okay. We'll figure it out." His lips pressed into my hair.

Dane waited until the quivers settled, and then he released his hold. I inched back, eye-level with the tears and snot that soaked his shirt.

"I'm sorry," I groaned. If the ground opened and swallowed me at that moment, I'd thank it for saving me from my mortification.

"This is what we're gonna do," Dane said, taking control. He pulled me to the couch and tugged at my arm until I sank into a cushion. "First, we're going to stop apologizing to each other. And then we're gonna get some *real* food. Okay?" He nodded, and I found my head bobbing along.

"I need to shower, and—" I gestured toward my tear-streaked face when he cut me off.

"Take a shower. Take your time. I can hang out here until you're ready." He patted the armrest, then motioned toward the television. "Did you cancel cable yet? I haven't gotten to watch TV since I moved in. Take your time, Nov. I'll be right here."

WITH THE WATER temperature turned to hot, I scrubbed my scalp, desperate to wash away the ominous feelings and dark ideas in my head.

It's leftover shock from a horrible accident. Post-traumatic stress.

I knew I had to move on, to let go, but until I found out

what happened to the woman and the other driver, I feared the unsettling thoughts would continue to haunt me.

The hours surrounding the accident slipped in and out of my memory, just like my consciousness after impact. Images would float to mind, then evaporate before I had the chance to absorb them. The woman's face. The driver's eyes —which in my muddled memory had morphed to my brother's. The darkness that took over. The fog. The fear.

After impact, I'd fought to keep my eyes open. My vision was too fuzzy to focus on any one thing. But through the haze, I felt it.

Death.

Maybe it hadn't claimed me, but what about the young woman? She stood next to the pole, right where my car had landed seconds after I spotted her.

I didn't have the courage to read the police report or ask about her status. Maybe my conscience needed that closure.

Shutting the water off, I stepped out of the shower and quickly towel-dried my hair and body. The bruise above my eye had all but faded, now a yellowish smudge, and the glue had finally made its way off. I pictured it washing down the drain, wishing it would have carried along those horrid thoughts.

One closet was located within my bathroom, holding my casual clothes, while the other in my bedroom kept my professional wardrobe. The old Nova certainly had a lot of extra spending cash based on the extent of her designer apparel.

My fingers stroked against the buttery fabric of a pale pink cashmere sweater. Its seven-hundred-dollar price tag still hung from a sleeve. I had thought I deserved such luxury. Now it only evoked guilt. Life was so much more than fancy cars and designer clothes.

You'll be tempted, Novalee, but profit and gain aren't worth the forfeit of the soul.

"What have I done, Aunt Lu?" I whispered, pinching the edge of the price tag. Somehow, I knew the question wasn't referencing my affinity for haute couture.

Pushing it to the side, I plucked a long tank top from a hanger and pulled leggings from one of the shelves. I slipped into them and gave myself a once-over in the mirror before exiting the bathroom. Peering over the balcony of my lofted bedroom to the living room below, I found Dane stretched across the sofa. His head rested against a thin accent pillow while his feet hung off the opposite armrest.

"I didn't figure you for reality TV," I called from the stop of the stairs.

"Seriously? It's just getting good—see that girl, the one with the big boobs? She slept with her best friend's ex-boyfriend. I'm pretty sure there's gonna be some hair pulling and drink throwing any minute," Dane teased. He sat up and glanced over. "I don't know how you do it."

"Do what?" I asked from the landing.

"Make everything look sexy." His eyes flashed from me back to the TV screen.

I didn't reply. What could I say? He'd drawn the line—we were *friends*—and as far as I knew, friends didn't call friends *sexy*. I exhaled, then moved in front of the television, blocking his view.

"Dane," I said with a sigh.

"Hmm," he murmured. His eyes again flickered over me.

The plain sleeveless tank fell mid-thigh. I'd seen girls wearing the same shirt as a dress, but I paired it with black leggings. Hardly a sexy look, but Dane's expression said otherwise.

"Let's go," I suggested.

He stood up, and his large frame soared over me. When he looked down, his gaze was so intent, so focused, he felt centimeters away.

"I need to make a quick stop at my apartment to change my shirt before we go."

The tears and snot. A fresh wave of mortification blushed my cheeks. I silently followed him out of the apartment.

After our quick stop at Dane's, we stepped onto the city sidewalk. Music from the jazz band still flittered through the air. I suggested we walk to Cathedral Park where we could catch the last part of the outdoor performance and check out the food carts that lined the square.

Dane kept a safe distance on our walk. The deliberate space eased our strange tension. He asked about my family just as we passed Juneau Street. I was glad for the distraction.

"I'm a twin," I offered—the easiest answer of my complex youth. "Our Aunt Lu raised us, although she's not really our aunt."

"Twins? Every man's fantasy!" Dane's eyes twinkled, and he suggestively wiggled his eyebrows.

"Dane, eww!" I gave him a playful punch to his bicep.

He chuckled. "Seriously though, there's *two* of you running around?"

"My twin is a boy. A brother," I explained. "Neal."

A smile still tugged at his lips. "I can't picture a dude version of you."

The music grew louder as we neared the park, and I hummed to the distinct sound of the saxophone. Growing up, dance and music had centered my world. Along with ballet, I'd learned to play the violin and harp while Neal reluctantly took on the cello. He'd begged for a drum set, eventually winning the battle by getting a guitar.

Clusters of people walked in varying directions, coming and going from the numerous bars and restaurants that littered our neighborhood. We passed DiSuro's Italian Restaurant, the location of my last real date—the disastrous ending to my relationship with Beck.

"This place is amazing." I nodded toward DiSuro's door. The date may have gone sour, but the food was always fantastic.

"I was thinking we'd eat outside?" Dane shrugged his shoulders. "Although I do love pepperoni pizza."

"I'm more of a sausage girl." *Well, that sounds bad.* I shook my head, waving off any innuendo. "But I meant for future reference, you know, being new to the area and all. They have amazing pizza and pasta."

We maneuvered through a throng of people lugging coolers and picnic baskets. One of them held what looked to be a large bakery box, probably a birthday cake. I had a twinge of jealousy.

In my twenties, even with work being hectic and demanding, I maintained a great network of friends. Our group seemingly drifted apart as we entered our thirties, many marrying and starting families, while another part got more wrapped up in their careers. Just like me, work took over. Now, without that, I felt more than a little alone. Lost.

No friends. No family. Only Cami and Neal, but I didn't even know where he was these days.

If I weren't so lucky the evening of that terrible accident... if my guardian angel had looked the other way... if I had died, how long till the memory of me is forgotten, wiped away? No one to mourn my loss. No husband, no children, no legacy to leave behind.

"So, tell me about Neal. Does he live around here?" Dane asked.

"I think he's somewhere in California." Sadness coated my voice. "Let's just say Neal and I might look alike, but that's pretty much where the similarity ends."

"You don't know where he is?" Dane cocked his head. "I thought twins had some weird twin-bond thing? Feeling each other's pain and stuff?"

"We did, when we were young. Neal and I kind of grew apart. Aunt Lu—" I stopped, not wanting to evoke long-buried, complex issues. But maybe talking about it would relieve the guilt. I knew I needed to reach out to my brother, to rekindle our relationship.

The warped vision of Neal, his face behind the wheel of the car that almost killed me, I needed to put all ghosts to rest.

"Aunt Lu, the aunt who raised you..." Dane offered. I realized I'd stopped walking. He watched as I gave a limp smile and began to move toward the square.

"She wasn't our biological aunt, but she raised us," I explained. Cathedral Park stood before us, and I again stopped walking, looking off into the distance to Saint John's —the church that anchored the square. "She met us when we were just a few days old. Abandoned newborns." I gestured toward the building. "That's Saint John's. I'm not religious, really, but I come here sometimes—when life seems a little chaotic, a little off. It's calming."

Dane looked to the domineering church, taking in the expansive stained-glass windows and towering steeple.

Saint John's was located two blocks from Loft and Associates. The rare times I had a free lunch hour, I'd drop in, appreciating both the silence and peace that instantly washed over as I stepped through its tall, carved wooden doors.

"Aunt Lu was—" I stopped, unable to conjure words to describe her, my head still not working right following the accident. Memories were too fuzzy to form solid, congruent thoughts in my mind. I searched, but her memory ebbed from my reach, like swimming to the shore with a current pulling me back.

"She's gone?" Dane asked quietly.

"Yes. She passed away when I was in college." I glanced to Dane. "Neal and her were my only family. I don't know where Neal is these days. The only other person tying me to my childhood is my friend Cami. I was walking to see her this afternoon when I saw that... that *bird*."

Dane nodded, urging me to go on.

"Maybe I should go see her." My voice came out sad and small.

"Your friend? Cami?" Dane attempted to piece together my chaotic chain of thoughts.

"Aunt Lu—" I hesitated. "I should visit Aunt Lu. Her grave." I stared absently at the church, hardly noticing Dane's arm that had snaked around my waist.

We stood, gazing at the cathedral while pedestrians maneuvered around us. Something warm settled over my shoulders. Warm like the sun, like a blanket. Like a prayer. I felt its strength traveling through my body, up my spine, bringing me taller, as if pulling me closer to heaven itself.

I released a breathy sigh—the kind I'd usually make when finishing yoga or a good workout. Looking up at Dane, I gave a small smile.

"Let's get dinner," he grinned back and jutted his chin toward the row of food trucks.

The breeze carried a whiff of barbeque. Dane claimed I

ate like a rabbit; I'd prove him wrong.

We each ordered the rib platter from Smokey Sam's—an iconic vendor in Milwaukee. Anyone who'd spent any time in the city knew Sam. At closing time, the long-retired original owner walked Brady Street, selling smoked sausages from a cooler. People claimed he had gone senile.

Dane, against my wishes, handed over a cluster of bills to the clerk and took the two heaping plates. Spectators and diners packed both the park and blocked-off street. I suggested we grab an open space on the curb—not the most ideal place to enjoy ribs—but Dane motioned to an occupied picnic table. The young man seated at the end stood up upon our approach.

"You guys leaving?" Dane asked politely.

"Yes, we are." The guy glanced over to his companion who appeared confused as she still chewed. "It's all yours." He collected his plate and plastic cup and offered the space. His lady friend reluctantly followed suit, looking stunned.

They had walked several feet away when she nudged his arm and scolded him. "I was still eating!"

Dane smiled. "Ah, young love."

We ate our dinner in companionable silence as the band took their intermission. I glanced to Dane. Barbeque sauce smudged the corner of his lips. I smiled into my plate. There was no way Beck and I could sit through a meal like this. Beck ate pizza with a fork and knife—barbeque sauce would give him a panic attack.

A mountain of soiled napkins later, we finished. Dane licked his fingers, making obvious sucking noises, then peered at me.

"Ah, she really does eat!" he delighted. His hand reached over to wipe sauce from the corner of my cheek, and his finger lingered. "Messy stuff, huh?"

My stomach fluttered. How could a simple gesture feel so... seductive?

The band regrouped just as I tossed the final bone onto my plate. Smooth jazz soothed, and I tried to suppress a yawn.

"Should we head back?" Dane asked. "You look tired."

"Sorry, I have to admit, I am. But they just started playing again." I motioned toward the music. "I don't want you to miss out."

Dane gave an absent wave of his hand, then stood and collected our plates and the pile of napkins. I followed him to the large plastic blue bins where he tossed them away.

"Why don't you go see your Aunt Lu?" Dane said, ushering me toward the sidewalk.

"My car's totaled." I took a deep breath. "Guess I could get a rental."

Dane stopped walking. "I'll take you."

"That's nice, Dane, but you don't have to keep proving how right *your* aunt is," I joked lightly. The offer was tempting. The accident was still too fresh, and I dreaded getting behind the wheel again. "Besides, it's not a quick trip. She's buried outside of Chicago."

"Well, that's perfect." Dane rubbed his hands together. "My territory includes Chicago. I was planning on taking a drive down there to get a feel for the route. Let's make a deal. I'll take you if you agree to come with me for some meet and greet thing next Thursday."

"Meet and greet?" I asked.

"Yeah, some cocktail-hour thingy. Networking, blah, blah, blah." Dane gave a slight eye roll. "Not my thing, but I gotta go."

Thursday. My stomach flopped.

"At Bar Continental?" I asked, although I sensed the

answer.

Dane nodded.

"I'm going." I sighed.

"Oh." Dane paused and cocked his head. "Good, we can go together then."

"With Pete," I clarified.

The small jerk of Dane's head was so slight, I'd almost missed it. He continued to walk, and the companionable silence from earlier was now replaced with an awkward, obvious quiet.

We passed the Metro Mart—the store where Dane had offered to carry my bags and invited me to bake cookies. He had a way of pulling me in and then casting me out.

Now he seemed to be reeling me in again.

"Well, as your *friend*," Dane broke the silence, "I think Pete seems nice. My offer for Chicago still stands. How about Tuesday?"

"Dane, you don't have to do this," I said.

"I want to," he replied firmly. "I want to help you."

"Why?" I couldn't help but ask. Being new to town, I could understand his desire for friendship, but offering to take a near stranger to visit her dead aunt's grave seemed beyond the normal, neighborly scope.

Dane again stopped walking. Turning toward me and leaning in, he studied my face. His eyes dropped to the freckles at my collarbone, making my cheeks blush, before shifting back up. "You went through something traumatic. I just want to help. I've been in your shoes before. I get it. You're looking for something. Answers, closure, peace." He shrugged.

Answers, closure, peace. He hit the nail on the head. I wasn't sure how he knew—before I realized it myself—how desperately I sought all three.

TEN

Pre-accident, yoga was my outlet when life seemed unsettled. Cami had gotten me hooked on the practice in my early twenties, at a time when I struggled juggling college, internships, and relationships. She always looked out for me, like a big sister, somehow knowing I'd need a healthy way to ground myself.

Since I still wasn't up for an in-person class at her studio, Sunday morning I streamed a session on my laptop. I finished with a breathing exercise, sighed breathy and content, then lifted from the carpet to switch off my computer and push the coffee table—which I'd shoved against the wall to make room—back into place. Dropping onto the sofa, I shot Cami a quick text, then headed upstairs to shower and dress.

As my foot hit the top step, the suitcase came into view. Still occupying half my bed, still bulging with power suits and matching pumps from the London project. I knew I needed to unpack it. It'd become the elephant in the room, signifying life pre-accident. The "me" I used to be. And maybe I wasn't ready to say goodbye to her just yet.

Peeling off my clothes, I whispered, "Baby steps."

After a quick rinse-off and change of clothes, I returned downstairs with a notebook in hand and fresh determination.

"Baby steps," I said firmly, staring out the patio door. Cautiously, I pushed it open and stepped outside, holding my breath as I waited for something ominous to pop out. Chatter floated from the park below and emerald-green leaves rustled in the warm breeze.

Flowers and giggles.

Like the memory of Aunt Lu, the image was there and gone. Try as I might, I couldn't recall it.

"Baby steps." I repeated the mantra, sighing as I tossed the notebook to the floor. A freshly sharpened pencil had been tucked into its metal coils.

"You again," Dane called over from his patio. He plopped onto his lawn chair with a beer in hand. "Can't get a second away from you, can I?"

I grinned back, giving a small wave.

"I asked yesterday, but you were still mad at me then. Now that we're friends again, can I please get you a chair? Your tiny, invisible one just looks so uncomfortable."

"I will not take your chair, Dane," I replied.

"You won't be; I have an extra." He stood up. "I'll be right there."

The knock came a minute later. Dane stood outside my door with a folding chair in one hand and a six-pack in the other.

"Here." He handed them over. "I'll be right back."

Seconds later, he breezed through the open door with another chair in hand.

"Yes, sure, come on in," I teased.

"Thought you'd never ask." Dane smiled coyly. He

carried the chairs to the patio while I followed behind with the six-pack.

"I normally don't drink this often," I said after he'd taken a seat, popped open two beers and handed one over to me.

"That's funny because I normally don't drink this... *little*." He clinked his bottle against mine. "To *friends*." Dane nodded toward the abandoned notebook. "Writing?"

"I have so many things I need to sort through. I need to find a job. I need to reach out to Neal," I explained. "And I want to write memories of Aunt Lu. She's been gone so long I can hardly picture her." I glanced over to Dane. "I miss... I miss my family. I guess I'm feeling a bit guilty."

"Why would you feel guilty?" Dane's eyes softened. They could change from sarcastic to silly to serious with a blink.

"Near death experience? I don't know. I can't make sense of anything. It's been so long since I've thought about Aunt Lu and even longer since I've talked to Neal. Since the accident, I feel like I need to reconnect."

Dane looked out to the park, then back. "When did Neal move away?"

"It's been fifteen years. He didn't even come home when Aunt Lu died." I stopped as my voice cracked.

An unwilling tear traveled down my cheek, and I brushed it off. The old Nova rarely—*never*—cried. Decades of holding it in, and now, since the tears started, I couldn't seem to turn them off.

"Sorry," I said into my bottle, taking a slug.

"Don't apologize. As hard as it is, grieving, those emotions—they're necessary." Dane reached out but then drew back his hand, snaking it around his beer. "I'm glad I'm here, that I get to go with you," he said more quietly.

"I'm glad I get to be the one to help you find closure. Or whatever it is you may be looking for."

Dane's phone buzzed from within his short's pocket. We both flinched, startled by the sound.

"That'd be the pizza. Half pepperoni, half sausage. I took your suggestion to try DiSuro's. And, I remember you're a sausage girl." He winked, then popped up from his seat and glanced over the balcony. "Yep, they're here. I'll be right back."

He slipped out of my apartment, leaving me to once again question his intentions—the mixed signals. The kindness in his voice and sincerity of his actions felt more intimate than neighborly friendship.

I didn't know why he wanted to keep things platonic when we both knew there was something more. An undeniable chemistry, an indescribable connection. Being with him felt too right to be wrong.

Dane and I finished the pizza and six-pack while watching the sun set. Under a silver moon, we talked until nearly midnight. Sweet and simple, intimate yet innocent, it was the best non-date—or date, for that matter—I'd had. Throughout the evening, we kept our distance. No lingering touches or glances. Yet forces beyond our control continued to play, drawing us closer.

Dane helped me gather the plates, pizza box, and bottles before he left. With the bag of trash in hand, he stopped just short of the door, turning around and tilting his head. He studied my face, then said, "Tonight was..." He trailed off, but I knew what he was going to say.

Tonight was perfect.

I knew because I felt it too.

The evening went beyond sharing pizza and a sunset. Beyond a silver moon. Beyond an undeniable connection.

Something happened over the course of a few days, something that led this stranger to become more than a neighbor, more than a friend.

Dane departed with a soft, regretful smile, leaving me to fall asleep wondering why he held reservations. We both wanted more, so *why* was he fighting it?

ELEVEN

I lay in bed the next morning, mulling over Dane's intentions when my cell ignited. Pete's name flashed on the caller ID, and I sighed. Instead of sending him to voice-mail, as I'd done numerous times, I tapped the screen and connected the call.

"Morning Nova. Did I wake you?" Pete politely greeted.

"No, I'm up," I replied, pushing upright in bed.

"Oh, good. I'm on the train, on my way to Milwaukee. Are you free for lunch tomorrow? I have a break in my schedule around noon."

"Tomorrow?" I closed my eyes. "Sorry, Pete, I'm heading to Chicago tomorrow."

"Chicago? I'll be there, and you'll be here." Pete laughed. "What's going on in Chicago?"

"Family stuff." I hesitated. Talking to Dane about my complex childhood was seamless, like chatting with an old friend. I hardly knew Pete.

"Oh." Pete sensed my reluctance. "Well, what about tonight? Maybe we can grab dinner?"

My mind flashed to Dane, our attraction undeniable, but he'd drawn the line in the sand.

Pete, on the other hand, was straight-forward and professional, no games. If he wanted a proper date, maybe I should give him a proper chance. Besides, I had already committed to joining him for the happy hour on Thursday.

"Sure. Where are you thinking?" I squeezed my eyes shut.

"Well, I'm fairly familiar with Milwaukee. Table Top Five is always good, and it's close to my hotel, but I'm open to suggestions."

"Oh right, if you're taking the train, you probably don't have a car? Table Top Five is perfect. It's just a few blocks away, so I can walk."

"You don't have a car either, huh? Has an adjuster spoken with you yet? Let me know if I can help with that. I know your car's totaled; I read the report."

The reference to the accident quickened my pulse. I breathed in through my nose, releasing it from pinched lips before asking, "You've read it? The police report?"

Before Pete could answer, I interrupted, needing to change the topic. "What time are you thinking?"

We firmed our plans for the evening before clicking off the call. I'd meet Pete at seven thirty, which seemed very late for dinner now that I wasn't working. How quickly I seemed to forget the demanding schedule of an attorney.

PUFFY white clouds and blue skies held no hint of rain, yet the forecast called for strong afternoon thundershowers. I closed the blinds and then dressed quickly, throwing workout shorts and a tank top on before lacing up running shoes. On this second attempt to visit Cami, I'd take the longer route through the city streets. And I'd remain on the sidewalk, no venturing off to explore. I wouldn't allow my imagination the opportunity to outrun me.

Earbuds pumped music into my ears, masking the hub of traffic and chatter of fellow pedestrians. I navigated down Ogden Street to Brady, turned onto Humboldt, then swung a left on Commerce Avenue. The route added a few extra blocks to my walk, but the presence of people calmed my nerves.

Spirit of the Sky Yoga's lobby smelled of tea tree and lavender. I instantly relaxed as I stepped through the entrance.

"Nova!" Cami squealed, hurrying from behind the registration desk to embrace me.

Cami had a youthful appearance with a rosy complexion and always-happy, yet intense, amber-brown eyes. They were staring squarely into my own, probing with a gentle kindness. Her thick hair was cut into a long bob. While mine could be considered beach blond, Cami's was *bleached* blond—a snowy white that would've looked highly unnatural on anybody else.

"Hey Cam!" I greeted, my voice enthusiastic but not quite as happy as hers.

Looking me over like a mother hen, she clasped my hands in her smaller ones. "You look so much *better!*"

After my last attempt to visit Cami, I'd sent a text asking to reschedule but didn't divulge the details of my panic attack. She worried enough about me, especially following the car accident.

"I am." I nodded. "I should be back in the studio next week. At least, I'm hoping to be. I've done some online classes in my living room. Feels good."

"So where are the promised cookies?"

"Oh. I, um, ate them all," I confessed.

"Look at you, baking! Honestly, I thought you were kidding." Cami giggled and dropped her hold on my hands. She tilted her head, studying me. "You seem... different?"

"Yeah, Cam, I feel different. Thankful to be alive."

The door burst open and a few people shuffled in. Cami looked down at her watch, then pulled me in for a quick squeeze. "I'm so sorry, but I have a class starting in a few. Maybe we can grab lunch? Tomorrow?"

"Oh, right. I have plans with my neighbor tomorrow. Another day?"

"Your neighbor?" Her amber eyes narrowed.

"My new neighbor." I smiled. "We have *a lot* to catch up on, but I don't want to keep you."

Cami's nose scrunched, like she was confused, but she gave a little shake of her head, brushing it off. "Oh, there's a professionals' cocktail event at Bar Continental on Thursday. I hope to make it, although I might be late. You should come with me!"

Of course, she'd be at the cocktail hour. Cami, the social butterfly, never missed those types of events. She thrived off other's people energy.

"Actually, I'm planning on it. I'll see you there," I replied.

I'd hoped to fill her in on Dane and Pete, but it appeared she'd be meeting both soon enough.

HAVING ARRIVED at Table Top Five a few minutes early, I ordered a gin and tonic at the bar and waited for

Pete. Just as the bartender set the glass down in front of me, he hurried through the door with his briefcase in hand.

"Hey." Pete grinned, settling into the stool next to me while placing the briefcase at his feet. "I was hoping to drop this off and change before meeting you, but my last appointment ran late. You know how it goes, I suppose. Is that a double?"

Taking a quick sip, I glanced at my drink. "Yes, and not to sound like a lush, but I need it. It's been a weird week. Weird month. Since the accident, everything's been... weird."

"Right." Pete's eyes rounded in sympathy. "You look great. How are you feeling?"

"Better, for the most part. Almost all healed." *Almost*.

"I know you didn't want to talk about it when we met last, but before you quit Loft, Darrell gave me a run-down of your situation. You know he needs to make someone pay. I think you might have a case against the construction company."

"The construction company?" I asked, absently running a finger around the rim of my glass.

"Yeah, and after digging a little deeper, I agree. It's a strong case. My buddy with the Milwaukee PD was able to get me an expedited copy of the police report."

The police report. I swallowed the lump in my throat as heat crawled up my neck. Now was the time to ask. To find out what may have happened with the driver and that woman. Put those ghosts to rest.

To heal, I needed the closure.

"About the report..." Pete's eyes were on mine, and he nodded, encouraging me to continue. "How is the woman?"

"Woman?" Pete cocked his head.

"By the telephone pole, where my car hit." My voice wobbled.

"There was no woman." His head gently shook. I found mine following suite.

"What about the car that side-swiped mine?" Neal's face flashed in my head, and I resisted shivering. "The other driver. How is he?"

"Other driver? There wasn't another car." Pete's puzzled tone and raised brow had my heart pounding. I looked down to my drink. "Nova, do you remember what happened?"

"No other car?" I repeated, my voice echoey and fuzzy. The sounds of the people around us—the clink of silverware and the bustle of waiters and diners—buzzed, growing as loud as a swarm of bees.

The noises around us pitched, jolting my vision as I tried to recall details of the accident. I squeezed my eyes shut.

A flash of lightning. Neal's stricken face. The woman's worrisome eyes. Touches as soft as feathers. A guardian angel.

"There was a lightning storm. I was side-swiped driving home from the airport," I whispered, eyes still tightly closed, "and I hit a telephone pole."

"No, Nova," Pete rested his hand over mine, and I finally opened my eyes to meet his curious gaze. "There was road construction at that intersection. The crew was required to put up flashing lights on the barricade, and they didn't. You swerved to miss it, and with the storm, you spun out. That's how you ended up hitting that pole."

I pulled in my bottom lip and dropped my eyes to my feet, focusing on my pedicured toes that peeked from my sandal. "It's in the police report? No woman? No other car?"

"No woman. No other car," Pete reiterated.

"No woman. No other car." I blinked.

"I can drop off the report tomorrow, if you'd like?"

"That's okay," I replied softly. "Thanks though."

"Are you okay?"

"Yes, I am." I downed the rest of my cocktail, and then slipped from the barstool. "Let's grab a table."

Pete closed our bar tab while we waited for the hostess to seat us. Weaving through the restaurant, I tried to let the thoughts of the accident slide away. The gin dulled my aching nerves, yet I couldn't help but think something was wrong. *Terribly* wrong. Every time my mind wandered to the accident, I pictured Neal and that woman.

The rest of our dinner passed with laughs and good conversation, even though questions about the wreck lingered in the back of my head.

I had to admit, there was an undeniable attraction to Pete, which only confused me further, and my unsettled head certainly didn't need any more of that.

Pete rode with me in the cab, then had the driver wait while he led me to the double doors at the entrance of my apartment building. Standing beneath the flood lights, my stomach grew nervous as our awkward goodbye played out.

Perhaps sensing my hesitation, Pete leaned in and placed a gentle kiss on the side of my cheek. "I never thought I'd be thanking Darrell Loft for anything, but I'm glad he gave me your number."

Pete's smile softened the boyish features of his cute face. He was kind, smart, and handsome. When I looked at him, I could envision a perfect future. White picket fence, two kids, a dog. On paper, Pete was everything a woman could wish for. Safety, security, a good job. Clean cut and straightforward. Dane, the exact opposite, was a little rough around the edges. Silly, sarcastic, and spontaneous. Mysterious and exciting.

I should not have compared the two men, but they came into my life at the same time, making it impossible not to notice their vast differences. Pete, a sure thing, versus Dane, an unknown. For reasons I couldn't seem to decipher, I gravitated toward the latter, even knowing the risks.

Sometimes the unknown, while a greater risk, offered the greater reward.

Sometimes the risk wasn't worth the reward.

TWELVE

Tuesday morning, I opened my apartment door at the agreed upon departure time. Dane stood with his fist raised, ready to knock.

"Very punctual, Ms. Nixon. I'm impressed."

"Do you ever wear anything other than black?" I teased. He looked effortlessly cool with a black polo shirt and grey trouser shorts.

"I'm going for dark and mysterious." He chuckled, sweeping a thick forearm down his body. "Better than camo. You ready?"

Right. Dane had been in the military. Hard to remember with his shaggy hair and low-key, relaxed persona. I always pictured soldiers to be fresh shaven with crew cuts and serious, no-nonsense dispositions.

I followed Dane to the parking garage and was slightly surprised when he led me to a blood-red Audi TT. I'd fully envisioned him riding a Harley.

"Nice car," I praised, slipping into the black leather seat.

"Thanks. It was a present to myself. A gift following my last mission," Dane explained.

"Oh, right." I pulled at the hem of my blue silk shorts, adjusting to the buttery leather. "I think you might be the first Army guy I've met, in person that is."

"Soldier." Dane glanced my way, a smile tugging at his lips. "We're soldiers. But, yeah, I thought I'd feel a little guilty spending all that money. Nope, no regrets." He revved out of the parking garage.

"I had a Beamer. The Bermer Beamer." I looked out of the window, watching for traffic as Dane pulled onto the street. My fingers dug into my thighs. "This is my first time in a car since the accident. Well, except for the trip home from the hospital, but I was kinda out of it for that."

"Oh, good to know. I'll keep that in mind." Now he had a full-on grin, yet I noted true sincerity in his tone. "One of the reasons I bought this sucker is for its pick-up, but I'll be extra careful. Precious cargo and all." Dane glanced at me before checking his blind spots, using both the side and rear-view mirror, then giving an extra look over his shoulder before switching lanes. "Is the Bermer Beamer the car that got wrecked—wait, *what* is a Bermer Beamer?"

"The BMW I bought after a big project—the Bermer deal—with my bonus. Now all that money's sitting crumpled in a salvage lot."

Unlike Dane, I felt the guilt. So much money over the years spent on high-end clothes, purses, and a ridiculously priced car. Unnecessary extravagances. Aunt Lu taught me better. I should have done better. I *could have* done so much more.

You'll be tempted, Novalee, but profit and gain aren't worth the forfeit of the soul. I stiffened in my seat.

Dane turned on the radio, switching stations before

settling on country. His fingers tapped in tune on the steering wheel. I wouldn't have guessed him to be one for songs about honky-tonk bars and tractors, not with his urban-metro edge—the black clothes and the sports car were a stark contrast to cowboy hats and pick-up trucks.

"Country, huh?" I asked, curiosity getting the best of me.

Dane kept his eyes on the road, but I could see the corners of his eyes crinkling as he spoke. "Not my first choice."

"Oh, what is?"

He glanced my way before fidgeting with the buttons on his steering wheel, accessing his playlist through Bluetooth. Instruments sounded, a gentle teaser before picking up in tempo.

And then a rich baritone voice sang foreign words.

"Opera?" I cocked my head and suppressed a giggle. And here I thought country was farfetched. "Really?"

He enthusiastically nodded his head. "Not to brag, but I've been to nine out of ten of the largest opera houses in the world. Austria, two in Italy, two in France, Sydney, and the Lincoln Center—of course. Oh, and Russia. The Bolshoi may be my favorite. If only for the fact that it's survived wars, fires, and a revolution. I'm only missing Argentina, and that was due to unforeseen circumstances."

"Wow," I said under my breath, feeling quite uncultured. "You've traveled quite a bit then?"

Dane sneaked a look, catching my eyes before glancing to check the right-hand lane. The Audi moved like a knife through butter. "Yeah, the military is rough on a guy's personal life but great for adventures."

Army guy, right, almost forgot. No, *soldier*. I reminded myself.

"I can relate to having a job interfering with my social life, but definitely not on the adventures. I traveled a lot for projects, but even if I went someplace cool, I was given zero time to sightsee." I huffed, thinking of all the working weekends I spent in London, New York City, and San Francisco.

I didn't have a lot of stamps in my passport, but even when an opportunity to work abroad arose, Loft kept me so busy I hardly had time to eat, let alone explore.

All work and no play. My prior life never seemed to belong to me, never my own.

"Honestly, I can't think of the last time I took a personal trip. A real, honest-to-goodness vacation," I said, my voice a bit deflated.

I leaned back, racking my brain, pulling up a series of flights, schedules, hotel rooms, and rental cars.

"Oh my gosh, Dane." I looked at him wide-eyed. "I've never had a vacation! I'm thirty-three years old, and I've *never* had a vacation."

Dane chuckled, shaking his head. "Well, now that you're voluntarily unemployed, maybe you'll have the time?"

"Yeah, except I'm also now voluntarily *not* receiving a paycheck."

"There are lots of ways you can do it on a budget. Trust me, the military isn't that generous when it comes to pay." He glanced to the GPS screen on the dash. "Hey, can you plug in the address? We'll be crossing the border soon."

THE TWO TOWERING, limestone pillars at the entrance to Saint Rita Cemetery loomed with the clouds. Dane pulled to the side, allowing the car behind us to pass. I stared at the life-sized, marble statue of the cemetery's namesake saint.

"Saint Rita." Her name slipped out in a whisper. I watched a bird land at the base of the monument. It plucked its beak into seeds that must've carried with the wind, then hobbled back. As if sensing my eyes on it, it looked up. I didn't know it was possible to make eye-contact with a bird, but our gazes locked. Several seconds passed until it severed the connection, jerking its little head toward Dane before taking off.

As it flew out of sight, I released an anxious sigh. Unlike the ominous black birds that had scared me witless with their shrill caws, this little bird was silent and unassuming. Even so, it left me unnerved.

Dane placed his hand over mine. "Are you ready to see her?"

I solemnly nodded. "Follow this road. When it comes to a fork, we take a left and go straight until we see the Mother and Child statue. You can't miss it; it's massive."

Dane maneuvered back onto the path and followed my directions to the impressive statue. Seeing it again took me back to that day, when wind and rain whipped my cheeks, and I stood, feeling more alone than I thought imaginable, burying the person who may not have given me life, but gave me light. A home, history, devotion. A woman who loved me like a mother when my own was taken so young.

We stepped from the car, and an intense sense of shame consumed me. I could hardly picture Aunt Lu, her face a black hole in my memory. Since the car accident, many of my memories seemed blurry, as if looking at an out-of-focus picture.

Tears already swam in my eyes. I wordlessly walked

down the trail of headstones, counting to the third, stopping at Aunt Lu's.

Edmund Pearson, Loving Husband and Father

I took a step closer, studying the words.

"It's the third headstone," I said into the air, then spun around to check the one behind me. "No, it's on this side." I ran ahead, reading plot names as I made my way down the row. "Something's wrong."

Dane caught up to me, taking my elbow and turning me into him. Tears trickled down my cheeks, and my breath caught in my throat. I couldn't meet his eyes.

Humiliation and fear mingled in my belly, churning so violently I thought I might be sick.

"What's wrong?" His eyes were soft and wide.

I closed mine, desperate to pluck images from the day I had said my final goodbyes. All I could muster was the vulnerability of the moment, feeling utterly alone, as if the world itself had turned on its axis and changed. The innocence and security of childhood had been stripped away along with Lucille, my mother-figure.

I eyed the statue. Aunt Lu's final resting place should have been three headstones away. *Mother and child.*

My stomach twisted. The cemetery suddenly felt so strange and foreign, I couldn't trust my recollection. I squinted at the statue, reaching for it with an outstretched hand, reaching for the shaky memories...

An end to your innocence, your eyes will be opened. Humanity will challenge you. Choose wisely child. You'll be tempted, but profit and gain aren't worth the forfeit of the soul.

Aunt Lu's words illuminated in my blackened memory like a shooting star in a dark sky. It was the last advice she'd given before she'd left me, before my whole world *had* turned on its axis and changed.

Next thing I knew, I was hunched over, dry heaving into my knees.

~

THE DRIVE back to Milwaukee stretched on in uncomfortable silence. I kept my jaw tense and my fingers clenched into tight fists in my lap. My mind worked feverishly to understand my muddled memories.

Dane glanced my way every so often, his concern palpable. Even worse, his obvious pity. He put on classical music, turned it low, and gave me space to decompress. Halfway through the trip home, I groaned. It just kind of slipped out.

"Nov?" His eyes remained on the road. "You want to talk about it?"

No, I don't, my inner voice pouted. I didn't want to talk about the two hours we spent searching headstones or the near-breakdown I had as I desperately tried to remember one of my life-defining memories.

Opting to change the subject, I said, "I just remembered, we were supposed to stop at that bar. You were going to deliver some sample bottles."

"It's no biggie. Are you hungry?"

I shook my head back and forth.

"I know you're—" Dane snapped him mouth shut. He gave an assured, gentle smile. "You're upset, but we'll figure this out."

What was there to figure out? I knew the spot, the *exact* spot. Saint Rita's Cemetery. The Mother and Child statue. Three markers. There was *no* figuring it out.

"When we get back, check your records." His voice trailed off, and he remained silent for a few minutes before offering a last piece of advice. "Don't be so hard on yourself, Nova. You suffered a serious accident, a severe concussion. You're not yourself. I may not know you well, but I know you well enough."

Again, silence consumed the car. It wasn't until we pulled into the parking garage that I offered an explanation.

"Thing is, I don't have anything else to go on. No records, except my birth certificate. Everything else is gone. I was only nineteen when Aunt Lu died. I lived in Milwaukee, was in college at Marquette—I didn't have a car. I had to take the train to get to her funeral. An auction house came and cleared everything away. Maybe it was my own way of grieving, just to let go, forget, and move on. I have nothing tying me back to her. I have nothing tying me to my family."

And then, for the umpteenth time, I cried in Dane's arms.

THIRTEEN

The next afternoon, I yanked open the suitcase and began pulling out its contents. After the last few weird days, facing the luggage felt miniscule. As I sorted through the clothes, making separate piles for donation and laundry, I found it surprisingly therapeutic to put that part of my life to rest.

By late afternoon, I had the emptied suitcase tucked back in to my closet, a garbage bag ready for Goodwill, and a vow made to never, ever wear a suit again. I then canceled cable, meditated in the living room, checked in with the insurance company, and reviewed my finances.

The busy work kept my thoughts off Aunt Lu and the trip to Chicago, but as night fell, my mind wandered back to her. I sat at my desk, nervously strumming my fingers over my computer keyboard. Why couldn't I find her grave? The one tangible link to my family was nonexistent.

I'm wrong. My head's messed up. The wreck caused some serious damage to my long-term memory recall.

If only I could contact Neal. To my knowledge, he never owned a cell phone. My last email to him years ago had bounced back as *user unknown*. He'd not only stopped responding to my messages, but had closed the account, destroying our final link in communication.

I doubted Neal had social media accounts or an online presence, not with his vagabond, off-the-grid lifestyle. Regardless, I pulled up Google and typed his name. Nothing populated.

"Where are you, Neal?" I whispered, leaning back into my chair, absently gazing at the computer screen. Last I knew, he was in California. I had received a postcard around our shared birthday—the first one we'd spent apart since birth.

The postcard! I'd kept it, cherishing his words, not knowing they would be the last he'd write to me.

Popping up from my desk, I searched my closet, finding the small, floral-printed box tucked away on the highest shelf. Instead of getting my desk chair, I stood on tip-toes and swatted at the box, watching it skid sideways with each jab until it inched over the edge and fell to my feet. The lid popped off, and its meager contents spilled out.

I gathered the measly reminders of my childhood and clutched them like precious jewels. Aunt Lu died before digital cameras and email were prevalent, and she didn't waste money on frivolous things such as film and stamps. There were only a few pictures of Neal and me.

As I flipped through them, memories flooded my head. The outside of a house, rose bushes lining the driveway. Neal and I wearing plain dress clothes and wide grins. Then I came to a weathered postcard, its edges rubbed raw. On the back of it was Neal's handwriting, his first message after hightailing it out of my life. *When the sea goes still, you'll find me here, singing under a half moon bay.*

Tears leaked from my eyes. My brother, filled with so

much soul and spirit, wanted nothing more in life than to write songs and strum his guitar. Aunt Lu would have none of that, pushing him to do more, to *be* more. In the end, he followed his free spirit, leaving me alone to pick up the pieces.

I set the postcard aside and unfolded a fragile sheet of paper that was covered with my own sprawling handwriting.

When Neal took off, I sorely missed his soulful words and angelic voice. I'd written down the lyrics of a song he frequently sang to me. After he left, I didn't want to forget them like he'd forgotten me.

Now, those words—the lyrics that were once my lullaby —stroked my sad soul. I allowed the memory of my brother to fill a space that had been vacant for way too long.

When the sea goes still, you'll find me here
Singing under a half moon bay
When the stars lose their shine,
you'll find me here
Singing under a half moon bay
Singing a song so sweet, as sweet as the fruit,
the fruit of the land
Singing a song so bright, as bright as the light,
the light of the sky

I softly sang the words out loud. And for the first time in years—since Neal's abrupt departure—I *felt* him. A sadness that seemed to connect us over countless years and miles.

And somehow, I knew he felt me too.

FOURTEEN

Thursday afternoon, as I stretched and twisted during a session of yoga in my living room, my cell pinged. I finished the video, grabbed a glass of ice water, and sat on the couch to listen to Pete's voicemail message.

He'd laid out a detailed agenda for our evening date, including the cocktail hour at Bar Continental and dinner to follow at a new Italian restaurant. Pete had back-to-back meetings lined up for the rest of the day and wasn't sure he'd have the chance to check in again. I shot a text back, suggesting we meet at the bar once his last appointment wrapped up.

Pete's voicemail drove home another fine distinction between himself and Dane. While Pete ran by a well-ordered schedule, Dane seemed more impulsive, as exhibited by his multiple last-minute invitations to me.

Dane would be at the cocktail "thingy" as he called it. Everything slid off him so easily. His cool persona, the ease in which he moved, like he didn't have a care in the world. Or, at least a care that couldn't be cured or masked with alcohol or a joke.

I was bound to run into him tonight. Part of me flushed from embarrassment. I'd made a fool of myself one too many times in front of Dane.

But an even bigger part of me tingled with excitement from the idea of seeing him, being near him.

Uh oh. This isn't good. I needed to set thoughts of Dane aside, and quick. Tonight was for Pete. I should give him an honest chance.

Later, as I pulled a designer dress from my closet, my thoughts again wandered back to the two men. Dane, dark and sexy with a mysterious edge, carried himself with assurance and a protective stance. Being former-military gave him a dangerous vibe. On the other end of the spectrum lay Pete, the all-American boy next door, possessing a classic handsomeness. A well-educated professional who seemed more at home in a suit and tie, or polos with chinos.

Running a hand along the shiny black chiffon skirt of my chosen cocktail dress, I brushed away those thoughts. I couldn't—*I shouldn't*—compare them. I pulled the dress on, slipping the straps of the silk tank over my shoulders. The hem of the skirt floated around my legs, skimming my calves and showing just enough leg to be considered appropriate for a summer cocktail hour with colleagues.

Ex-colleagues. I swallowed the instant lump that formed in my throat. Associates from Loft were certain to be at Bar Continental.

By five forty-five p.m., I had my hair twisted into a neat chignon, my make-up set, and my patent-leather clutch packed. Uncomfortable, but sexy, strappy heels waited by the front door. I padded barefooted down the steps to the kitchen and poured a splash of wine into a glass.

Moving to the patio, I carefully balanced the

chardonnay as I pulled the sliding glass door open. I had at least fifteen minutes until I needed to call for a cab.

Dane's voice carried from his own balcony. "Yeah, well things are a bit more complicated now. No, you didn't explain that."

Although I was still hidden within my apartment, something about his tone had me taking a step back.

"This was supposed to be an *easy* job, that's what you said. Well, I have it on good authority there's another agent in town." I couldn't see him, but his voice grew angrier with each word. A different side of Dane emerged as I continued eavesdropping on the one-sided conversation. "Lots of shit going on. I have that thing tonight. Yeah, I'm keeping an eye on her. Pretty easy considering the proximity."

Another agent? Keeping an eye on her? I put a hand over my lips. *Pretty easy considering the proximity.* Did he mean *me*?

"No, she doesn't know a thing."

My heart thudded, and I took another step backward, but my trembling hand caused wine to slosh over the side of the glass. I grabbed a towel from the kitchen just as my phone lit with a text from Pete.

"Shoot," I mumbled, dropping the towel over the wet stain on the carpet. I snatched my phone from the countertop and quickly read Pete's message. His meeting was wrapping up and he'd be to Bar Continental shortly.

Slipping the strappy heels on with one hand, I grabbed my clutch with the other. Hurrying out of my apartment, I locked the door then pivoted around in such a rush I didn't notice the dominating second body in the hall. My face smacked into a tower of muscle.

"Whoa!" Dane laughed, his eyes twinkling from a wide grin. "In a hurry?"

I peeled myself from his chest. My heart pounded, and a tingle shivered over my skin—now caused by anxiety instead of desire.

I'm keeping an eye on her. No, she doesn't know a thing.

I nodded, unable to find my words.

"Where's Pete?" Dane pointedly looked over each side of my shoulders.

"I'm, um, meeting him there."

"Ah, on your way now?" he asked, motioning toward the clutch. I nodded in response. "Me too. Wanna share a cab? Mine's here." Dane waived his phone, flashing his confirmation from Uber.

"That's okay, I, uh..."

"Everything all right?" His eyes softened. "You okay? Hey, I hope you don't feel weird about Tuesday, really, Nova."

Dane's entire face transformed—the sharp edges rounded with compassion, his head tilted protectively toward me—and my fear quickly faded. I'd spent most of the last week with him, and other than the yo-yo signals, he'd shown nothing but kindness and compassion.

Why would overhearing a private conversation make me think something sinister? Maybe "her" referred to a competitor?

I shook my head again, looking more and more like a bobblehead. Forcing myself to make eye contact, I smiled. "Sorry, yes, sharing a cab would be great. But my treat this time."

Dane gave a firm nod, took my elbow, and guided me into the elevator where we stood side by side. I caught his appraising glance in my peripheral.

"You look stunning, as usual," he said softly.

I bit my lip. Having no good read on him, I couldn't

distinguish between friendly chatter or flirtatious vibes. We exited the building, and Dane's hand again went under my elbow as he led me into the waiting cab.

Minutes later, the taxi pulled up to the curb outside of Bar Continental. We easily could have walked. *Well, not in these shoes.* My heels clicked along to match Dane's stride as we entered the crowded lounge. I recognized a few faces, nodded and smiled, but made no effort to mingle. No, then I'd possibly have to explain why I'd left Loft.

What would I say? The truth? A near death experience made me realize being unemployed was better than working my life away for a jerk boss, and I wanted more from life.

"So, where's Peter?" Dane leaned in, his warm breath tickling my neck. He turned to fully face me. "Can I get you a drink while we wait for our *friend?*"

"White wine, please," I replied flippantly.

Dane strutted to the bar. I took the opportunity to check my cell. Pete should've been here by now. He'd messaged that he was on his way, and his hotel was practically attached to Bar Continental. I sighed, wishing I was anywhere other than here.

Maybe I'll feign sickness. But Dane was to my side seconds later, two drinks in hand.

"Your wine, madam," he said, giving a slight bow as he handed over the stemware. He straightened, took a sip, and nodded toward my clutch where I'd hastily stashed my phone. "Any word from our friend?"

"He's on his way—" my voice faltered as the air suddenly thinned. An instant dizziness had me leaning into the strength of Dane. His free hand flew to my waist.

My pulse pounded. Heat flushed my neck and cheeks. I closed my eyes as the background chatter seemed to amplify.

"Are you okay?" he asked.

The feeling that had just rocked my body quickly disseminated with the sound of his voice.

It's a panic attack, Nova. Breathe. Breathe through it.

Taking a step away from Dane, I fought the urgent need to flee. I started to open my mouth to reply, but a gruff voice sounded from behind.

"Well, well, well... if it isn't Dane *Kill*-bane."

Dane turned slowly, his eyebrows rising as he responded in a surprisingly annoyed tone, "Big, *bad* Liam. I heard you were in town."

"Did you?" Liam replied. The man wasn't extraordinarily tall, but he stood with a confidence that seemed to add a few inches. The stubble from a few missed shaves—not quite a beard, but beyond a five o'clock shadow—along with his eyes, which had narrowed to slits, gave him an indignant air.

They didn't shake hands, instead they eyed one another. Tense silence hung between us as we stood in a jagged triangle. Dane's hand remained protectively under my elbow.

I smiled awkwardly, then offered my hand. "Hi, I'm Nova Nixon."

"No-va," Liam said, enunciating my name in the same manner Dane had at the Metro Mart. He cocked his head. "Dane, you speak Spanish, right?" Not waiting for an answer, he then turned to me. "Sorry, Miss Nixon, it's a pleasure to meet you. Dane and I are... old friends, work in the same field."

"Tequila?" I asked dubiously. Although, this might be the mysterious agent Dane had referenced in the call I overheard. Sales reps certainly had come up with creative, benign names—ambassadors, guides, advisors—to overcome their pushy stigma.

"Something like that." Liam's tight smile remained planted firmly in place.

"Liam and I worked together—"

"We *still* do, Dane. Don't forget that," Liam interrupted before giving a final nod to Dane, tipping his glass toward me. "Miss Nixon, enjoy your evening." He walked away, leaving me more confused than before.

Several quiet seconds passed before Dane shrugged and grinned, diffusing the strange tension. "Well, that was weird. Sorry about Liam. I heard he might be in town. He's a bit rough around the edges, but a decent guy. We kinda hit a snag a few years ago. Friendship hasn't been the same."

"Yeah." I gave a forced laugh. Glancing over Dane's shoulder to catch a final peek at the mysterious Liam, I noticed the large clock located on the bar's far wall flanked by smaller clocks baring the time of various cities around the world.

Central time zone read seven fifteen p.m.

"I should check if Pete's messaged. Do you mind?" I handed my glass to Dane, then fished in my clutch for my cell.

"Ah, pokey Peter, losing points for tardiness." Dane smirked, blinking rapidly, as if holding my glass was a taxing favor. I shot him a look—the raised eyebrows, shut-it type.

The only message was from Cami, who was on her way. I slid the cell back into my handbag.

"Ten minutes. He gets ten minutes, and then I'm leaving," I declared, snatching my glass from Dane. I brought it to my lips, tipped it back, and sucked it dry. "Mind getting me another?"

"Of course." Dane spun and made his way to the bar. I watched, appraising his broad shoulders and muscled arms as he reached across the bar to grab a napkin. Fabric stretched over his thick bicep. I still didn't know what his tattoo was...

I'll show you mine if you show me yours.

Who should appear to sour my flirty thoughts... none other than sugary-sweet Lori, sauntering up to Dane and batting her eyes like a lost kitten. Before I realized it, I was between them, cutting Lori off mid-screech.

"Thanks, Dane." I smiled sweetly at him, lifting one of the two glasses set in front of him, and jutting my chin to Lori. "Oh, excuse me."

Lori glared back, sneering through gritted teeth. "Dane, I'll see you tomorrow. Looking forward to it." Her eyes flashed pointedly to me before she pranced away.

"Lori, was it?" I asked sweetly, sipping from the wine. "Hot date lined up?"

"Something like that." Dane sighed, then glanced over my shoulder to the clock. "Any word from *your* hot date?"

With a clenched jaw, I slugged my wine. *How humiliating.* Not just being stood up but being stood up with Dane in the audience.

Just as embarrassment threatened to engulf me, there Pete was, standing across the lounge and scanning the room. I gave a little wave when his eyes roamed over the bar area. He nodded back with a wide grin.

"Well, well. Speak of the devil." Dane eyed him, then returned his focus to me.

Pete was to us seconds later. "Nova, I am so sorry. I sent you that text then got wrapped up in a hell of a call." He brushed back his hair, then loosened his tie.

"No prob, Pete. I've kept your date well occupied."

Dane smirked. "You look like you need a drink. What'll it be?"

Oh no, this is not turning into a date with a third wheel.

Pete politely nodded back. "Thanks brother. Hey, have we met?" He extended his hand. "Pete Mackroy, with Carbondale. You with Loft?" He noted Dane's puzzled expression. "Nova's firm?"

Dane seemed to assess Pete's hand before firmly shaking it. "Dane Killbane, Nova's neighbor." He swiveled in his stool and gave a nod. "Well, I should go mingle, I suppose. I'll leave you two to it. Nova, Pete, you kids have a nice night."

He walked away, muttering under his breath, "And I'm *not* your brother."

"Right, your neighbor. He was at the coffee shop. Is he always that pleasant?" Pete's eyes crinkled as he joked.

But an overwhelming urge to defend Dane slipped from my lips. "Actually, he's wonderful."

Pete's smile froze. Uncomfortable seconds passed before we slipped from the bar and moved to the far end of the room where a few of his colleagues had congregated.

"I'm surprised I haven't run into anyone from Loft," I said, trying to rekindle the conversation with Pete. He'd barely said a word since Dane's departure.

"Yeah, well, I think they're working late tonight," Pete replied off-handedly. He sipped at his cocktail, then paused. "Hey can you hold this?" I took the glass from him as he pulled out his cell. He scanned the message, his eyebrows twisting and his lips flattening into a tight line. "Nova, I gotta go. I'm really sorry. This night is definitely going to shit. Can I call you a cab?"

"That's okay, Pete. A friend of mine is stopping by, so I think I'll stay a bit. Hope everything's okay?"

He replied with a shrug, "We'll see... Okay, I really got to fly. I'm sorry. I'll call you tomorrow."

The night was still young, but besides a quick hello to Cami, I had no desire to stay. I scanned the crowd for her, but instead found Dane immersed in conversation with the ever-present Lori. Although tempted to again interrupt them, I opted to save face and leave. He didn't need to know just how poorly my date had gone.

I pushed through Bar Continental's glass doors. July's sticky breeze kissed my cheeks. The sun was starting its descent, hanging over the horizon like an orange creamsicle.

So many thoughts swam in my head, but in that moment, jealousy from seeing Dane engrossed in conversation with Lori overwhelmed everything else.

Leaning against the railing of Bar Continental's wide concrete steps, I closed my eyes for a minute, thinking back to the kiss Dane and I shared a few days earlier. His lips would forever be seared into my memory. Like fireworks, an explosion, he ignited something in me I couldn't extinguish. Even with the arm's-length approach he tried to maintain, I had a feeling he was as bewildered by these uncontrollable feelings as me.

If I'd thought starting something with Dane was a bad idea before, now I knew. He'd be my downfall.

I should stay away, but like a moth to a flame, I couldn't seem to resist. Spinning on the heel of my strappy sandals, jealousy swept me up the stairs and back into Bar Continental to look for him.

As I neared the bar, I spotted a familiar crop of near-white hair. I must've missed Cami when I scanned the room before. Her bob had been curled into loose ringlets, looking like the swirl of soft-serve ice cream and contrasting with her deep summer tan.

Approaching, I stopped in my tracks as the figure behind her came into view. The man Dane had introduced me to, *big bad Liam*, spoke heatedly to a clearly frazzled Cami. Her chin tilted defiantly as she began to step away, and his arm shot out, firmly grasping her elbow.

"Cami!" I exclaimed, the need to protect her rushing with urgency from my lips.

Both sets of eyes snapped from one another to mine, and Liam's arm fell away.

"Nova," Cami spoke calmly. Her eyes shifted from me to Liam and back again to me. "Hey, girl. I'll meet you at the bar in a minute." She turned her back on me and reengaged Liam.

Ignoring her instructions, I remained planted in place, curiously watching their exchange. Liam gave a firm nod to Cami, then looked over her shoulder to me, giving me the same nod, clearly his way of bidding farewell.

Cami shook her head as she turned away.

"Everything okay?" I asked when she reached my side. "Who's that?"

"Liam?" Cami's voice came out small, no hint of her usual spritely tone. "Oh, yeah, don't worry about him."

"Seemed kind of heated?"

"Liam operates at one level—intense," Cami said. She sipped her drink. "He's, uh, an old friend, helping me with Celia."

"Really? Is he a PI or something? Think he could help me find Neal?"

"Trust me, you don't want his help." Her amber eyes narrowed with warning, causing my brows to rise. When she spoke next, her demeanor reverted back to her usual chipper self. "I tried to call you; I can't stay long tonight."

"I was about to leave, but..." I trailed off, feeling silly

about my surge of jealousy at seeing Dane talking with Lori. Peeking around the room, I didn't spot either of them. Did they leave together? He could start something with her, but not me? I sighed, certain my face had turned an ugly shade of green. "I'm ready to call it a night."

"Let's get out of here." Cami linked arms with me.

We remained silent as we waited for a cab. It wasn't until we were safely tucked inside that she turned to me with a small smile.

"I do have some news on Celia." She smoothed her skirt, then nervously picked at the hem. "There's a lead I need to follow up on. I hate to leave you so soon after the accident—"

"Cami, that's great. Don't worry about me. I'm feeling pretty good actually." Cami had been searching for Celia for years. I didn't want her fretting about me when she had greater fish to fry.

"Yes, well, hopefully if I actually find her, she'll talk to me." She stared ahead, watching the cab driver as he turned onto my street. "That guy you saw me with—Liam—he's, um, well, I don't think he'll be in town long, but wherever he goes, trouble seems to follow."

Big bad Liam somehow knew both Dane and Cami. The coincidence seemed beyond strange, but after the crazy few weeks I'd had, I wasn't the best judge. Both Dane and Cami's reaction toward Liam led me to not question her opinion. He was bad news. Before I could ask her more, her arms were around me, pulling me into a tight hug. She was like a dose of hot chocolate on a cold day; she warmed my soul.

"I won't be gone long." Her arms loosened, and I leaned back. Worry etched her perfect features, and her amber-brown eyes clouded with caution.

"What's going on, Cam?"

"Nothing I can't handle. Stay safe, sweet friend."

As soon as the cab carrying Cami pulled from the curb, I felt her loss like a security blanket being yanked from my shoulders. Vulnerability had me spinning on my heels and digging out the key fob for the front door.

I stopped to grab my mail from the row of mailboxes in the entrance, then stepped further into the lobby to wait for the elevator. The door creaked open, and Mrs. Cooper, an elderly neighbor who also lived on my floor, stepped out.

"Hello there, dear," she said. A fluffy, white kitten was clutched to her chest. "I was hoping to run into you."

"Hi Mrs. Cooper. Who's this little guy?"

"Oh, this little princess is Nellie." She looked adoringly at the kitten and nuzzled her chin into its furry head. "Can you help me a minute? With my mail?"

"Sure, of course." I took the key, which dangled from Mrs. Cooper's knotted fingers, and opened her bin. A few large envelopes had been stuffed so tightly into the box that it took a few strategic wiggles to free them loose without tearing into the edges. I could see why Mrs. Cooper would have difficulties, especially with her arthritic knuckles.

I helped Mrs. Cooper into the elevator, listening half-heartedly to her ramblings, and a pang of guilt stabbed my heart when she spoke of Jasper, the cat she'd recently put down. Everyone on our floor knew how much she adored her feline friend.

"Lots of changes around here, dear," Mrs. Cooper said, unlocking her apartment door. She leaned over to set Nellie down, then looked toward Dane's unit, glancing to the newspaper pile that had once again accumulated at his doorstep. "That young man is such a gentleman. He's been bringing me my mail every day, but he must not be home today." She shook her head and kneaded her swollen fingers as she stood upright. "He brought me homemade cookies. Even ran out to buy me creamer yesterday when I told him I was out. Such a nice boy." Her wrinkled face lit in a smile, and her eyes twinkled. "Everything is going to be fine, just fine."

Mrs. Cooper took the pile of mail from my hands and thanked me before shutting the door behind herself. With the sound of her lock clicking into place, I moved toward my unit, but stopped outside Dane's door. For all I knew, he was still at Bar Continental, chatting up Lori with her sugar-syrup voice.

Or maybe he'd gone somewhere else with her, back to her place.

Clenching my jaw, my mind raced down jealousy lane. I took a deep breath and decided it was time to shift gears. Both times Dane and I had run into Lori, he appeared annoyed by her which was easily accomplished with her garish nails and high-pitched voice. I couldn't fault Dane for Lori's interruptions, especially when he didn't give any hint of interest toward her.

After hearing all the kind deeds Dane had done for Mrs. Cooper, I had to agree with her sentiment. Dane was a good guy. The concern and care over the last few days—not just for me, but old, sweet Mrs. Cooper—showed his true colors.

Actually, he's wonderful. I'd said it myself.

My jaw relaxed as I stepped away from Dane's door, but the address label on the paper caught my eye.

Mirabel Merano.

Of course, her name is Mira. An image of the young woman, inky black hair and big brown eyes, came and went, along with a resounding memory... *Flowers and giggles.*

FIFTEEN

The next morning, as I lifted into a side plank, my left hand reached toward the ceiling. I attempted to regulate my breathing and my thoughts.

Big breath in... hold... big breath out.

The buzzing of my cell nearly had me toppling over, my mind obviously not in the exercise. Scrambling to my feet, I grabbed my phone from the coffee table. The leasing office for my apartment complex flashed over Caller ID. Swiping across the screen, I breathily mustered a greeting into the mouthpiece.

"Ms. Nixon?" a chipper voice asked. "This is Holly from East Point. Just a friendly reminder your rent was due on the first."

"Shit," I muttered. "I mean *shoot*, sorry. It totally slipped my mind. I know it's no excuse, but I was in an accident a few weeks ago and everything's been a bit out of order since."

"Oh, wow, I hope you're okay?"

"Yeah. I'm much better. I'm so sorry; I'll get the check to you right away."

"No problem, it happens. I would have called you sooner, but we've had issues with our accounting software and manually tracking these payments has been a mess. I'll waive the late fee if you can stop by with a check today. The office is open until five, otherwise there's the drop box outside."

"I'll be over in a bit." I ended the call with a promise. The leasing office was located in the adjacent building, an easy walk over.

Grabbing the checkbook from inside my desk drawer, I glanced at my copy of the resignation letter to Loft before hastily writing out July's rent. I'd always been organized, on top of things, but once again, the accident proved to do more damage than a knock on the head and a jolt to the ribs.

Another reason to pull yourself together. No more excuses, people have weathered far worse. Stop feeling sorry for yourself.

Firmly nodding in agreement with my inner voice, I slipped into flip flops and rushed out of the door.

Another newspaper had been added to the pile at Dane's door. Mirabel Merano must've had a daily subscription. I picked up the top paper to bring along to the leasing office. Perhaps they could contact her for forwarding purposes.

Exiting through my building's rear door, my thoughts wandered back to Dane. Why hadn't he picked up the other paper last night? Did he *actually* go home with Lori?

More importantly, why did that thought make my blood boil?

Nearly seething with jealousy, I pushed the glass door to East Point's office with more force than intended, causing the lady standing within to jump back a step.

"Sorry." I sheepishly smiled.

She glanced to the check in my hand, then to the newspaper in the other. "Are you Novalee? That was fast."

"Yes. I'm so sorry, and honestly, a little embarrassed this is so late." I held the check out to her. "While I'm here, I thought I'd drop this off. Can you get in touch with my old neighbor, Mirabel Merano? She needs to forward her paper."

"Mirabel Merano?"

"Yeah, apartment 204. They're piling up."

"Piling up? Is she on vacation?" Holly eyed the paper.

"Well, she moved out."

"She did?" She stepped back and turned toward the desk behind her. "I just got her rent check a few days ago. Funny, it was late too; she's always been as punctual as you."

"A few days ago?" Dane had been in the apartment for at least a week.

My stomach sunk as another wave of doubt crept up my spine.

Why would he lie?

"She must be on vacation," I said weakly. "Sorry, again, for being so late with my rent."

As I exited the leasing office, questions bounced in my head. Why wouldn't Dane tell me he was subletting? Was he lying? Or, there could be a simple, logical explanation. Maybe Mirabel moved for a job and her employer facilitated the sublet?

I didn't want to think something sinister was going on, but things weren't adding up and the possibilities had my stomach twisting in knots. The tense phone call I overheard, the odd conversation with Liam, and now this. I needed to clear my thoughts, so instead of retracing my steps home, I took the front walkway to the corner of Ogden and Cass

Street, then crossed the road to the opposite side where the park lay.

Following the crisscrossing pathway, I stopped at the center of the park, skimming my fingers along the smooth, stone surface of the fountain's basin. Water cascaded from the sculpture in the center—an angelic woman, face angled toward the sky. She held a bundle of grapes in one hand and a flower in the other. It reminded me of Neal's song lyrics I'd just uncovered.

When the sea goes still, you'll find me here
Singing under a half moon bay
When the stars lose their shine, you'll find me here
Singing under a half moon bay
Singing a song so sweet, as sweet as the fruit, the fruit
of the land
Singing a song so bright, as bright as the light, the
light of the sky

"When the sea goes still, you'll find me here, singing under a half moon bay." I sang the remainder of the song out loud.

"What'd you say?" Dane called from behind me.

"Oh! You scared me!" I exclaimed, clutching my chest. Avoiding him seemed impossible.

"What was that you just said?" he asked again.

"I don't know...song lyrics." I was already on edge and not feeling particularly chatty to offer a further explanation. "What're you doing here?"

"I saw you from up there." His chin nodded toward his balcony.

"Okay? You following me or something?" Before he could respond, I spit out, "Fun night with Lori?"

Dane's eyes widened then narrowed again. "Lori? Barely know that chick. She's annoying as hell. I need to talk to you."

"Actually, *I* need to talk to *you*." I wasn't planning on bringing up the newspaper, but he had me on guard. "Who's Mirabel Merano?"

Taking a step back, Dane sighed and rubbed his eyes. "What are you talking about?"

"The newspapers. They're addressed to Mirabel Merano, and according to the leasing office, she just paid this months' rent. She's still on the lease."

"Maybe I should be the one asking. Are *you* checking up on *me*?"

Now it was me taking a flustered step back. I hugged myself and looked to the fountain. "No, I was just in the office, and I asked them to—never mind, Dane. I have to go."

I couldn't explain myself further. None of it made sense. Besides, confronting Dane meant one thing—he'd been lying to me. I couldn't face that truth.

Rushing past him, I'd almost made it to the entrance of the park when his arm snaked around my waist. He pulled me against the solid wall of his chest. Within his hold, he twisted me around so my body was flush against his. Breathing heavily, either from distress or the nearness of him, I lifted my eyes to meet his. They sparkled and dark-ened. My chest heaved, and his gaze wandered down, settling on the trio of freckles near my collarbone.

"I don't care anymore; I don't have it in me to fight this." With his odd proclamation, he leaned down and captured my trembling lips with his own. His strong hands pulled me closer as he deepened the kiss.

As if sipping from my soul, his mouth drank from me, taking more and more until I was breathless. All my reservations and doubts slipped away, yet Dane's hand splayed heavily across my back, pressing me into him as if he were afraid I'd try to escape.

Finally, his grip loosened. Now it was me leaning into him, holding him tighter. My hands moved up his back and settled in his hair. Our lips no longer hungry and frantic, they began a slow, synchronized exploration. I no longer cared about a neighbor named Mirabel Merano or piled-up newspapers. I didn't care about Liam or agents. No, my only concern was the man who was kissing me and how his kiss made me feel.

Like heaven. Kissing him felt like heaven.

And like the gates guarding the kingdom above, my soul opened up to him, letting him in as I fully offered myself.

Just as I did, Dane pulled back. My eyes fluttered to meet his bewildered face.

"What are you doing to me?" he whispered into my still-parted lips.

What am I doing to him? The better question was, what in the world was *he* doing?

Neither of us had an opportunity to speak. A vibrating noise and pinging came from Dane's pocket, breaking the connection. He shook his head as if shaking himself back to reality, then stepped back and removed his phone from his pocket. Glancing at the screen, he slid a steady finger over the glass, then held it to his ear.

I looked down to my own hands, still shaking.

The person on the other end of the line was too quiet for my ears, but Dane's expression turned serious. His eyes narrowed, and his lips flattened into a firm line. My pulse quickened, now anxious from his somber vibe. He muttered a quick "got it" before ending the call.

"I have to go." His eyes lingered on mine as he searched my face. "We'll talk later."

Turning around, he walked away without further explanation, leaving me on the sidewalk wondering, once again, what the *hell* had happened.

SIXTEEN

E very time I closed my eyes, I relived our kiss. The memory pounded at my head like the migraine that hammered my skull following the accident. Once again, Dane reeled me in only to push me away.

The day stretched ahead, seeming long and heavy, and thoughts of Dane only added to the muddle. The confines of my small studio apartment suffocated me. Questions pinged off the walls, hitting me with a force that made me wince with each revelation. I could no longer deny it. Dane was lying to me. Something was up.

Tequila distribution. Agents. Mirabel Merano. Big bad Liam. Cami.

Slapping my palms against my bare thighs, I popped up from the white leather couch and grabbed my laptop from my desk upstairs before I lost the nerve. Punching the name Dane Killbane in the search bar, I waited impatiently for Google to run its detective magic. A page of results filled the screen, but none of the corresponding information fit Dane's description.

Dane Killbane Army

Dane Killbane Monterey

Dane Killbane tequila

Nothing. Each search result came up empty. There was no trace of Dane Killbane.

As if he didn't exist.

Holding my breath, I punched in Mirabel Merano. My finger lingered over the "enter" key before I released a sigh and clicked.

This time, a link for a Facebook account populated. My heart pounded with urgent caution as if I were about to discover something profound. I closed my eyes and waited a full minute before opening them again, blinking rapidly as the profile loaded. Two familiar faces grinned back at me from the screen.

Mother and child. Inky black hair. Giggles and flowers.

Similar to my memories of Lu, the thoughts of Mirabel and her daughter were too foggy to decipher, too far out of reach to bring to the forefront of my mind. I couldn't pinpoint it, but a deep sense of calm intimacy settled in my gut.

Although the memories were vague, I knew one thing was certain—Mirabel wasn't simply a random neighbor I'd run into in the hallway.

The rest of her profile was secure, but the profile picture was enough to pique my curiosity. I recognized the face that went with the mysterious name.

My thoughts switched back to Dane. Another mystery. An internet search should reveal at least one or two tidbits of the man. There had to be *some* digital footprint of him. I understood why I couldn't find anything on Neal—he'd lived the vagabond lifestyle since moving away at age nineteen—but Dane was a professional. There should be *something*.

Desperately wishing for more information, a small morsel to ease the confusion in my damaged mind, I returned to the living room to resume my internet sleuthing. Just as I lowered myself onto the couch, my cell phone ignited with a text from Pete.

Pete: I am so sorry for last night. I'll call you later to explain.

Instead of the much-anticipated apology from Dane, Pete was proving to be the more considerate man.

But he doesn't make your heart race. Not like Dane.

Hushing my inner voice of reason, I shot off a reply to Pete.

A few seconds later, the phone buzzed again. I assumed it was Pete, but instead, Dane's name flashed on the screen.

Dane: Sorry about earlier. Explain tonight. Dinner at my place.

No niceties, no asking if I was free for dinner. Did he just assume I'd come at his beck and call?

The difference between the two men vying for my attention grew glaringly obvious. Pete, eager and kind, versus Dane, who kept pulling me in only to cast me out. Again and again.

I wasn't giving in so easily this time. A simple sorry wouldn't suffice.

Me: No thanks. Busy tonight.

Dane: I'll have cake.

Me: Busy. Sorry.

Dane: Tomorrow?

Me: Busy then too.

My cell buzzed with a phone call from Dane, which I promptly sent to voicemail. A few seconds later, an indication for a new message pinged, and I chucked my phone to the sofa. My head hit the back cushion of the couch, and I winced.

Adding insult to injury, the migraine was back.

TENSION BUBBLED IN MY STOMACH; the mission at hand feeling strangely perilous. All I had to do was make the short walk to the Metro Mart, buy Tylenol for my pounding head, and make it back without allowing my nerves get the best of me.

The automatic double doors opened as I neared the entrance. Not bothering with a cart, I perused the produce department, stopping short at the bakery.

Unbelievable. Even with his back to me, I recognized Dane's formidable frame. It was as if the universe wanted to push us together. I shook my head, resolving to get this next encounter done and over with.

Dane looked up just as I approached.

"Well, well, now *who's* following *who*? I do believe *I* was here first." He grinned, nodding toward his basket which held a mishmash of groceries, including a six-pack of beer and a miniature frosted birthday cake.

"It's your birthday?" I asked, pointedly ignoring his obstinate question.

"Mm-hm. I told you there'd be cake. You didn't give me the chance to explain it's a birthday party." His tone was jovial, as if he'd completely forgotten about the scene on the sidewalk earlier in the day when he'd ditched me after kissing me breathless.

"A party?"

"Mm-hm." He picked up the cake and tilted it toward

me. "Offer still stands. My place at seven—I'll be grilling too."

"That's an awfully small cake for a party." I looked at the bakery box. Yellow and red globs of frosting created a bouquet of balloons, and a swirled Happy Birthday message was written along the bottom. The tiny cake could feed two to three people at most.

"It's an awfully small party. I'm new in town, Nov. I don't know *that* many people." His eyes were bright and mischievous. He set the box back into his cart and jabbed a finger at it. "That's buttercream frosting." His eyebrows wiggled.

"Let me guess, it's a party of one?" I *did* love buttercream frosting, but I wasn't about to admit it.

"Well, hopefully a party of two?" The smile that spread across his face was so sweet and sexy, I found the corners of my lips lifting as he reeled me in. *Again.*

"Okay. Fine. But only because it's your birthday," I relented. *Again.* "And you and I *will* talk."

"I'll even let you have the piece with the balloons. I can taste the frosting already." Dane smacked his lips and closed his eyes, making soft "yum yum" sounds. His eyes popped back open. "Do you have a lot of shopping to do? I'll wait and walk with you, although maybe I shouldn't... I'd hate to somehow put my foot in my mouth and end up losing my only friend again."

"More like put your mouth on my mouth." The words tumbled from my lips, and my fingers flew to cover my mouth. Based on the slight blush creeping along Dane's face, he wasn't expecting my call-out either. Finding his reaction oddly satisfying, I replied with a syrupy grin, "Actually, I'm just grabbing Tylenol for the whiplash you keep giving me."

Dane's eyes softened with concern. "Headache's back?"

"Yep." *Thanks to you.*

We continued walking, each looking ahead. When I stopped at the medicine aisle, I sensed his eyes on me.

"I am sorry for earlier," he said softly. "Not for kissing you, but for leaving. There's a lot going on behind the scenes... at work."

"Tequila distribution?" I watched his face intently for a reaction. As I suspected, the glint in his eyes faded, replaced by a guilty, sad smile. *He'd lied.*

If he lied about that, what else was he holding back? Who, exactly, was his co-worker Liam? And what about Mirabel? Things weren't adding up.

Suspicion and doubt traveled up my spine. He'd warned me over and over, yet here we were. I studied Dane's face, my heart sinking as I faced the truth. "Dane, is this a good idea?"

He peered down with solemn eyes. One of his hands gently brushed a loose curl off my shoulder. It then swept down my shoulder blade. "I'll explain tonight. Please, at least let me explain."

I found myself nodding in agreement. Just as he'd declared earlier, I also didn't have it in me to fight this.

SEVENTEEN

With the remainder of the afternoon to burn before dinner at Dane's, I busied myself with music and sunshine. The patio not only offered an escape from the confines of my apartment, but I hoped the fresh air would sweep away the fog of doubt in my mind.

Plopping onto the lawn chair with ice water and a notebook in hand, I started doodling along the edges of a blank sheet of paper. Light murmurs of the picnickers floated from the park below, making me feel less alone as I stared at my scribbles.

A Jarhead Junction album played from my phone, and I soon found myself humming along. My pen tapped against the paper. The next song began, and different lyrics sang in my head in tune with the slow ballad on my phone.

When the sea goes still, you'll find me here
Singing under a half moon bay
When the stars lose their shine,
you'll find me here
Singing under a half moon bay

Singing a song so sweet, as sweet as the fruit,
the fruit of the land
Singing a song so bright, as bright as the light,
the light of the sky

The song Neal had written long ago was one of his favorites to strum on the guitar and sing to me. The poignant words were a glimpse into his sensitive mind. I wished I would have enquired more about his passion, shown more interest in what drove the poetry he put to music.

Back when we were still close, I had asked about this song. His sad, soulful eyes darted to the crumpled piece of paper in his balled-up hands. Tossing it into the trash, he had explained, *"There are many stories that need to be told, but I have to be careful with my words, Novalee. This one, I wrote for you. It's part of your story. When it's perfect, I'll write it down again. Always remember, this one's for you."*

I didn't understand then, and I certainly didn't understand now.

The Jarhead Junction song ended just as my phone vibrated, scattering the memory of Neal.

I glanced at the screen. The promised call from Pete.

"Hey there," I greeted softly.

"Hey. Glad I caught you. I'm really sorry about last night—I'd like to make up for it. You free tonight?"

"Sorry, Pete. It's my neighbor's birthday today. I'm heading over there in a bit."

"Neighbor Dane?" he asked, then continued without giving me an opportunity to reply. "Do you and him have something going on?"

"I don't know." It was the most honest reply I could give.

"I don't want to pry, but how well do you know that guy?" Concern softened his voice, and my stomach dropped. Was Pete jealous... or did he sense something off about Dane?

Reigning in my thoughts, I replied in an almost defensive tone, "Well, I only met him recently, I mean, he just moved here from California. He doesn't know anyone else, and it's his birthday today."

"From California? What's he doing out here?"

"Yeah, Monterey. New job in tequila distribution. Think he just got out of the Army or something." Pete's line of questions had me doubting Dane further and further.

Pete hesitated, sighing before speaking. "You've been through a lot lately, and I don't want to see you hurt. You're a great girl, and he's lucky to get a chance with you. I hope he doesn't screw it up."

I smiled sadly, wishing in a way I felt differently about Pete. He was a sure thing—intelligent, considerate, honest, and straight forward. We had similar careers and mutual colleagues, commonalities which made us an ideal match.

Pete should have had me swooning, while Dane should have had me running.

But sometimes we have no control over who our soul seeks.

EIGHTEEN

As I raised my fist, ready to knock, I realized I'd arrived empty handed—no birthday card, no gift. The bottle of white wine in my other hand would have to suffice. Besides, Dane wasn't back on my good side quite yet.

Tonight would be a night of reckoning, birthday or not. He'd have to come clean on some of his half-truths. I came prepared with a list of questions in my head, most of which revolved around his job and how he'd secured the apartment. Maybe it was a sublet? If so, he should have known who Mirabel was and easily could have informed her of her ongoing newspaper delivery.

Deep inside, I felt Dane was keeping something from me. The logical lawyer part of me warned to take that gut reaction and run, but a bigger part of me—the woman part with heightened emotions and an undeniable sexual connection—lobbied for an explanation. There had to be a reason behind his little white lies. All I could hope was that they were made in good faith. The feelings I had for Dane were beyond my control. I wanted him, good or bad.

Something about him made me feel alive.

The door flew open, and Dane stood waiting. He looked at the wine, then threw out a casual, "Hey."

I offered the bottle and smiled. "Happy birthday."

"I have the SOLO cups ready," he joked. He took the bottle and stepped aside, allowing barely enough space to cross through the threshold without touching him. Sensing my reservations, he gently said, "Let's have a glass of this, and then I'll explain everything."

The moving boxes had been emptied and discarded. Minimal furnishings made his apartment appear larger than my mirrored unit. But similar to mine, no personal effects were on display. No knickknacks or pictures. I wondered about Dane's family, his upbringing, potential brothers or sisters. Unlike previous men I'd dated, I felt a keen desire to learn everything about him. We'd spent so much time over the last week together, but much of our conversations focused on the present versus the past, as if we both had secrets we were guarding.

Stemware had been set out, an upgrade from the promised SOLO cups. Dane uncorked the bottle and dispensed it evenly between the two glasses. Handing one over, his fingers brushed deliberately against mine. The current between us already had me feeling dizzy.

Dane held my gaze as he spoke. "Thank you for coming and for allowing me to explain. I've been a shit, and I know I don't really deserve this."

"Dane—"

"Let's sit. I'll start up the grill in a minute."

Nodding my head, I followed him to the sofa. The last time I was in his apartment, we sat opposite one another with me on the recliner and him on the sofa. Now, he sunk into the cushion beside me. Our knees touched, setting my skin on fire. Our chemistry was undeniable, if not palpable

—an electric current that crackled in the air, ready to explode by the slightest fuse.

My eyes shifted to the spot on my knee where we'd touched and remained fixated there when I addressed him. "I'm guessing whatever it is you want to explain... it's nothing nefarious. I mean, I just need to know there isn't anything shady going on, and then we can drop this, move forward. I need to know what your relationship is to Mirabel. I—" My voice faltered as a sudden wave of emotion rolled through me. "I knew her."

Dane's eyebrows rose at this admission.

"I don't know if it's the accident, the concussion, but some of my memories are a little foggy. But I know this, she was a wonderful person. A mother. She has a little girl. Do you know what happened to them?"

He sighed, leaning back. "Not really. I don't have details. My buddy set up this sublet. From what I heard, she got married and is spending time in Europe."

"Married?" Now that he said it, I remembered. *Mira had gotten married.* Of course. She was happy, content, *at peace.* Relief had me nearly sagging against the sofa cushion.

"She needed this place cleaned up and cleared out. Guess their trip to Ireland was pretty last minute. Mira had loose ends here, wanted someone to help Mrs. Cooper, keep an eye on her. She just lost her cat before Mira left, and I guess they were close. It was a trade-off; I'd help out around here, free of rent, until the lease runs out in October, and it gave me a break from California, new scenery before my next assignment."

Yeah, I'm keeping an eye on her. He was referring to old Mrs. Cooper during the conversation I'd overheard.

My mood turned hopeful as some of the ambiguity

began to clear. Yet, I had to ask, "Assignment? What exactly is your... line of work?"

A deep, troubled exhalation rumbled from Dane. He ran a hand through his hair. "That's a bit more complicated. This tequila gig is temporary, kind of a side job to pass the time until my next contract."

"With the military?"

"Never really bothered me, to drop everything for a mission... until now." Intense blue eyes bore into mine. "The truth is, my time here is limited. The offer to bring Samson's Tequila to the Midwest was an idea I threw out to help Sam expand. His shit is good, and I had free time to do something for him after all he'd done for me. All the hours I spent at his bar, drinking his liquor for free, never charged me, just thanked me for my service. I figured, what the hell, I'll see if I can drum up some business for him while I'm here helping my buddy with this apartment."

My time here is limited. He'd warned me before. Was that why he kept pushing me away? He was only here until the lease ended in October. My heart sunk, suddenly heavy by the idea that he could be leaving.

Reading it on my face, Dane leaned forward and took my hands into his own. I couldn't help but breathe in the subtle, intoxicating scent of his cologne mixed with wine as he spoke. "I tried to stay away, but from the moment I met you, you... you're all I can think about. All I want. And I can't walk away, not anymore. It needs to be you. Either we accept this—whatever it is—or we end it now. But I can't walk away. I'm putting the reigns in your hands."

I didn't need to reply with words; my body gave him my answer. Releasing his hands, I slipped onto his lap, and my mouth met his with the urgency of a starved man finding his bounty. We kissed feverishly, our mouths devouring each other's taste.

The pace changed abruptly when Dane's hands came to rest on my hip and at the back of my head. He broke away from our kiss, only to start again, this time slowly, deliberately working his way up my neck, nipping at my lobe before claiming my mouth once more. Now it was a sweet and purposeful exploration. The trail he left along my bare skin seared, passion lighting the flame that had started to flicker in my body the minute I had first laid eyes on him.

With every nerve ablaze, my body never felt more alive, as if my soul itself was set on fire.

His tongue swept along my lower lip, and I could no longer contain the breathy sigh that had built in my chest. Encouraged by my reaction, Dane reclaimed my mouth as his hands simultaneously claimed my body. His large palms cupped the sides of my hips, pulling me in closer so I could feel his erection, his body hard with need. Another sound escaped my lips, this time a groan that caused Dane to loosen his hold, and lessen the pressure building between us.

"Nova," he whispered into my hair. "I don't want to stop, but if we don't now, I know where this will lead."

Again, I let my body answer his unspoken question. I knew where I wanted it to go, and I was ready, regardless of the ambiguous amount of time we had left. Even if this was for only one night, he had ignited a desire that burned so bright, it felt like lightning striking through my veins. Blinding and scorching. I didn't know the outcome or what tomorrow might bring, and for the first time, it didn't matter. I wouldn't think things through or go the logical route. *I'd live*. I'd take what felt good right now, what I needed now, and live in the moment. Only heaven knew what the next moment might bring.

My blonde hair curtained his face as I hovered over him. His arms moved up my sides to sweep away the tendrils. He looked into my eyes, searching for my answer. I gave a resolute, firm nod, and he pulled me into him. His hands ran along the length of my back, then up my sides and into my hair. They wove through my tangle of curls and cupped the back of my head.

"You're more than beautiful. More than I deserve," he whispered before his lips moved over mine, then trailed down my neck. Feeling his need for me, I leaned back and pulled my shirt over my head to expose the lacy, red bra I'd chosen when dressing. Maybe it was a subconscious decision because the racy color and sexy cut pushed my breasts up and created a long line of cleavage screaming for his eyes' attention. Down they went, drinking in my body, devouring my skin. His mouth followed, tracing a path from my neck to my collarbone, where he stopped to gently kiss the trio of freckles speckling my skin. His fingers lingered over the back of my bra, hesitating for only a few seconds before unclasping it. I let the silk slide down my arms, and then gingerly plucked it away, leaving my upper body bare.

Never one to be ashamed of my body, I was surprised to find my cheeks flush as Dane's appraising eyes again got their fill. He took his time, studying each limb, each breast, every inch of skin, before returning to meet mine.

"Perfect." The hunger in his gaze and the honestly in his voice made my insides flip, my stomach flutter, my sex clench.

Next came my turn to explore. I grasped the sides of his T-shirt and pulled it upwards until his hands took over and he lifted it the rest of the way. A black lock lolled over his forehead, and I swept it away, my hand trailing down his cheek. He had strong features that only appeared harder from the thick tension between us. Strong and hard like the rest of him. My fingers wandered over his shoulders and to his chest, feeling muscles that had been defined by long hours in the gym.

A tattoo of a bow and arrow decorated his left pec. I traced it with a finger, and then kissed it. My eyes roamed to his bicep, and I finally saw the entirety of the one which I'd previously only been given a peek. Black, intricate lines twisted into a warrior's shield.

As my hands traveled lower, down his solid abs to the edge of his trouser shorts, his breath caught, and his weight shifted. He had me flipped onto my back and was hovering over me before I could react. One of my legs settled between his while the other wrapped around his hip. He pulled at my calf and pushed into me so I could again feel the strength of his hard body, the length his erection.

Our chests pressed skin to skin, limbs intertwined. He lifted his weight, but only to allow for his mouth to capture a nipple. I thought I'd melt, my insides turning to liquid as his mouth worked my body, giving it heavenly attention. My nails raked at his back, then moved to clutch his hair. I pressed into him, rubbing against his crotch.

"I need you." I didn't recognize the husky sounds coming from my own lips.

He looked up, an almost pleading look on his face. "Are you sure?"

A ghost of a smile graced my lips before I reached over and unbuttoned his pants, which he quickly slipped out of along with his boxers. He removed my stretchy yoga pants. I never wore panties under them. Inch by inch, my body was exposed as the fabric slowly slid over my hips and down my legs.

The sun had begun its decent, casting shadows along the living room. Even in the haze, I caught every expression of Dane's face as he lowered his body onto mine, entering me and filling me in a way that made me feel whole —complete.

An emptiness I'd lived with for far too long was filled by him, a man I'd known for only days.

A gentle curse slipped from his lips, his eyes meeting mine, and I saw the same look of surprise. He watched intently for a few seconds, not moving, just absorbing the moment, before he began rocking ever so gently. Each movement shot a current of pleasure through my body, the electricity in my veins building.

Our gazes locked.

"Nova," he commanded in a calm voice that betrayed the fury building between us. "Baby, I want you to come with me, but it's going to be soon. Can you do that?"

"Yes, yes." It slipped from my mouth in both a promise and a plea. I was nearly there myself. It'd never been this quick before, the journey to pleasure, to the top of the hill that I was about to tumble over.

Our bodies so in tune, we climbed together, our breaths and pace matching, synchronizing until we were at the top, hand-in-hand. I knew he was with me, as if he'd squeezed my hand at the edge of a cliff, encouraging me to jump alongside him.

We flew over together, catapulting to orgasms that burst like bombs within my body, within Dane's. The world seemed to detonate along with us. Lightning shot through my nerves, crackling the air around us, illuminating the darkened room. Next came the thunder, vibrating rumbles that groaned along with Dane and me. And finally, the aftershocks. Shudders that had my body trembling long after our release.

Dane held me until the tremors subsided. Loosening his hold, he whispered, "I don't know how or why, and I'll no longer question or deny it. You've taken me someplace I haven't been in a long time."

I understood what he meant, because he'd taken me there too.

A place that felt so good, so right, it could only be described as heaven. And if it were indeed heaven, then he was my salvation.

NINETEEN

We lay in a daze, each recovering from a moment of passion that had transported us away from Dane's tiny lofted studio in downtown Milwaukee. The storm that ravaged our bodies had transcended the walls of the apartment, evident by the steady rainfall pinging against the patio door.

Dane moved behind me and cradled my naked body in his own. His hand roamed along my side, stopping at my hip, just above the spot where a tattoo marked my skin. It reminded me to ask about his.

"I saw yours." I smiled, thinking of the warrior art on his chest and arm. I didn't know what they meant, yet they fit him.

"Hmm?" he murmured into my hair. His back was smooshed against the sofa cushions while I was cocooned in his body.

"I saw yours—the shield and the bow and arrow," I clarified. "Where your fingers are now, that's my one and only tattoo."

"Really?" This had him shifting. Try as he may to catch

a peek at my hip, two bodies sharing the sofa was too much. My butt began to slide away. Dane pulled me in and upright, so I was sitting on his lap. "Let's see. A Celtic knot. You're Irish? Any special meaning?"

"I, um…" I stumbled over my words. Was I Irish? I didn't recall Aunt Lu mentioning it. But the Celtic knot had meaning. It *had* to have meaning. Tracing over it with my finger, the ink beneath seemed to tingle. "I don't know."

With Dane's body so near, I could feel his chest expand and retract with each breath. It calmed my racing heart as I desperately searched my muddled memories. *It means something. But what?*

So deep in thought, I barely comprehended Dane's words.

"—not that I regret them. Maybe the one on my back—"

"I'm sorry." I shook my head. "What did you say?"

"Oh." Dane titled his chin. "The skin art. I got them all a long time ago, each after something that, at the time, seemed very important. Now, well, I guess they've become a part of me, of my story. Glad for some of them, except the one back here." His thumb hitched toward his back.

They've become a part of me, of my story. Again, the knot on my hip tingled as if agreeing with Dane's words. If only my broken mind could pull up these memories faster than the turtle pace it'd begun to operate at after the accident. I'd gotten the Celtic symbol well over a decade ago… a drunken night in college…

I must've tuned out again, because I soon found myself being gently lifted and deposited back down while Dane stood. He stretched his arms above his head, then leaned over to snatch his boxer shorts. I got a peek of the aforementioned tattoo that ran across his shoulder blades.

"Why not the one on your back?" I asked, studying the

intricate dark lines that swirled from each blade, meeting in the center to create a small lotus flower.

He paused before slowly standing upright. Turning to meet my eyes, he explained in a quiet voice, "You're not the only one orphaned at birth. I was born under... unfavorable circumstances."

My eyebrows knitted. The sympathy must've been evident on my face because Dane lifted his hands and stopped me before I could speak. "My childhood was wonderful. Don't feel bad. I wasn't raised in the muck I was born into."

"So why do you regret getting it?" I asked.

He inhaled through his nose, then slowly released out through his mouth, considering his words. Face tilted, eyes hooded, he spoke in a manner that took him away, as if revisiting a time or place far from here. "Because I haven't lived up to its symbolic weight." As soon as the words left his mouth, his demeanor instantly changed, and he returned to carefree Dane. "Let's eat. I'm starved."

Tucking away his words, I committed to a web search of the lotus flower later when I was back in my own apartment. It was obvious he didn't want to talk about it further, and I knew better than anyone that sometimes we needed a break from reliving the pain of the past.

"Want to order pizza?" I asked, glancing toward the patio where a steady stream of rain continued to fall. My attention then shifted to the pile of clothes that had been discarded. Shimmying first into my yoga pants, I then pulled my tee over my head. "Where's my bra?"

Dane's eyes twinkled as his lip turned up into a mischievous grin. "What bra?"

~

AFTER EATING PIZZA, drinking wine, and watching the rain, Dane led me upstairs to his lofted bedroom and onto the mattress that lay pushed against the farthest wall. No box spring, no bedsheets, only an olive-drab sleeping bag spread over a thin mattress. With no other furniture in the room, it pounded home the truth that Dane's time here was short. He hadn't bothered with unnecessary things that would only need to be moved again.

Dane's eyes locked on mine, consuming me as he moved to the space beside me, breaking his stare as his lips covered mine.

We spent hours discovering one another, connecting in a primal way with our bodies and in a mental way with unspoken words—in a way that transcended lust and desire. I no longer doubted him, who he was, or why he was here. His body spoke silent promises with each soft caress, each tender kiss, each gentle breath, tethering me in trust.

Finally, after our expended bodies collapsed in the wee hours of the night—or early morning—sleep came easily. I didn't care the next morning when I woke with morning breath. It didn't matter that my hair was so messy I couldn't even run my fingers through the tangled curls. The only matter of importance was the man sleeping beside me.

Studying Dane's face, I noticed the laugh lines around his eyes were smooth in sleep, although I could still see their slight impression. I liked them. They said he smiled a lot. Stubble dotted his jaw, and his black hair fell across his brow. I resisted touching him, although the impulse to brush away the lock had my hands hovering over his cheek before dropping back to my side. His state of sleep allowed me the opportunity to unabashedly watch him. I did just that, taking in and memorizing each feature of his beautiful face.

I could stare at him all day.

Dane shifted in bed, pulling me into him again, and my eyes quickly snapped shut. I attempted to regulate my breathing, pretending to still be asleep. His fingers brushed against my cheek, yet I kept my eyes closed. A test to see what he'd do next. Would he study me? Was he as fascinated by me as I was of him?

"Next time, Nova," he whispered, and when my eyes popped open, a devious glint lit his face. "Take a picture. It'll last longer."

With his last jab, I gave him a push, and in return his large palms reached out to tickle the sensitive skin below my rib cage. I giggled, gasped, and squirmed but was no match against his strength. He pulled me closer, continuing his tickle assault until I played dirty—planting a deep kiss on his lips. His hands went still, then he lifted me up and over him, placing my legs over each side of his torso.

"You are going to be the death of me, woman." He palmed my cheek. "You hungry? I'm starving." His eyebrows wiggled.

"Dane! Is that all I am now? Not even going to feed me?"

"Baby, I'll treat you to steak and lobster, but dinner isn't for a few more hours, and we have no time to waste. Breakfast in bed?"

No time to waste... My time here is limited... I froze as his words pounded in my head.

"Hey, don't think about that now." His teasing grin faded to a half smile. He ran his fingertips up my arms, then to my back where he pulled me into him so I was flat against his chest. His lips brushed against my forehead, and his heart beat steadily beneath my cheek. I relaxed into him. Dane stroked my hair, and then trailed his hands to my bare shoulders where he traced circles over my blades.

"I've imagined moments like this, but I sure as hell never thought I'd experience them. It feels... right." I didn't move, but my breath hitched at his whispery words. Raw, honest, and real. "I wanted you from the moment I saw you, something fierce, like nothing I've ever felt before. I think about you all day, all night. I find myself staring at your wall, wondering if you're on the other side. Wondering —*hoping*—you're thinking about me too. Last night I said I can't walk away, and I mean it. I'm not giving you up."

My chin lifted. "You're leaving. The lease is up in October."

"Come with me," he suggested simply.

Before I could read too much into the request, he had me flipped on my back with my arms pinned above my head. His eyes twinkled, obviously pleased by my surprised squeal, keeping me on my toes. His head bobbed down, catching my lips before he sprung away. "Let's eat."

BESIDES COFFEE AND CREAMER, Dane didn't have other breakfast foods on hand, so I suggested he come to my apartment. While the contents of my fridge were hardly robust, I knew I had at least a few eggs and a half loaf of bread to make omelets and toast. I left him to brew a pot of coffee, and returned to my apartment to freshen up.

My door clicked behind me, and I beelined up the stairs and into my bathroom. Splashing cold water over my pink cheeks, I couldn't stop grinning. I'd never cooked with a man before, besides baking cookies with Dane. I'd experienced more "coupley" things with him in the last week than I had with all my previous relationships combined. Other men in my life had been kept at arm's length. No sharing wine while watching the rain, no cuddling after sex, no cooking breakfast the morning after.

Over the course of the last—I counted quickly in my head—twelve days, Dane had slipped—*no, barreled*—into my life.

"Come with me." He'd put the offer out there, and while I didn't know the where or when, it still was tempting.

The clang of my front door shutting had me spinning. I quickly dried my face, tugged my shirt smooth, and stuck my head out of the bathroom door. "I'll be down in a minute!"

Dane called back an unintelligible response. I squeezed paste onto my toothbrush, gave my teeth a quick scrub, then pulled my hair into a knot on the top of my head and secured it with a black band. With a final sweep of the tendrils off my neck, I slipped out of the bathroom and down the stairs. Dane dispensed the pot of coffee he'd brought over into two mugs.

"Let me guess, black?" Dane asked over his shoulder.

"You are correct," I replied, brushing past him to open the refrigerator door. I pulled out the carton of eggs and a bag of shredded cheese. "You too?"

"Nope, lots of cream, lots of sugar. You'll come to learn, if it's bad for me, I like it."

"Interesting. Sounds pretty complex for a self-proclaimed 'simple man' though?" I teased, reaching for a mixing bowl. With my back to him, he pivoted and placed his hands on either side of the counter in front of me, boxing me in.

"Simple needs, Nova, not simple tastes." His voice was thick and husky, his breath hot on my lobe. His nose traced around my ear and up my hairline. "Let's cook."

Staying behind me, his right hand reached for an egg,

bringing it in front of us to break into the bowl. He cracked a total of six eggs and mixed them with a fork, all while his arms caged me.

Each brush of his arm, each accidental graze of his fingers, each puff of his warm breath against my skin caused my heart to pound faster and my cheeks to burn hotter. Tingles flickered in my belly, and I thought I would combust when I caught a whiff of his scent—a musky combination of soap and coffee. I pushed back with my butt and flipped around to face him. He grinned down at me, looking devilish and pleased with himself. I reached behind to shove the mixing bowl out of the way before hoisting my butt onto the counter. Dane simultaneously moved in as my legs snaked around his waist, pulling him closer.

"Nothing simple about you," he murmured before claiming my mouth. Placing his hands under my butt, he lifted me from the counter and carried me to the white leather couch, our lips connected the entire route.

After depositing me on a cushion, he lowered himself, and I tugged at his bicep. The edge of his tattoo peeked out. Using one hand to lift his sleeve, I traced along the bottom of the shield with my other.

"Tell me about this one," I said.

He shifted into a sitting position, placing my legs over his while I leaned my head against the armrest. Baring his arm to me, he looked at the art while solemnly explaining its origin. "I got it before a particularly rough mission. One which came to define me. I failed it on some levels, succeeded on others. Now it's always with me. Helps me remember, even though I know I'll never forget. That day sealed my fate, changed the direction I was headed, and led me on a new path."

"In the Army? Were you in Iraq?" I didn't know how

much he was willing to discuss, or how appropriate it was to probe.

"I've seen war. I've fought. Sometimes it feels like I'm still there, fighting." Finally tearing his eyes from the tattoo, he looked at me. "This may sound crazy, but last night... I felt peace. Now," he stopped, placing his hand over his heart, "I feel it again. With you, I feel like I did before this. Before I saw the ugliness of humanity. I feel like the person I used to be."

"Well, I like the person you are now," I said earnestly. I pushed up with my elbows and studied his face, seeing a new depth to Dane. He'd always come across as dark and edgy or silly and sarcastic. Now I saw an innocence and vulnerability.

He kept my gaze and inhaled. My eyes flashed to his chest, watching it deflate as he released a long, calming breath. "Let's eat, and this time, don't distract me, woman."

Playful Dane returned, but I itched to probe the sensitive side he kept tightly guarded.

AFTER OUR BREAKFAST of cheese omelets and buttered toast, we cleaned the kitchen together in a companionable silence. As Dane placed the last plate into the dishwasher, I wondered what came next. Would we return to the sofa and pick up where we'd left off before we'd gotten sidetracked, or would he bow out and return home? Looking down, my fingers clenched the dish rag. I didn't want him to leave.

"Do you want to—" I began as Dane simultaneously asked, "What do you have going on—"

"Go ahead." Dane grinned.

"Want to go for a walk?" I asked, nodding to the patio door which illuminated with the summer sun. "Looks like a nice day. We could walk to the lakefront."

"Yeah, sure," he said, swiping his hands against his shorts. "I haven't been to the lake yet. Then how about tonight we have steak and lobster. I'll grill."

"Like you grilled last night?" Now I wiggled my eyebrows suggestively.

His eyes dropped to my chest, then flickered back up. "You're absolutely right. If I get you back over to my place anytime soon, I'll be skipping the grill and going right for dessert." My cheeks flushed, and his grin widened. "I want to take you out, show you off, and then deliver you home with a kiss at the door. A proper date. Let's get dressed up and have a night out on the town. What's the best steak joint around here?"

"I'd have to check online," I stuttered. My heart thumped wildly from his words. He wanted more than the physical; he wanted to *show me off. A proper date.* "I'm going to change before, um, we go."

"Right, our walk." Dane moved next to me. His arm circled my waist as his chin lowered. "I'm going to take a quick shower. I'll be back in a few." He leaned in and brushed his nose against my forehead. "I mean it, Nova. I'm not walking away."

His hands dropped, and he silently stepped out of my apartment.

I hurried upstairs to grab a quick shower. Stepping under a cool stream, I rubbed soap over my body. My fingers pressed into my ribs. With all the activity of the last few days, I hadn't felt a single twinge or jolt. I tapped against them, testing for pain. Nothing. With a shrug, I turned off the water and stepped out. I towel dried my hair, then slid into fresh yoga capris and a clean tank top.

Before heading downstairs, I grabbed my cell to recharge. Alerts for a few missed calls and a text from Pete flashed on the screen. A small pang of guilt hit me as I plugged the phone in. I hadn't really given Pete a proper chance.

Who could when a man like Dane comes careening into your life?

DANE HAD CHANGED into athletic shorts and a tight grey shirt. The thin material stretched across his chest like a second skin. He was tall and broad, and next to him I felt small but safe. Linking arms with me, he led me to the elevator.

"Where to?" he asked as we pushed through the front door.

"Let's head to the lakefront path. There's an ice cream stand and a coffee shop near Bradford Beach."

"Can't remember the last time I had ice cream," Dane said. I could believe it; his stomach was flat and well defined.

A breathtaking specimen of a man. Like a mythological Greek God, Dane was almost too perfect to be real.

We bypassed the park across from our building and turned onto Ogden Street, passing row after row of condominiums and apartment buildings. A whiff of dryer sheets wafted from a building's vent. Fresh linens used to be my favorite aroma, now replaced by Dane's distinct scent—the mingle of his cologne and unique male pheromones.

Dane grasped my hand and laced our fingers together. "Lead the way, milady."

My body hummed, his touch like a drug I was quickly becoming addicted to. I led him down Ogden, which ended at a T intersection. We crossed the street and stopped at the top of the steep staircase that led to the walking trail.

"Want to race?" Dane challenged as we stared down the stairs. Without answering, I dropped his hand and pushed past him, skipping down the stairs to get the head start I knew I'd need if I had any chance of winning. By the time I hit the bottom step, Dane had not only caught up, but was in front of me, waiting to pick me up and pull me into his arms. Sweat had formed between my shoulder blades, and his nearness only caused my skin to flame hotter.

"Cheaters never win," he scolded with a smile as he set me back on my feet.

I tried to catch my breath before speaking. There I was, glistening with sweat and panting while he looked fresh as a daisy. "I was leveling the playing field. Unfair advantage—you have like a foot on me."

"Well, as they say, life isn't always fair, is it?" His playful tone turned solemn, not a bitterness but a sadness, as if he'd been given an unfair advantage at another point in time. Although he always seemed so self-assured, in control, I realized vulnerability lay beneath that tough exterior. He knew so much about me, yet he kept much of his past hidden.

We walked in silence until I broke it by asking, "Where'd you grow up? Tell me about your childhood."

"I was raised by an uncle, but unlike your Aunt Lu, he was my biological uncle, a brother of my mother. A solid man. Took me fishing, hunting. Taught me to be a man. He did it on his own too. No help from family. He was the only one willing to step in, step up, and raise me. For a long time, I wanted to know them, the people whose blood I shared. But I quickly found that they didn't want to know *me*, the bastard child. The auntie I spoke of before—Josefina wasn't my real aunt, but she took on that role. Besides the two of them, no one gave a shit. Never called him uncle, though, he was always Jake."

"I'm sorry—"

"Don't be. Like I said, I had a great childhood. Every boy's dream. Camping, hunting. Jake was an outdoorsman, taught me survival skills that today's youth are severely lacking."

"Did he encourage you to join the military?"

"Yeah, I guess, but it wasn't really encouragement, it just *was*. It was my calling."

"Wow." I thought back to Aunt Lu, and why I became a lawyer. To fight for justice, to fight for...

You have always been logical... it is why you became a lawyer... but you are neither judge nor jury... you revere faulty courts of law dictating good and bad, guilt and innocence... sin and temptation are a part of humanity... as I have always said, you will be tempted, Novalee, but profit and gain aren't worth the forfeit of the soul.

"Whoa, where'd you go there?" Dane asked.

I realized I'd not only stopped walking, but had closed my eyes. And for a long second, Aunt Lu's face lit in my memory like a flash bulb.

It can't be.

But with one hundred percent certainty, I recognized her. The same cobalt-blue eyes, the same strawberry-blond hair, the same sad smile. A picture-perfect memory of Lucille—*Aunt Lu*—an identical image of the woman from my muddled rendition of the accident. The young lady whose eyes had locked on mine just seconds before impact. Watching, waiting, standing by the telephone pole as if she'd known the course I'd travel, where my car would land.

Dane must've noted the color draining from my face because his hand was instantly under my elbow, steadying me as I swayed into him. Allowing a few minutes to regain my bearings, he remained quiet until I pulled away. Then his worried eyes searched my face before he asked, "You okay? Need some water?"

The sun blinded, heat emanated from the concrete path, and I did feel lightheaded, a touch dehydrated. I gave a nod, and he led me further up the trail to the coffee shop. Depositing me at a table, Dane got in line which gave me a minute to recollect the memories that had raked my nerves.

Was she a vision? A mirage? Had my mind created a memory of Aunt Lu to help me through the trauma of the car accident? But the woman by the pole was young enough to be my sister, not the old lady I'd buried when I was barely nineteen.

Dane returned with two water bottles and two scones.

"Maybe you need a little sugar?" He slid the plate over, and then unscrewed the top of the bottle. "Are you okay?"

"Yes." I hesitated, blinking as I focused in on the water bottle. "I just remembered something Aunt Lu used to say. Kind of the reason I went into law. My head's been so fuzzy since the accident, but it came to me, like she was speaking right between my ears."

"What was it?" he asked, his blue eyes bright with curiosity. He made me feel like everything I said or did was important. "By the way, that one is blueberry, the other is cinnamon chip."

Picking at the one closest to me, I absently pinched off a bit and rolled it between my fingers as I tried to recall the words. "Lucille used to talk about temptation ruining the soul."

"Nova?" he asked again, his head cocking with thought. "Is Lu short for Lucille? You've never called her that before. Guess I figured her name was Louise."

"Lu? Yes, it's short for Lucille." My voice held a mixture of question and revelation. I closed my eyes again, conjuring the image of Lucille. The woman in my memory—the woman I saw standing by the telephone pole—with the same cobalt blue eyes and the same soft smile. Young versus old, yet one and the same.

"Dane? Do you believe in ghosts?" I whispered. "Because I'm sure she was with me during the accident."

TWENTY

"Angels, saints, heaven... yes," Dane answered, eyeing me. "But not ghosts."

"She was an angel then, my guardian angel, like the doctors said." *Here I go, sounding crazy again.*

"How do you mean?" Dane leaned in closer.

"Can we take this to go?" I nodded toward the door.

We silently gathered our goodies and deposited the plate into the bin by the trash, then walked out, each carrying a water bottle and a scone. We continued north, taking the sidewalk up the hill to Prospect Avenue instead of returning to the lakefront trail.

We walked a few blocks in silence before I spoke. "The night of the accident, I was coming home from the airport."

"The airport?"

"Yes. I returned from London late. Cami left my car at the airport for me earlier in the day. She borrowed it while I was traveling, and couldn't pick me up that night, so she left it for me and took a cab home. We'd been emailing back and forth, and I told her it was no problem for me to get a cab. It didn't really make sense for her to drive my car to the airport only to have to cab it back herself, but she insisted. I was flying in late, and she said it was easier for me to hop into my own car instead of waiting in the taxi line with all of my luggage. Parking spot 514—May fourteenth is her birthday so it was easy to remember."

Dane stopped walking. He took a big gulp from the water bottle, then turned to me. "Who's Cami again?"

"Oh, my friend. We've been friends... forever. Anyway, she left a really sweet welcome home note on my driver's seat along with chocolates and flowers. Calla lilies." I grimaced, just now remembering the beautiful flowers—my favorite—that obviously didn't survive the accident. "It was storming that night, really bad rain and wind, and I remember exiting—" I pointed in the distance, toward Interstate 794, although we were too far away to see it. "I was at the bottom of the ramp, heading onto Lincoln Memorial Drive."

"Near Clybourn Street. I was at the Hilton that night—my first night in Milwaukee." Dane nodded, still making no effort to continue on the walk.

I closed my eyes as I continued, and my voice lowered to a near whisper. "I came to the intersection, and the sky was blowing up—I mean, I just missed the fourth of July here in America, but I got my own fireworks display that night—so I was kinda taken off guard when lightning hit the water, and..." Now it was me taking a gulp from my water. "And, I saw a woman standing by the telephone pole, right where my car landed when it spun out. I was side-swiped. Another car came through and, well, hit my car."

I shuddered, and Dane's arm instinctively went around my back, rubbing away the horrible memory.

"But Pete read the police report. No car, no woman."

"What?" Dane's eyebrows shot up. "Huh?"

"The whole thing is crazy. Honestly, until Pete told me there was no woman, I thought... I thought she'd been crushed... killed. I swore, I felt... I saw *death*."

"Nova, the human brain can be a mysterious muscle."

"It's actually an organ, not a muscle," I corrected, and he chuckled. "So, there was no other car, no woman, yet every time I think of the accident, I see *her*, and... *him*." I paused, now taking in a gulp of air. "I see Lucille and Neal."

"Your aunt and your brother?" Dane was nodding now, as if agreeing. "Nova, it's trauma, it's only natural for your brain to create something to comfort you during a moment of trauma. You're not crazy, you're normal. Completely normal."

"But Dane, you don't understand. Aunt Lu was an old woman when she raised us. The woman I saw was her, but younger—my age. And I haven't seen Neal since he was a teenager, but in my memory of the accident, he'd grown into a man."

I didn't realize until the moment I spoke out loud how fast my heart was racing or how nervous my stomach felt. Dane stared at my face for a minute, as if taking my words into serious consideration, inhaled long and deep, then blew out. It soothed over me, his breath a calming blanket that fell over my shoulders, settling my nerves. Taking my hand, he titled his head, again studying my face.

"Tell me the rest. How did the accident really happen?"

"Well, it was storming, and I guess there was road construction without proper barriers and signage. Negligence, I suppose. That's why Darrell gave Pete my contact information, in case I wanted to take legal action."

"But you don't remember that?"

I shook my head. "No, but I must've given the police a

statement. Cami said I was really out of it for a while, so who knows what exactly I said."

"Cami, the friend who you lent your car to?"

"Yes. Actually, Dane, I've been meaning to tell you, because this is such a weird coincidence, she somehow knows your friend Liam."

If I hadn't been paying such close attention to Dane's face, I possibly could have missed the sudden look of surprise in his eyes. He glanced to the couple walking past us before meeting my gaze. "That is a weird coincidence. Then again, Liam has been in and around this area for years. It's a... much smaller world than we think. We're all somehow connected in some way. Seven degrees of separation or something."

"Yeah, I kind of wonder if they hooked up or something. She didn't seem too keen on him."

"Liam can be... intense." Dane linked his arm through mine, and we began to walk down Prospect. "Let's head back. I have a couple errands before our big night out. And I think I need a nap; someone kept me up way too late last night. Want to join?"

I snuck a peek, and as I suspected, he was grinning that devilish smile that not only made my heart skip a beat, but also made me realize how deep I'd fallen.

TWENTY-ONE

As tempting as lying in bed with Dane sounded, I realized I legitimately needed rest. Instead of following him into his apartment, we parted ways at our respective doors with a kiss and a plan in place for the evening.

After a quick search on my cell for a restaurant, I reserved a table for two at Milwaukee's finest steakhouse. With that out of the way, I shuffled upstairs to crawl under the thin layer of my purple duvet for a catnap.

Placing my cell on the nightstand, I hesitated before clicking it off. Pete had left numerous texts and a voicemail, but I didn't check them. I wasn't ignoring him per se. After the previous night with Dane, and an upcoming date at one of the city's best restaurants, I knew I needed to have an honest discussion with Pete and let him know Dane and my relationship was progressing.

Sleep came quick and easy, and I woke over an hour later feeling sweaty and stifled under the duvet. Yanking it off, I climbed out of bed, only to stop as my feet touched the floor. I don't know if it was a sound or a sensation, but my head jerked toward the window, which from my lofted bedroom was a wide arching pane above the sliding glass door. Noting nothing amiss, I swiped hair off my damp neck and grabbed my cell to check the time.

The phone powered to life, and a text notification popped on the screen. Another message from Pete. Sighing, I chucked the phone onto my bed and padded into the bathroom. I knew I should return his call. He deserved better than being ignored.

Although I'd taken a shower earlier in the day, I stepped under the stream to wake up and wash off the sweat from my hard nap. I used a loofah and bath gel over my legs while a conditioning mask soaked in my hair. After rinsing, the scent of coconut lingered on my skin, making me think of sun and sand. I dried off, rubbed on a layer of body cream—also coconut scented—and then an anti-frizz serum through my long curls.

With a round brush, I dried my hair straight, running the barrel from root to ends until it spilled down my back in a glossy sheen of silk. The vanity light illuminated my skin, and I studied the blemish above my left eyebrow. The bruise had faded, and the scar had lightened to a wisp. A barely-there reminder.

Slipping into a black, lacy cocktail dress, I returned to the vanity to add the finishing touches: blood-red lipstick and leather jewelry. The knotted bracelet and matching earrings—feathers cut from leather—created a hard contrast to the soft lace edging on my dress. I pulled open my closet to pick out a pair of heels, choosing the Manolo Blahnik stilettos that hurt like hell but defined my calf muscles.

Dane's knock on the door had me rushing down the stairs, shoes in hand. Before answering, I clumsily stepped into the heels, and then stood tall, brushing my dress of any imaginary wrinkles. It fit like a glove, smoothly draping over my curves and falling just above the knee. My breath felt rushed, my pulse pounded. I'd spent almost twenty-four hours with Dane, minus the last few hours napping and primping, but as I opened the door and saw him standing under the frame, looking sexy as sin in dark trouser pants and a charcoal button-down, butterflies fluttered deep in my belly.

"Wow," Dane murmured. His eyes slowing devoured me, eating me up like I was dessert—and the main course.

My cheeks reddened, and I resisted covering my face with my hands. I was a thirty-three-year-old successful woman, yet the appraising eyes of my suitor had me gushing.

Before I could return his compliment—because Dane looked damn good with his black hair, tanned skin, and striking blue eyes—he swooped in, leaning close to my ear and whispering, "You're stunning." Then his lips brushed my cheek.

I shyly smiled. "Ready?"

"As I'll ever be." He winked back.

"Oh! My clutch!" The shiny patent leather clutch I'd used for our night at Bar Continental still sat on top of the kitchen counter, already packed with gloss, a comb, and cash. I snatched it, grabbed my keys, and led Dane out of my apartment.

As the elevator descended, I glanced to Dane and caught his eyes on me. No longer hungry and lustful, they'd softened to sweet and focused. Gentle and consuming. The elevator door creaked open, and Dane placed his hand under my elbow, leading me to the front entrance. I assumed a yellow cab would be waiting at the curb, but instead there was a white stretch limousine with a tuxedo-clad driver parked in front of the building.

I grinned at the driver, then up to Dane. With a giggle, I asked, "Really?"

"Your chariot awaits, milady," Dane said with a fake accent and slight bow.

The driver delivered a polite greeting as he opened the door. I scooted in, followed by Dane.

Inside there were two champagne glasses, a bottle chilling in ice, cheese, crackers, and a platter of chocolate covered strawberries. I looked around the limo, taking in the soft music that lulled in the background, the champagne, the food, and the man sitting beside me. A light, airy sigh escaped my lips.

"This is amazing." My breathy voice came out light and airy. I *felt* light and airy, like a princess being taken to the ball or a teenager going to prom. "I've never been in a limo."

"I'm glad you like it." Dane beamed, then divulged, "I've never been in one either."

Like two giddy teenagers, we both giggled. Dane filled the champagne flutes.

"We don't have much time before our reservation." I leaned into the leather cushion and looked up at the moon-roof. "This is amazing. Look at the sky. Maybe I should change our reservations, or maybe we can get something to go? Eat in the limo?"

"What are you thinking?" Dane replied. The partition separating us from the driver rolled down.

With a big grin, I requested the most absurd option. "McDonald's! Oh, the drive-thru?"

Dane twined our fingers together as he called to the driver, "Louis, the lady would like a Big Mac. Can you take us through the nearest drive-thru?"

As directed, Louis navigated to a restaurant a few blocks away, pulling forward enough so we could deliver our order through the back windows. Once we had our bags of greasy hamburgers and fries, Dane directed him to take us down Lake Drive.

The sun started to set. Through the moonroof, a haze of colors fell over the plush leather interior. Dane distributed the contents of the McDonald's bag, and we ate in serene silence while light music murmured in the background.

Night slowly began to fall, and the stars twinkled in a clear sky. We finished the bottle of champagne, and Dane opened a white wine. Glancing at the label, I recognized the name of the local vineyard I usually bought. Dane must have noted my preference and stocked the limo with my favorites. The cheese was the same variety of sharp cheddar, Gouda, and Butterkäse I'd picked when we first bumped into each other at the grocery store. A tingle rushed through me from a mixture of happiness, sweet wine, and the man sitting beside me.

Louis didn't ask for additional direction, but followed Lake Drive, a twisting road that hugged Lake Michigan. Moonlight bounced off the waves like little firecrackers. Feeling more and more like a princess, I took in everything —Dane, the silvery sky, and the music that seemed to be singing just for us.

At some point, Louis must've turned us around. The city's skyline grew closer as we approached Lincoln Memorial Drive. I tensed, but Dane squeezed my hand and calmly spoke. "You're okay, Nova."

I took a deep breath as we passed the scene of the accident, but for the first time, thinking about it didn't cause an ounce of anxiety or panic.

Dane hit the button for the intercom. "Louis, can you please stop at the art museum?"

A few minutes later, the limo turned onto the frontage road leading to the Milwaukee Art Museum. Since it had closed hours before, the streets and walkways were empty. In the dark of evening, spotlights glimmered along the criss-crossing walking pavers of the plush, manicured forecourt. Tall evergreen hedges dissected the expansive lawn. Intricate flowerbeds ran the distance of the garden and were flanked by large water fountains. Lake Michigan's waves shone in the distance.

Dane shifted in his seat as Louis cut the engine.

"Want to go for a walk?" he asked. Under the stars, he looked boyish, less rugged, bashful. Almost unsure of himself.

I nodded as Louis opened the door. Dane climbed out and extended his hand, which I accepted as I tried to gracefully exit. Leading me onto one of the paved walkways, music from the limo notched up.

"Tonight is perfect," I softly said. Inside, my stomach turned to mush and my heart swelled with the effort Dane had put into making this one of the most memorable evenings of my life. "Everything is perfect."

Dane gave a lopsided smile, and his eyes fluttered down. "I'm glad you like it."

Heat traveled through me, watching *his* reaction to *my* reaction. The pleasure and happiness *he* emitted from making *me* happy. In that moment, everything felt right; everything made sense.

I'd only known Dane for a short time, but he'd made his way into my head and into my heart. For the first time, I could envision a future. A future that included love. The

kind of love that was tangible. A love that led to perma-
nence. Marriage, children. *A family*.

The feelings may have been irrational—Dane and I
hadn't known each other long—and love certainly wasn't
something I was looking for. Marriage, children, and family
weren't on the horizon prior to my car accident. So focused
on my work, I never looked that far ahead. I hadn't thought
of anything beyond the present.

Now I realized how desperately I wished for more—for
a family.

*Mother and child. Brothers and sisters. Husband and
wife.*

Dare I hope for such things?

The song in the background came to an end, and a slow
ballad started. Dane extended his hand. "May I have this
dance?"

My eyes lifted to meet his, and every feeling that had
just run through my head and heart reflected in his eyes. I
didn't respond with words but took his hand and let him
pull me in close.

The sweet ballad serenaded us, singing of the moon and
sea, magic and love. Under the silver haze of the evening
sky, and surrounded by the lull of Lake Michigan's waves,
the song was ours, articulating everything that remained
unspoken between us.

Hope, peace, joy. Heaven on earth.

Tucked into Dane's chest, his arms held me with his
promise—they weren't going to let me go. He wouldn't walk
away.

After several slow minutes, the song faded, yet I
remained in Dane's arms. His chin dropped to rest against
my forehead. Endless seconds passed before his arms
loosened.

"Nova? Will you come away with me?" His breathy question hit my cheek like a kiss.

"Hmm?" I looked up to catch the moonlight dancing across his strong features. Still feeling dizzy from the dance, I asked, "Away?"

"I need to return to Monterey," he explained. "Will you come with me? We'd be gone only a week or so." Dane stepped to the side, holding my hand and leading me along the path toward one of the fountains. "Will you think about it?"

I bit my lower lip, looking at his hopeful face, and gave a slight nod.

We stared quietly at the fountain, enjoying the calm sounds of water splashing into the basin. Dane glanced at his watch and then toward the limo.

"Time's up?" I asked, feeling a bit like Cinderella. The night was beyond perfect, and I didn't want it to come to an end.

Noticing our return, Louis hopped from the front seat of the limo and hurried to open the passenger side door for Dane and me. I entered first, sliding along the u-shaped seats, followed by Dane. After the door closed, Dane leaned in, his eyes serious.

"So, you'll think about it?" he solemnly asked again.

"I'll think about it," I agreed softly.

Inside my conflicted head, the words *yes* and *no* echoed simultaneously. Traveling while unemployed hardly seemed prudent, but the more I tossed around the idea, the more it made sense. Hadn't I recently proclaimed I'd never been on a vacation? And sure, I hadn't known him long, but we connected in a way that defied sense and reason.

The limo maneuvered onto Lincoln Memorial Drive, carrying us from the most magical moment I'd experienced in my lifetime. I closed my eyes, committing every second to memory. By the time I opened them, we were in front of our building. Louis cut the engine and came around to open our door. My stomach sunk.

After guiding me out, Dane dropped my hand to shake Louis's, and then escorted me inside and up the elevator. The door creaked opened to our floor, and Dane said what I'd been thinking.

"I don't want the night to end."

"It doesn't have to," I replied. From my clutch, I extracted my keys, and Dane followed me inside.

The air conditioning had been set to cool earlier in the day, and the chill brought goose bumps to my bare arms. I went to the thermostat, clicked it off, then pushed open the sliding glass door. The humid evening air instantly warmed my skin. As I turned around, Dane stood an arm's length away, intently watching me.

"Tonight—" he began, but my mouth cut him off as I rushed the few steps to him, wrapped my arms around his neck, and sought his lips. Dane's hands flew to cup my cheeks, holding my face in place as our kiss deepened.

He leaned back. "I wanted—" Dane was cut short again, this time by pounding sounds at the door, followed by an urgent, masculine plea.

"Nova!" the voice called and the pounding resumed.

"What the hell?" Dane's head swiveled from me to the door. "Is that the douche lawyer from the bar?" Dane jerked away. A combination of confusion and annoyance had his brows drawn as he yanked the door open. "Christ Pete, you're going to have that old cat lady down the hall calling the police."

"Nova, are you okay?" Pete pushed past Dane.

"Pete! *What* are you doing?" My lower jaw dropped, and my hands flew to cover my mouth.

"I've been trying to reach you since yesterday. This guy's lying to you. I told you I didn't get a good feeling from him, and my buddy confirmed my suspicion."

Dane leaned against the door, his arms unfolding to wave Pete further inside. "Now it's a party. Sure, come on in, Pete."

Pete kept his focus on Dane's face as he moved toward me.

"Did you have him do a background check on me?" Dane asked, rubbing a hand through his hair.

"Of course not." The internet search didn't count, and I certainly hadn't involved Pete.

"So, tell us, Pete, what did you find?" Amusement tinged his voice as if he found this horrifying, embarrassing situation funny.

"I don't know what kind of sick prick you are, but your name's not Dane Killbane, that's for sure. There was a soldier with that name stationed at Fort Ord in Monterey, California, with the birthdate of July twenty-fourth, but—" Pete glanced at Dane, who appeared more formidable than usual, and took a discernible gulp before continuing, "He was killed during World War II."

Dane nodded, as if agreeing with everything Pete had said. "Is that all?"

Another gulp gyrated over Pete's throat. "Is that *all*? You're a freaking liar. You stole someone's identity!"

Pushing from the wall, Dane prowled toward Pete who visibly shrunk as he neared. Dane wasn't much taller or stockier, yet he dwarfed Pete. Barely three feet separated them, but it seemed they were chest to chest when Dane looked down and spoke to him in an eerily calm voice.

"You are mistaken. Nova appreciates your concern, but you're wrong. You've worried yourself over nothing. Forget you had this conversation. Forget you ever heard the name Dane Killbane. Forget about Nova. Go, leave. You've interrupted a very important evening for us. Do you understand everything I've said?"

"I understand," Pete replied in a flat tone. Without looking at me, he stepped around Dane and let himself out of the door.

The huff from Dane brought my stunned eyes from the door to his face. I couldn't speak. I had no words for what I just witnessed. My mouth opened but snapped shut again.

"You're not afraid," Dane said calmly as he neared me. He watched for a reaction before taking a seat on the leather couch. "You're not afraid, are you?"

"No," I whispered. "I should be, right?"

Dane nodded, then motioned to the space next to him. "Have a seat. I'm going to get you some water." I obeyed without question, taking the spot on the sofa he'd just vacated. He rummaged through the cabinets, pulling a pint glass and filling it with tap water. "Here, take a sip."

Again, I obliged, moving the glass to my lips and taking a small drink. Pulling the glass away, I asked, "Why can't I help but do as you say? What did you do to Pete? Why did he leave like that?"

"When I met you, I knew something was different. There's something special about you. You're special, of course, but in a *unique* way. Running into Liam only adds to my confusion. I've learned over the years that *nothing* is a coincidence. There's a reason he's here, just as there's a reason I'm here. And I'm certain there's a reason I was meant to meet you. I just can't put my finger on it."

My throat turned dry, and my heart pounded so hard I

feared it'd thump right out of my ribcage. I couldn't blink, couldn't move.

The guy vacating his table at Dark Beans. The two patrons at Winetopia who slid from their stools offering us a place to sit. The couple at the picnic table eating barbeque who gave up their seats. Pete rushing off at Dane's command.

Just like them, I couldn't help but follow his spoken— and unspoken—commands.

"I'll answer your next question, but please drink." He motioned to my glass, and I instantly had it to my lips. Nearly all the water disappeared down my throat as Dane watched approvingly.

Whatever spell Dane had used on Pete and the others also kept me captive. Instinctively, I knew it should be setting off alarm bells, yet I felt no fear.

"Are you okay?" He waited for me to nod before breaking eye contact. As soon as his gaze left my face, my hold on the glass loosened, and it fell into my lap. A splatter of water landed on Dane's forearm. We both stared at it.

I should be afraid, but I'm not.

"I don't want what Pete said to factor into your decision to come away with me. I want you to come of your own accord. I'm not a bad guy, Nova," Dane said softly. Hope thickened his voice, and for the first time since meeting him, I witnessed complete vulnerability from him.

"You want me to go away with you." Repeating the request out loud made the idea sound less crazy considering the circumstances. Almost reasonable. "When?"

His eyes flickered from his knee to my face. "Soon. Tomorrow or the day after. I need to secure a flight."

"Is your name really Dane Killbane?"

"Yes. And yesterday really was my birthday. I haven't

celebrated it in a long time." He blew out a long breath and shrugged. "Look how that's turned out."

I was about to ask more questions about Pete's tirade, but Dane held up his hands. "Honestly, I'm not sure if I can explain."

The panic I should have been feeling all along rushed up my spine, but Dane quickly placed his giant palm against my cheek, stroking with his thumb and instantly settling my pounding heart. "There are some things I simply can't explain, Nova. They won't make sense to you, but I can show you something."

Dane pushed from the sofa and took the few steps to the sliding glass door where he stepped through to the patio. Hesitating, I waited a few seconds before joining him. His forearms rested on the banister, and he looked ahead to the park.

"The things you've sensed—the birds, the confusion—they're no coincidence either." My gaze was trained on the park, but I knew his eyes were on me. "There's something inside of you that is like me."

"What?" I whispered.

"Something special."

Special how? I wanted to scream.

"I don't think you'll believe it unless I show you." Leaning over the banister, he focused on the park, then blew out a gentle puff of air. The leaves, bushes, and flowers below rustled, only settling once Dane's pursed lips relaxed.

My jaw dropped.

He then looked to the night sky. With a flick of his chin, a groan of thunder rumbled in the distance.

A breathy gasp escaped my lips, yet I didn't speak. I didn't move. I was paralyzed.

"Nova?" Dane asked in a low voice. "Do you understand?"

"No," I whispered, afraid to meet his eyes. *No*, I didn't understand any of it. None of it made sense.

"I'm sorry our night is ending like this. But you *will* remember it for what it was—a perfect evening untarnished by this odd detour." His words were calm and soothing. I stood frozen. "I'm going to let myself out. Get a good night's sleep, sweet Nova."

TWENTY-TWO

My eyes popped open as I jerked awake. Pulling the duvet off, I climbed out of bed only to stop as my feet touched the floor. The sound of birds chirping had my head jerking toward the arched pane, then fell to the wide-open sliding glass door below. Hurrying down the stairs, I shoved it closed, and then checked the thermostat. No wonder humidity stifled my loft.

Right. I had turned it off after my date with Dane when he deposited me at the door with a kiss to the cheek. *A proper date.*

The night was something out of a fairytale, perfect from start to finish.

I began to pivot, only to stop as a black flash and loud plunk came from the glass pane. My hands flew to my chest.

Did a bird hit the door? The door I'd just shut?

"Oh my gosh, oh my gosh," I whispered, rushing to the door, where, indeed, a dazed blackbird perched unsteadily on the wood planks. Its head twitched, and it looked at me before hopping a few steps closer, stopping again as if in pain.

The bird watched me as I lowered to my knees. Our eyes remained locked. My breath hitched. Fear soured my stomach when it cocked its head.

"What do you want?" I whispered.

The bird bounced a step closer. The hairs on the back of my neck stood up.

"Leave me alone," I pleaded.

Its head began to frantically twitch left and right as if shaking its head *no*. Gasping, I shuffled backwards, and then scrambled to my feet.

Still clad in my sweat-dampened pajamas, I spun on my heel, rushed out of my apartment, and banged on Dane's door. Seconds later, it flew open, and he stared down, wide-eyed as his hand clenched the edge of the towel wrapped snugly around his hips. Water drops speckled his broad chest.

"What's wrong?" he exclaimed.

"A bird flew into my window!"

He inhaled, his shoulders tensing. "A bird?"

"It hit my freaking door literally seconds after I closed it!"

"Okay, okay, it's no big deal. Birds see their reflection and want to attack. It's probably just dazed." Now he exhaled, long and steady. "No big deal."

"Dane! It was *staring* at me," I said, my voice pitching. I didn't care if I sounded hysterical.

"Let me throw on some clothes... or not?" He shot me a devilish grin, but I was not in the mood for flirtation. "It's okay, Nova, I'll take care of it."

"Now, please." I nervously balled my hands.

"Of course. I'll be right back." Dane hurried up the stairs to change while I waited in the doorway with my arms crossed protectively over my chest. He was back, wearing an athletic T-shirt and shorts, within a minute.

"Let's go," he directed.

My apartment door was wide open. I hadn't closed it in my rush to get Dane. The blackbird sat outside the sliding glass door. Its little head jerked, and it hopped a few steps back.

I remained a step behind Dane as we slowly approached, and then crouched alongside him when he stopped outside of the door. The blackbird's eyes, tiny as they may be, appeared focused on Dane as it hobbled further from the glass door. Dane's chin slowly moved upward and out, just as the bird's wings began to flutter.

"Shoo, get out of here," Dane whispered.

The bird's wings began to flap violently, and it took flight, croaking with a shrill sound that had me gasping for air. Dane's arms were around me, stifling my cries as he pulled me into his chest.

Minutes later, when I finally pulled away, tears streamed down my cheeks. "What was that?" I asked hoarsely.

"Nova, I know you're upset, but we need to talk." Dane guided me to the sofa where we sat side-by-side, knees touching. "Being here, meeting you, and knowing Liam's here—" he looked at me, taking his sweet time to absorb each feature of my face, as if committing it to memory. "I'd like to think it's a coincidence, but I've come to learn nothing is ever a coincidence."

The conversation sounded eerily familiar.

Last night... Pete banging on the door. Dane's paralyzing voice...

"I remember," I whispered. "I remember last night."

Dane nodded. "Are you afraid?"

The rustling bushes, the groan of thunder.

"What are you?" I asked. Sweat beaded the back of my neck. Heat consumed me, flushing my cheeks and making me dizzy.

"I can't answer that."

"Dane, please." I teetered on hysteria. He shifted from the cushion to a crouched position with one knee bent to the floor. His large palm gently covered mine, firmly grasping my hand. He closed his eyes.

Touches as soft as feathers, hushing my fears, sheltering me as I slipped into the dark confines of unconsciousness.

No, it isn't possible.

"You were there. You were with me after the accident," I squeaked out.

A bubble of bile burned in my stomach, and I bolted from the sofa to the bathroom upstairs. Clutching the toilet, I heaved into the bowl. Tears and snot ran down my cheeks. Dane came through the door, concern fierce in his eyes.

"I'm sorry, Nova, I'm so sorry. I hate seeing you in pain," he whispered as he helped me stand. "You're not ready to face the truth yet, but you have time." I had no idea what he meant. Confusion and fear churned in my stomach. Dane cocked his head, watching for my reaction. "I want you to know me... what I am." He tapped his chest. "And I want to find out more about you. Who you are. But you're not ready... you're not ready."

My mouth opened, but I didn't know what to say. I didn't know what to do. I was paralyzed by a fear so great, it began to shutter my vision, making the edges black and fuzzy.

Dane's words turned to a whispery echo as I faded into

unconsciousness. *"I know I should walk away. It'd be best, but I can't. I can't leave you. Not yet. Will you come away with me? Please come... please come..."*

PART TWO

I will restore your fortunes and gather you from all the nations and all the places where I have driven you, and I will bring you back to the place from which I sent you into exile.

(Jeremiah 29:14)

TWENTY-THREE

Having slept in obscenely late, I woke Monday morning to the crisp chill of the air conditioner. My purple duvet cocooned my body, securely tucked from my chin to my toes. I wiggled out of its hold when a resounding thought popped into my head.

Yes, I'll go away with you.

After our fairytale date the night before, I wanted nothing more. Dane had left me at the door with a proper kiss and a question—would I go away with him?

Now, I knew my answer.

I slid from bed, made a quick trip to the bathroom, then changed into a tank top and athletic shorts. I found myself knocking on Dane's door minutes later.

He opened it, a sexy grin lighting his face. "Morning, sleepyhead."

Suddenly shy, my eyes shifted to my toes. "Uh, hey."

"What brings you by so early?" He glanced at his watch. "Actually, not that early. Want coffee?"

The scent of freshly brewed coffee percolated the air as Dane ushered me in. On the countertop, two mugs had been set out along with a paper plate piled with pastries from Dark Beans.

"I'm sorry, am I interrupting? Were you expecting someone?" I asked, nodding to the food as I slid onto a barstool.

"You, silly. I was expecting you." Dane poured coffee into the mugs, then pushed one toward me. "I was about to text you to see if you were hungry."

"Oh," I said, bringing the offered cup to my lips. "Thank you."

Dane cocked his head and looked at me expectantly. "So, have you thought about—"

"My answer is *yes*."

We spoke simultaneously, then stopped, both giggling.

"Did you do all this to butter me up?" I waived at the countertop.

Dane nodded. "Did it work?"

"I was going to say yes anyway." Grinning, I pinched the edge of a chocolate-filled croissant and popped it into my mouth.

"Thank you, Nova." Dane cupped my face with both hands and placed a quick kiss on my nose. "This means so much to me, showing you where I grew up, where I come from. I spent my childhood up and down California's central coast. I want... I want you to know me."

My cheeks flushed. Last night when Dane and I danced under the moonlight outside of the art museum, I felt something move deep within my soul. Hope for the future. Planting roots, planning a family. I'd been without one for so long that the idea always seemed foreign, out of reach. When I thought of Dane, how perfectly we fit, I could see that future. I hoped he saw it too.

"How soon can you go?" he asked.

"Well, you caught me between gigs, so my schedule is fairly open."

"How about tomorrow? I'll look into flights. I don't need to check-in with my commander until Friday, and that's a simple debriefing. It's contractual. I can't do it by video conference. Pretty much a quick in-and-out, get-my-signature kind of deal."

"You want to leave tomorrow? Airfare will be crazy with that short of a notice." I set the mug down, frowning as I considered the outrageous cost of a last-minute ticket.

"I have a gazillion frequent flier miles. Don't worry about it."

The timing seemed rushed, but Dane's eagerness melted my reservations. I couldn't help but find myself nodding and smiling in agreement. "Okay, tomorrow."

"It's one of the most beautiful landscapes, Nova. You're going to love it, at least, I hope you do. I'm kind of tethered to the area."

Right. After the lease was up here, he'd eventually return to Monterey for good. I needed to remember that as my heart filled more and more with pieces of him. I couldn't relocate... *Or could I?* Nothing really tied me to Milwaukee. I didn't have a job anymore. No family anchoring me here.

"What should I pack?" I asked, thinking about the luggage I'd *just* unpacked.

Dane went into a detailed explanation of the vast temperature range along the coast. But I only half-listened, instead musing about the many mornings I woke up spooning the suitcase, and realizing in the days ahead, it'd be Dane in its place.

TWENTY-FOUR

"So, what do you prefer—scenic or fast? Personally, I wouldn't pass on the opportunity to drive along the Pacific Coast Highway. Wait, do you get carsick?" Dane talked a mile a minute, hardly stopping for air. Navigating through the winding rows in the rental car parking lot, he stopped in front of the attendant's booth, rolled down his window, and handed over a thick stack of paperwork.

"Do you need a map?" a scruffy-haired man asked as he scribbled furiously over the top of the receipt.

"Nah, thanks." Dane grinned, then nodded toward me. "Think we'll head along the PCH, see the Pacific in all her glory. Sound good?"

"Sure." I giggled. Dane hadn't stopped beaming since I had agreed to take this impromptu trip with him.

I still wondered how he'd pulled it off so quickly. Twenty-four hours later, here we were, pulling from the rental car lot at San Francisco International Airport.

Dane followed signs for the 101 heading south. I watched with fresh eyes as San Francisco rolled past my passenger side window. I'd been to the city a few times in the last decade for work but never experienced the sites.

"Can we see the Golden Gate Bridge?" I asked, craning my neck to get a peek of the skyline. My smile widened, ear to ear, when Dane glanced my way with a confirming nod.

"We can do whatever you want. This part of the trip is all about you."

"Okay," I said.

"I'll put the roof down as soon as we get out of the city," Dane suggested. The rental car was a black Mustang convertible. Dane claimed it'd "enhance the experience" driving along the coast. "You hungry? What about music?" He tossed his phone to me. "Here, pick a playlist. Or maybe some local stations are preprogramed on the radio."

"No opera?"

"You choose. Where we go, what we do, you get first dibs."

"Wow, Dane, what did I do to deserve the princess treatment?" I held my palms up. "I mean, I won't argue."

"Nova." His voice turned soft and serious. "I don't think you realize how much this means to me. The time I've had with you... they've been the best days of my life."

My insides melted. My skin tingled. And my heart soared. I wanted to scream "mine too." Instead, I clasped my hands on my lap and stared out the window. I'd never experienced feelings like this. I wasn't quite sure what to make of it.

Beyond primal lust, beyond blinding passion, I'd fallen. Fast, hard, and deep.

∾

AFTER DRIVING over the Golden Gate Bridge, roof down and hair blowing, we stopped at Muir Woods to stretch our legs. The mighty redwoods towered high into the sky as the Mustang wound down the mountain side to the park's entrance.

"We have to make it a quick hike, but it's worth it," Dane said, pulling into the crammed parking lot. A pair of women decked in yoga gear walked from their car toward the welcome center. Rolled-up mats were tucked under their arms. Dane asked from our open-air seats, "Hey, you guys coming or going?"

"Just leaving," the woman called back. "Hang on a sec."

Dane put the car into park, and we watched the women talk to an attendant before turning back in our direction. The lady signaled to a silver Jetta.

"Looks like we got lucky," I said, watching them climb into their car. "They must have a yoga class in the park. Cami would flip for something like that. Yoga and nature are her two passions."

"Cami? Your friend in Milwaukee?" Dane asked. His fingers strummed against the leather steering wheel. "You haven't told me much about her. What's her story?"

"Oh, she and I have been friends forever, since we were kids. I grew up with her. Neal, Cami, Celia, and I were four peas in a pod until, well... until we weren't. Guess we all kind of drifted apart."

"Celia?" Dane asked. He glanced my way before pulling into the newly vacated spot and cutting the engine.

"Celia is practically Cam's sister. They were raised like siblings, although they couldn't be more different. Cami's always been a breath of fresh air, and Cece's more serious, quiet. Cami's kind of in the same boat as me. Cece dropped out of her life, left town for some guy that was bad news.

They haven't spoken in years." A subtle sadness tinged my voice. I hadn't thought of Neal in a few days. Dane had preoccupied all my time and energy. "I think she hired a private investigator to find her."

"Wow," Dane said, pushing his sunglasses to the top of his head. He unclicked his seatbelt, exited the car, then came around to my side and opened my door.

I slipped from my seat, heavy in thought. Dane took my hand and led me toward the entrance to the park. Dropping his intertwined fingers from mine, he pulled his sunglass back down then scratched his chin.

"Thinking about your brother, huh?" he asked.

"Last I heard, Neal's here—well, somewhere along the coast. Maybe while we're here..." I trailed off. I knew it was a long shot.

"I know some people that may be able to help. When we get to Monterey, I'll ask around."

The welcome center had a large sign listing its hours of operation and park usage fees. Dane pulled out his wallet just as I reached into my purse for mine. I couldn't have him bankrolling the entire trip; he'd already insisted on securing our airfare.

"Military gets in free," he explained, sliding his identification card to the attendant. "One of the many perks for signing away your life."

"I didn't think you were still active duty."

"Retired. Now I do contract work." He slipped the card back into his wallet.

"Wow, retired?" I didn't know Dane's exact age, but he looked to be around mine. Early-to-mid-thirties at most. "Aren't you kind of young to be retired?"

"It's a complicated situation. I'm considered 'medically

retired.' Had an injury a few years ago that made me unde-
ployable. So, I got into contract work."

"Oh, I'm sorry to hear that."

"Eh, life has a funny way of working itself out. I wasn't
ready to give up the good fight, so now I do what I can,
although it's not ideal. Not exactly the route I would have
gone, but, well, it is what it is. I can have all the regrets in
the world, but it doesn't change the past. No use dwelling or
overthinking. I learned that a long time ago."

We walked along a winding path, damp and dark from
the towering redwoods. Patches of sunlight streamed
through sporadic openings. The treetops towered so high
above, some got lost in the misty fog.

"Amazing, aren't they?" Dane asked, looking up to the
soaring crowns. "Big, old giants on land. Some of these are
over two thousand years old."

The scent of nature thickened as we pushed further
into the woods. Fresh, clean, and earthy. I inhaled deeply,
closing my eyes and allowing my senses to take their fill of
the land. Exhaling in a long, slow breath, I leaned into Dane
as his arms came around me, pulling me close against his
body.

"Years ago, my uncle and I would come here often,
before it got so crowded and touristy. He took me camping
almost every weekend. Not always here, but Muir Woods
was one of his favorites. He said the redwoods embodied the
beauty and miracle of life. They're the tallest in the world,
closest to heaven, connecting all elements of creation. Feet
planted in the soil, roots drinking from the waters of the
rivers and streams, crowns in the clouds. He said one day
I'll understand the symbolism of the redwoods, their physical and spiritual strength. The healing, protection, and

peace they bring to the soul. One of the greatest connectors of life."

Protection, healing, strength. My soul desperately needed to hear those words, the promise that reverberated in Dane's words. The promise that even among life's obstacles, peace existed. Peace *was* possible.

"I'm glad I get to share this with you," Dane said quietly. "My uncle's been gone a long time now, and it's been a while since I've known... peace."

My eyes shot up to meet Dane's, but his chin was angled upward, toward the tall towering limbs that rustled above us. Shadows mingled with sunshine, dancing over his face like a tango between light and dark.

"Come on, let's find a banana slug before it gets too late. They're the grossest, but coolest little critters you'll see in these parts."

AFTER SPENDING ALMOST two hours at the park, we never did spot the bug. We made a pit-stop at the gift shop where Dane bought me a rubber version of the slug before we headed back to the car.

Sinking into the Mustang's leather seats, I nestled against the headrest and closed my eyes. "Where to now?"

"Let's get out of the city. It's overpriced and overcrowded, and there are lots of options south of here. Maybe we can find something on the ocean."

We again crossed over the Golden Gate Bridge. The city passed slowly as we sat in stop-and-go rush hour traffic. Exiting onto Highway One, it lightened from heavy congestion to a free flow. Signs for Moss Beach greeted us.

"Ready to stop, or should we push a little further?" Dane asked.

"Think I'm ready to stop, if you don't mind. I can check on my phone for a hotel," I said, tapping the screen. "What city's next?"

With his eyes trained on the road, Dane answered, "Half Moon Bay."

TWENTY-FIVE

Although he didn't look at me, I'm certain Dane caught the sudden jerk of my body.

"Nova?" He reached to clasp my hand, giving a squeeze.

"He used to sing about a half moon bay," I whispered, more to myself than Dane. "I didn't know there was a place along the coast with that name."

"Hmm?" Dane glanced my way, then returned his focus to the road. "It's known for a big annual surf event. Other than that, not much to the city. We can press on to Santa Cruz."

"Neal used to sing about a half moon bay," I said louder. "We have to stop."

Eyes still focused ahead, Dane replied, "What a coincidence. Can you check your phone for a hotel?"

I tapped the Hotels app and turned on my locator, but before the search results could populate, Dane pulled off the highway and onto a frontage road leading to an inn. In the distance, a vacancy light blinked on and off in front of a weathered, three-story building. Rows of balconies overlooked a small parking lot. A sandy beach and the ocean lay beyond the sidewalk.

As Dane cut the engine, the gentle lull of waves caressed the evening air. I closed my eyes, not only from the long day of travel and the hike through Muir Woods, but mental exhaustion. My mind raced with possibilities.

Could it be a mere coincidence?

I'd like to think it's a coincidence, but I've come to learn nothing is ever a coincidence.

"How's this place look?" Dane asked, interrupting my thoughts. He pressed the button to close the convertible roof. "Might not be the Ritz, but looks kind of charming."

Snapping back to reality, I grinned. "Did you seriously use the word charming?" Big, tough men like Dane didn't use words like that.

"Well, it's called Charming Inn, so, yeah, *charming.*" He shrugged his shoulders, then helped me from my seat.

The building in front of us, worn from wind and salt, had an understated, beachy allure. Dane pointed toward the matching grey sign bearing the name of the inn. "See?"

"Charming Inn." I read the sign out loud.

Dane clasped my hand and led me into the lobby. Inside, a gentle fire crackled in a stone-bordered hearth. Several skylights made the compact space appear cozy yet open. A haze cast by twilight sprinkled the room.

"A fire in July?" I asked Dane.

"There's a famous saying about summers in San Francisco. Mark Twain or someone. 'The coldest winter was a summer spent in San Francisco?' Something like that. You go inland a few miles, and it'll be ten degrees warmer," Dane explained, gazing around the room. "This *is* charming."

Two plush chairs faced the fireplace, while a wide

buffet with a coffee station, tower of cups, wooden box of teabags, and a pitcher of water sat below a portrait of the sea. Fruit had been set out, along with a small stack of napkins.

"Oh, hello," a soft, feminine voice called from the door behind the desk.

"Hi." Dane grinned. He planted his palms on the teak-wood countertop. "Any rooms available?"

The clerk's brown eyes snapped from Dane to me, warming as she smiled. "Aren't you just lovely. You remind me of someone."

Self-conscious, my hands patted at my tangled hair. The convertible might have been a fun ride, but my hair felt like a rat's nest. Probably looked like one too.

The clerk snapped her fingers. "She was a ballerina, floated around like a graceful little bird even when she wasn't dancing."

"Oh, well, I have two left feet." I laughed. "Definitely not graceful."

"Ah, you're not that bad. A few glasses of wine, and I'd almost say you've got skills." Dane winked, then added with a shimmy of his hips, "But no one can keep up with these moves." I gave a swat at his butt. We had danced together twice in the last few weeks, already making special memories in our short relationship. And I had to admit, I was more than impressed with *all* his moves.

"Oh, you two are adorable! And you're in luck. I had a cancellation this afternoon. It's a king suite with a fireplace, balcony, and small kitchenette. How long are you thinking? They had it for the week." She tucked a chestnut-brown curl behind her ear. Turquoise beaded earrings dangled from her ears, and her long, flowy, floral cardigan nearly swept the floor, making her appear like a modern-day hippie.

"A couple nights." I spoke before Dane had the opportunity to answer. As futile as the attempt may be, I wanted time to look for Neal. The song lyrics and the name of this city could be just a simple coincidence. But...

I'd like to think it's a coincidence, but I've come to learn nothing is ever a coincidence.

The words again echoed in my head, the faint memory almost a warning.

"I can do that. Two? Three?" the clerk asked.

Dane lifted a shoulder in a half shrug. "Let's start with two, if that's okay?"

The woman punched the keyboard in front of her. "Fantastic. Where are you two love birds from?"

I blushed, averting my eyes to my hands which I'd wrapped around Dane's thick bicep.

"Just flew in from Wisconsin, but I've been in and around these parts for years," Dane answered. The thick cording of his muscles tensed under my hold. He had a body made of steel, strong and unyielding.

My pulse suddenly quickened, the thought of sleeping next to Dane for a few nights bringing heat to my belly. We hadn't touched one another intimately—outside of chaste kisses here and there—since the weekend. Now we'd be sharing a bed and inevitably one another's space for a week.

Deep in thought, I hardly noticed as Dane's credit card and the keys to our room were exchanged.

"Hey, I was going—"

Dane cut me off with a wide grin, his hand patting the top of mine. "We'll worry about that later. Josie was just saying they offer complementary wine and cheese every evening from five to seven. Looks like we missed it tonight, but she's graciously offered to pour us a glass if we want to sit by the fire for a few minutes."

"You can bring them to your room if you don't mind plastic cups. The sun will be setting in a bit, and the view from the balcony is out of a dream," she offered.

"Red SOLO cups?" Dane asked in a serious tone, eyebrows raised. I giggled, the joke lost on Josie.

"In wine country? God no." She scrunched her nose and shook her head. The turquoise beads danced in her hair. "I have plastic wine cups. Hold on, let me grab the bottle. Oh, I don't want to forget to mention—we offer a continental breakfast every morning, seven to nine, here in the lobby."

She turned on a wedged espadrille sandal, her flowing cardigan waving behind her as she pushed through the door again. Josie reminded me of the free spirit I used to be before I morphed into a stuffy lawyer.

"How thoughtful." I grinned to Dane. Fatigue began to settle in my shoulders, and a glass of wine on the balcony sounded more than perfect.

"Here you two birdies go," Josie said, coming through the door again with two glasses in hand. "I'm just so tickled this worked out for us. For me to get a cancellation, then have you two show up. Must be kismet. Let me know if you need anything. If you want recommendations for dining, music, beaches—call the front desk. Half Moon Bay is small, one of those everyone-knows-everyone kind of towns, so I can personally attest to the hidden gems."

Tucking away that tidbit of information, I took the glass from her outstretched hand. "Thank you, everything is perfect."

"Nov, let's take these up to the room. I'll grab our stuff later," Dane suggested.

"Goodnight, darlings. Enjoy that beautiful view of the sea," Josie called with a warm, knowing smile.

I followed Dane through the front entrance and around the building to an exterior stairwell where we carefully climbed to the third floor, wine glasses in hand. Signs made of driftwood adorned each door. Dane stopped outside of 314 and pushed an old-fashioned key into the knob. The door swooshed open to reveal a spacious studio.

Stepping inside, two oversized lounge chairs faced a fireplace, while the king-sized bed was pushed against the farthest wall. The kitchenette was to our immediate left. Nautical accents in varying shades of blue sprinkled the room.

"Charming, huh?" Dane nodded to an aqua colored hand towel that had been molded into the shape of a heart and placed on top of the bed. Two gold foil-wrapped chocolate candies sat in the center. He set his wine glass on the wooden mantle and flipped the switch to the gas fireplace. It flickered to life, casting a yellow glow against the cream-colored carpet. "Want to check out the view?"

I followed him to the sliding glass door that stood a few feet from the foot of the bed. Assessing the placement of the bed and the patio door, I guessed we could see the sunset from bed.

The small patio held a black metal table with two matching chairs and overlooked the frontage road. The beach and ocean were in the distance, beyond the parking lot and sidewalk.

Dane pulled a heavy iron chair out for me and positioned it to face the sea. The sun had begun its descent, igniting the sky with streaks of pink and red over the ocean's white caps. I glanced to Dane, who'd taken a seat on the other chair.

"Beautiful view," I whispered.

"It is." His eyes locked on mine as he brought the plastic cup to his lips. He then abruptly pulled it away. "Wait! We haven't toasted yet." He sat still for a few seconds. "To you, the woman who has brought... goodness to my life."

"You too, Dane," I whispered.

Clinking glasses, we each took a sip from our cups. The wine was a dessert red, the kind I could only have a few tastes of before it became overwhelmingly sweet. I swirled the glass and brought it to my nose to sniff, thinking back to the first time Dane and I shared a glass of wine together on the night we made cookies. Only a few weeks in, and we'd already made a series of cherished memories.

I'd never forget a minute spent with this man.

I took another sip, then noticed Dane had set his glass down. "It's good. You don't like it?"

He watched me carefully, studying my face with an intensity that made my skin warm. I averted my eyes. When he spoke, his voice was so low I had to watch his lips as he formed each quiet word.

"You're a kind of goodness I haven't seen in a long time, not since I was young. Childhood seems so long ago. I'd forgotten what it's like, what goodness feels like. Being with you takes me back. Makes me believe again. God, I want this. I want *you*, but—" He blew out a long breath of air.

"But?" I asked quietly.

"You're a bright light. A bright star in a dark sky. My life has been dark for so long. I don't want to be the one that burns you out, steals your light. But I can't walk away."

"Then don't."

"Nova, we haven't known each other long, but I know you. I know myself. For the first time in far too long, I'm thinking about more than just me."

"I don't understand—" I snapped my lips shut, unsure what he saw in himself that made him feel so wrong for me, unsure whether I *wanted* to know. I stared ahead and sighed. "I don't understand what's holding you back. You've also brought goodness to my life. Two weeks, that's all it's been, but—" Now it was me hesitating, stopping because I couldn't find the proper words to express myself.

Beyond goodness, Dane ignited passion, a deep stirring in my soul. A desire that transcended lust. He made me feel *alive*. He made me want more. A future, a family. Roots and plans.

Dane picked up the abandoned wine glass and gazed at the setting sun. "The tat on my chest—the bow and arrow— my buddy and I got them together before a mission. Nick's is crossed arrows, a symbol of friendship. Mine's a bow and arrow, signifying protection, a primitive way to eliminate a threat. I was Nick's right-hand man, and the arrow on my shoulder pointed to him. I would have given up my life for him. As soldiers, we take an oath, but Nick and I went beyond brothers in arms. We were closer than brothers."

The emotion on his face told as much of his story as the words he spoke. He stared ahead to the water which sparkled under the sun's fading shine. The briny wind picked up, making Dane's low, quiet voice even harder to hear. I leaned closer as he continued.

"Nick and I got these before a mission, a particularly tricky mission. One of the most important seaborne inva-sions in history, and everything had to align to make it a success. Strategists detailed strict requirements, silly as it sounds—the phase of the moon, the strength of the tides, the time in which we'd act. If any one of those factors weren't perfect, the mission would be postponed. But, as fate had it, everything went as planned... until it didn't. I'll spare you the details, but war-time planning, no matter how detailed or strategic, doesn't take into consideration human reaction, human emotion. Planning on paper doesn't translate to planning in action. Nothing can prepare you for that chaos. The chaos of humanity."

The sadness in Dane's eyes brought tears to my own. I wanted to reach over, to grasp his hand, or cover his body with my own and take away his pain. But I feared the slightest move would break the spell, and I desperately wanted to hear more, to learn more.

"The mission was a success, yet I look back with regret. So much passes through you when you are thrust into the middle of war, when you witness death and destruction, when you are the *cause* of death and destruction. Following orders without question, doing what's necessary to protect your brothers and yourself. At what cost? Being evil to defeat evil? How do I justify it? Those are the questions I can't answer. Acting on emotion rather than logic—that's the sin I cannot forgive."

Sparse streetlights barely provided enough illumination to see beyond Dane's face as the sun set. A single tear rolled down my cheek. A tear for him, his pain, and his regrets. I held no judgement, no fear or condemnation, only compassion for the man who was so obviously hurting from his past.

"After that mission, this tattoo," Dane said, thumb jutting toward his chest, "came to represent something else. No longer my buddy's protector, it came to symbolize the hunter I became. The need I felt on that mission to find and destroy, rather than serve and protect. Nick is the only one who knows this; he's the only one I've been able to talk freely and openly to. Until today. Until you."

"He's alive?" I whispered. I had assumed Dane's deeply

rooted pain stemmed from Nick's death. I breathed in, then delicately asked, 'Your friend Nick, do you and him keep in touch?"

"I owe him a lot." Dane turned to fully face me. A small smile graced his perfect face. "He's the one that set me up with the studio in Milwaukee. He married your neighbor."

I blinked upon Dane's reference to Mirabel. Suddenly, clear as day, I recalled a conversation.

"You took a strange guy home? He's there now? Some weirdo you met at the Metro Mart?"

"Weirdo, no. He's like a freaking Greek god. I mean, seriously, you should see him. I could bounce rocks off him."

I lifted a finger to my temple. The words grew louder and stronger as I closed my eyes.

"Mira, being good looking does not make someone a good person. This sounds really creepy. Who picks up women at a grocery store? Wait, did you say he's a soldier? Mira, he's trying to get laid. You know it, come on. Ditch him and meet me."

"I, um, I warned her about him. I didn't know him, but Mira and I were friends. Oh Dane, I remember now, a conversation I had with her. The day she met him, I told her to ditch him and meet me instead. He was a soldier on leave in Milwaukee, and I told her... I thought he was trying to get laid. Now they're married," I said in awe, then frowned, thinking back on how I brushed off her excitement. So wrapped up in myself, my career, I didn't make the time or effort to meet my friend's boyfriend. "I never really got to know him."

"Well, to be fair, I've never met Mira. Tell me more about her," Dane directed, watching my face as excitement flushed my cheeks. Talking about Mira brought a sense of security and contentment that warmed me. "You couldn't remember her name a few days ago; now you're recalling conversations. Did you guys have a falling out? Nick hasn't told me much. They're overseas. He warned internet and phone service was spotty. I haven't been able to get in touch with him the last few weeks."

"She's—" I stopped, cocking my head in thought as my right hand gingerly swept along the scar at my temple. It trailed to the trio of freckles on my collarbone, then further down to my hip, stopping at my tattoo.

"She's happy," I said, rolling her name over in my head. *Flowers and giggles. Mother and child. Peace and contentment.* Try as I may, I couldn't pull up more. "We didn't have a falling out. We must've drifted apart."

"It happens. There's always time to reconcile, reach out and close the gap." Dane pushed up from the chair. "I should grab our bags from the car. Let's move inside. We can get delivery and eat by the fire."

After Dane left to retrieve our suitcases, I sunk into one of the oversized lounge chairs and stared blankly at the crackling fire. I wondered whether Dane was right. Was there time to reach out to Mira? To close the gap? She'd just gotten married and was starting a new life with her new husband. What purpose would it serve, especially now, while they were in the honeymoon phase?

"You're happy, Mira, and it gives me peace knowing that you're finally happy." I whispered the words into the fire, hoping that somehow, through the many miles, she'd hear my message.

TWENTY-SIX

After a late dinner of cashew chicken and egg foo young, Dane and I were too full and tired to do anything more than slip into pajamas and climb into bed. I woke the next morning tucked in Dane's arms.

So, so much better than a suitcase.

"Morning," Dane murmured into my messy mop of hair. "That's the best sleep I've had since Monterey. Something about the wind and waves. Salt in the air. It's a powerful force. I slept like a baby."

Wind and waves. Salt and air. A powerful force. I stiffened, the reference feeling strangely ominous, oddly familiar.

"You okay?" Dane asked, loosening his hold over my rigid body. He shifted to peer at my face. "What's wrong?"

Shaking my head, I closed my eyes, desperate to fill the blank spaces in my mind. The flashes came and went too quickly to decipher. My finger traced the faded gash at my forehead. "The doctor assured me there'd be no lasting damage from the concussion, but I keep having these weird memories. Snippets, here then gone before I can really grasp them."

"Healing takes time," Dane said. Now he traced a finger over the barely-there scar. "Your mind will mend. Don't rush it. Vacation is a time to slow down."

"No, no rush." The world could stand still, and I'd be fine stuck in place with Dane.

"Oh, I take that back; I think Josie said breakfast is served until nine—looks like we have ten minutes. I'll run down there and bring some pastries up. And coffee. Can't forget coffee." He leaned in, placed a kiss on my forehead, then jumped from bed. "Be back in a minute."

The door closed behind him, and I rolled to my side, eyeing the sun-filled patio. Sighing from sleepy contentment, I smiled at how perfect my first vacation was going. The simplicity of coffee and pastries in bed with the man I... loved?

I love Dane.

Flipping onto my back, I grinned goofily at the vaulted ceiling. *I love him.* The fan spun, blowing over my face and making the wispy hairs along my forehead tickle my flushed skin.

It might've been quick using a word as strong as love, and things might've been a bit messy with Dane, yet I could not deny it. I *loved* him. Sure, we had obstacles, but did love ever come wrapped in a perfect package? My life was anchored in Milwaukee, and Dane had a long-term commitment in Monterey. It would require give and take.

I'll take the good with the bad.

The door swung open, and my head jerked in its direction.

"Josie told me to take extras," Dane called. A tray with two coffees and a plate piled with at least five pastries balanced on one hand as he pulled the key from the knob with his other. "I got one of each."

Hoisting to a sitting position, I scooted back against the headboard. Dane set the tray at the foot of the bed. "In bed or outside?"

"Let's stay inside," he said, nodding toward the door. "The sunshine is deceiving. There's still a fog over the sea. It's pretty chilly out."

He climbed next to me, and then reached to hand over a cup of black coffee. Steam rose from the liquid. I put it to my lips to savor its rich aroma and taste.

"It's just not right," Dane said, shaking his head. "You make everything look so damn sexy. Drinking wine, sipping coffee. I could watch you all day."

My cheeks pinkened. I knew I was an attractive woman, but Dane made me feel so beautiful, so wanted, like a treasured piece of artwork. The way he studied me, not just my face, but each feature, as if trying to commit every detail to memory.

As if he worried, I'd someday be just that, a memory.

"After breakfast, do you want to hit up the beach? We can check out the Mavericks surf spot," Dane asked, oblivious to the effects of his compliments.

"Mavericks?"

"Yeah, although Josie said the waves are unusually tame. With the current surf conditions, might not be worth the drive. We can check out some of the beach trails around here. Up to you. She gave me a few maps, circled some cool spots." He shoved half of a chocolate donut into his mouth.

"Sure, sounds good." I took a bite of a vanilla frosted long john.

"People usually come here for the big waves, but Josie

said when the sea goes still, you find peace in Half Moon Bay."

I stopped chewing.

"I guess I see her point. It's calming." Dane shrugged and took another bite.

"Say that again?"

"It's calming." He popped the rest of the donut in his mouth.

"No, the other part. What did Josie say?" I whispered, heart thumping.

Dane watched me carefully, taking a moment to swallow his mouthful of food. He cocked his head. "When the sea goes still, you find peace in Half Moon Bay."

I'D LIKE to think it's a coincidence, but I've come to learn nothing is ever a coincidence.

The words echoed in my head again, but instead of heeding it as a warning, I pushed into the inn's lobby, certain weird forces were at play.

Josie was hunched over the refreshment station. Her turquoise and white chiffon cardigan floated over a short sundress. Gold bangles at her wrists clinked against one another as she continued to pile coffee cups.

"Josie?" I asked. My stomach twisted into knots. "Sorry to bother you."

She turned around, smiling with a knowing tilt of her chin. "Good morning, darling. Sleep well?" Her chestnut eyes matched the curls that drifted over her shoulders. In the daylight, she appeared a lot younger than I originally thought.

"I did, thank you. But, um, I'm wondering, is there a

place around here with live music? Someone who sings... Do you know..." I trailed off, hesitating.

"Live music?" Confusion creased her brow. "Sure, there are a few places. I have my favorites, of course—"

"Do you know someone named Neal?" Dane interrupted.

After an obvious pause, she said, "I didn't realize it last night, but now I see the resemblance." She began to smooth the pile of napkins, turning so her back was to me. "I know Neal."

And Neal... I fear far greater for him. Words from the past echoed in my head, along with a vivid yet quick flash of Lucille, the caution in her tone and the concern written on her face as crisp as a picture. I gasped, and my hand shot up to press against the scar at my temple.

"Nova, are you okay?" Dane's hand touched my elbow, steadying me. "Here, sit. Josie, do you mind getting some water?"

Inhaling deeply, I closed my eyes, desperate to calm myself. Over the last few weeks, memories seemed to flutter nonsensically in and out of my head, but now they were coming quicker and harder. The voices and images becoming clearer and stronger.

"Here, darling." Josie offered a glass of water. She leaned in to hand me the cup. Her trio of gold bangles slid down her arm to her hand, exposing the inner part of her wrist where I could see three dots that formed a perfect triangle.

Instead of grabbing the offered cup, my hands flew to cover the matching freckles on my collarbone.

Josie studied me, eyes round with remorse and concern. She set the cup down.

"Nova?" Dane crouched beside the chair. "Come on, let's get you up to the room."

"Oh, darling. Are you okay?" Josie asked, her fingers gently skimming my bare arm.

"Where can she find Neal?" Dane cut her off. They locked eyes before both turning to me.

"He sings every night at the Broken Board Café," Josie replied softly. "Every night, Nova. I hope you can help him. And maybe he can help you too."

Dane led me back up the stairs. My legs shook from the weird images that continued to plague me.

But more so, my entire core shook from the knowledge that Neal was *here*.

NEITHER DANE nor I acknowledged the bizarre exchange with Josie. We crawled back into bed where Dane held me tightly until my body released the tension that had built up between my temples and shoulders.

Once my breathing leveled, Dane spoke. "Do you want to see him?"

"I need to. Oh, Dane, how did he and I drift so far apart? He's my brother for goodness-sake, my *twin*! Did you see how Josie looked at me? He needed help, and I was too focused on my career to make sure my own twin was okay."

Dane drew in a breath, and then released it slowly. The cozy scent of coffee and donuts brushed against my cheeks, and I closed my eyes, immediately feeling less overwhelmed.

"Let's take a walk. You'll probably need a light jacket. The fog's starting to lift, so it should warm up soon. Fresh air will do us both good." He lifted my chin with his index finger, then leaned in to kiss my forehead.

Climbing from bed, I plodded to the closet to grab the fleece jacket I'd hung the evening before. Instead of pulling it on, I tied it around my waist, feeling way too hot and bothered to add the extra layer. Dane wordlessly followed me out of the room, locking the door behind us before taking the lead.

At the bottom of the stairwell, he pointed toward the beach. "Let's walk that way. I don't know how far we can go past that bluff."

To our left, beyond the sandy beach with its high dunes and smattering of succulents, a jagged rocky cliff jutted above the ocean. The briny scent of seawater carried in the breeze, brushing against my cheeks.

A combination of anxiety and peace confused my senses. Slowly, we made the short trek across the street and past the sidewalk, hitting the transition from concrete to sand. It felt familiar, as if I were stepping over the threshold to a home I hadn't occupied in years. Familiar, yet different. Changed in a way I couldn't put my finger on.

Coarse, high stalks of tall grass began to thin out among the loose sediment. I resisted the urge to kick off my ankle socks and sneakers so I could feel the sand beneath my feet, but even with the sun shining in the clear sky—the earlier fog completely dissipated—a chill floated from the sea. I shivered.

Releasing my grip on Dane's hand, I turned toward the bluff.

"I haven't been here before, but it reminds me of..." My words trailed off as a lone wave in the distance formed in an otherwise dead sea. Picking up in velocity, it quickly rolled toward shallow waters. Its white crest spilled over as it smacked into the jagged rocks just beyond the shore line. Liquid crystals sprung in the air, catching the sun's light as they cascaded through the air.

Wind and waves. Sand and salt. Land, sky, and sea.

More waves formed. Dane and I stood motionless. Faster and stronger, they continued forming and rolling to shore, crashing against the rocks with a ferocity that made the sandy ground beneath my feet shudder.

Reluctantly, my feet carried me closer to the edge of sand and sea until the gentle touch of Dane's hand on my shoulder stopped me.

"Your shoes are getting wet."

"Mesmerizing, isn't it?" I murmured.

"I've always lived by water. Couldn't imagine being landlocked. The sea has a healing quality, a peace that you can't find anywhere else. Well, I suppose that isn't entirely true. It also has been one of humanity's greatest natural threats—tsunamis, hurricanes. The ocean is a powerful force. Some say it's the bloodline of life."

The ocean is a powerful force. The bloodline of life.

"I've had this conversation before," I whispered.

"Hmm? Like deja-vu? Hate that feeling, so annoying and creepy." He shrugged, then took my hand, lacing our fingers. We continued along the shoreline.

"Looks like the sea isn't so calm anymore," I said, then stopped walking. Turning to face Dane, I asked the question that kept playing in my head. "Do you think this is awfully weird? I mean, the coincidence that we stop here, at this random inn, and Josie knows Neal? He's *here*."

"I've learned over the years that nothing is a coincidence."

There's a reason he's here, just as there's a reason you're here. And I'm certain there's a reason I was meant to meet you.

I had this conversation with Dane before. It wasn't deja-vu. I *knew* we had this conversation before.

"None of this makes sense. None of it." I shook my head.

He studied my face before leaning in. His chin dropped to rest on the top of my head. "I can tell you're suffering, and I wish I could take it away. But it's not that easy. Finding peace isn't something you can find from others. It needs to come from within. But you'll find it. Peace exists. We have to believe it still exists, because if we give that up, we'll never find our way back."

"Back where?" I whispered.

"Only you can answer that," Dane said solemnly. "Maybe seeing Neal will give you direction. I felt pretty aimless for a long time. War can wipe away hope. Hope for peace, for humanity, for the future. Hope gets lost so easily. I don't want you to lose your way."

I sighed. "Well, I can't really lose my way if I don't know where I'm going."

TWENTY-SEVEN

The sound of the sea settled to white background noise as Dane and I continued to walk along the shoreline. Each step brought a higher level of peace, an assurance I was on the right path, even if I didn't know where it led. The ocean's raw energy renewed my mental strength, readying me to face Neal, to face my past.

Dane and I came to a rocky outcropping that blocked our way, and we had to turn around. Instead of taking the same route back, we climbed up a sand dune, and followed a hiking path lined with purple wildflowers, blooming shrubs, and leathery succulents. Loose sediments and twists in the narrow trail made the trek cumbersome.

As we ascended a particularly steep dune, my shoe slipped against the sand. Flailing, I grasped Dane's hip to steady myself.

"Whoa there," Dane exclaimed as he looked over his shoulder and down to me.

"Guess I should have warned you, I don't exactly consider myself the outdoor type," I said sheepishly.

"Yeah, you've mentioned that." The corners of his eyes

crinkled from the wide grin spreading across his face. "Don't worry, baby, I've got you."

Dane's use of the endearment made my stomach flutter. Suddenly shy, my eyes dropped from his face to my hands which still gripped his hips. "Well, actually, it appears I've got you."

He pivoted to face me, moving so quickly that my fingers barely left his hips before they were placed back around him. Leaning in, his lips were suddenly on mine, and I felt unsteady again, shaky for a different reason.

Dane probed gently. His tongue slipped against mine, taking sweet tastes before pulling back, leaving me dizzy.

"Dang, I needed that," he said. The wide grin reappeared again.

But I needed more. His kiss only satiated a small part of the hunger that built when our tongues collided. With my hands still on his hips, I firmly pressed into him, confirming he needed more too.

"Let's go." The command tumbled from my lips, low and husky.

Dane didn't reply, instead he pivoted again, taking my hand in his as he lunged forward along the path.

Within a few minutes, the edge of the gray, weathered inn came into view. My stomach fluttered. Each step closer brought more heat to my core. When the key to our room clicked in the knob, a throaty sigh escaped my lips. Dane practically booted open the door.

As he picked me up, my legs wrapped around his waist and our mouths frantically met. He kicked the door shut behind us. Seconds later, he deposited me onto the bed. We momentarily came apart, and Dane hovered above me. We stared at one another, both breathing heavily. Lust hardened his face and darkened his eyes.

My hand reached for his cheek, breaking our spell. As soon as my fingers touched his skin, all preamble was lost. We turned desperate. Both sets of hands scrambled to remove the thin layers of clothing separating us. My shirt was gone, along with his—both tossed to the floor. We came together, skin-to-skin. Dane's mouth returned to mine, kissing me briefly before traveling to my jaw, down my neck, and settling at the trio of freckles that blemished my collarbone. He placed three soft kisses over each speckle, then moved slowly to my sternum, caressing the flesh between my breasts with his mouth.

My breath hitched from each kiss-dampened graze of his lips. The skin beneath his breath tingled as he mapped a trail down my body. Stopping above my belly-button, Dane looked to me with stormy-blue eyes.

"You're everything I've ever wanted."

My eyelids flitted down.

"You're the hope I've carried all these years. The goodness I need; the future I long for. I never thought it was possible until I met you, Nova. I plan to do everything in my power to keep you safe, to be here for you, to help you. We'll weather whatever comes together. This arrow on my chest now points to you, the one I will protect."

Dane then made the same pilgrimage of kisses up my neck before his lips settled on mine.

My hands moved to the back of his head, clutching his hair as I lost all shyness and deepened the kiss. The heaviness of his body crushed me, but I needed it—I needed to feel the security and weight of him.

With his body pressed against me, my physical need drew a whimper from our connected lips. Dane shifted, swiftly moving to his back while bringing me over him. His hands roamed down my sides, settling on my hips as I began to press into him, allowing a sweet pressure to build in my core.

Before it became too much, I rolled off him, and peeled the yoga pants that were like a second skin down my legs.

"Last time... we didn't use... are you covered?" Dane awkwardly asked as he removed his own shorts.

"IUD."

With my answer, his arms were pulling me back over him, positioning my legs over his hips.

"You're so beautiful," he whispered. His knuckles brushed my cheek, then slid down my neck to the sensitive skin above my breasts.

My hips moved of their own volition, moving against him until the sweet pressure in my core again built to a needy ache. Our eyes locked, speaking to one another silently, pleadingly. Dane moved his hands to my hips, slowly guiding me up and then back down, filling all of me with all of him.

TWENTY-EIGHT

The hours lazily passed as morning turned to afternoon. Dane ordered delivery for lunch while I turned on the TV and searched the stations. He flipped on the fire, and we crawled back under the covers.

After settling on a gameshow to watch, we shouted answers and ate pizza in bed. Dane declared himself winner of the first two rounds, although I questioned his faulty math in adding the final score. After the third episode ended, we hesitantly crawled from bed.

"I guess we should check out the area." Dane stretched his arms above his head. "Let's grab a quick shower. You can go first."

Not bothering with my discarded clothes, I padded naked to the bathroom, giving a little wiggle of my butt when Dane whistled. The bathroom, like the inn, was old, with a low-to-the-ground toilet and a small vanity that had barely enough room to hold a cosmetic bag. I turned on the shower to let the water warm up, then brushed my teeth before stepping under the stream.

The bathroom door creaked open, and Dane—who'd

dressed for the pizza delivery—stepped through, once again naked.

My skin bristled by the sight of his flawless body. The tattoo along his back rippled as he bent to pick up a fallen towel.

"Care if I join?" He flashed a devilish grin.

"Only if you answer a question first."

"Didn't I already beat you at Twenty Questions?" he asked, referencing the game show we'd just watched.

"What's the lotus flower mean? On your back. What does it symbolize?"

Dane's grin remained wide, but he blinked rapidly. "Sure. Okay, the lotus flower. Rebirth, resurrection, faith. A refusal to accept defeat. I can go on and on about its spiritual meaning, but I guess you want to know what it means to *me*." He nodded his chin toward the shower, and I stepped aside to allow him space to join. "A lotus flower grows out of mud, but somehow is able to protect itself, staying beautiful among the muck. No matter the hardships it faces, it returns each day. Unwavering, unscathed, unaffected by whatever it encounters. That's why I initially marked it on my body. A permanent reminder that no matter the trial, I can overcome it. Each day a fresh start, a new beginning." He eyed me. Water sprayed against his face and droplets dripped off his lashes. "After the war, it no longer made sense. How can I rid myself of that ugliness? Cleanse myself of my sins? It's not that easy. Sometimes humanity is just so damn evil, so bad, nothing can mask its filth."

A tear rolled down my cheek as Dane bared his soul. His words rang loud and clear—touching my soul. Through my dampened eyes, I caught a similar moisture in Dane's.

Each compassioned word drew us closer, kindred spirits who found solace in one another.

Dane leaned in and tilted his head down so his nose brushed my forehead. His warm breath mingled with the steamy water. "I'm starting to believe again. Maybe there is such a thing as second chances and new beginnings. Maybe I don't need to be defined by the past."

I couldn't help but wonder if the accident was my lotus flower moment, my rebirth. An awakening that would lead to a new beginning—one that included Dane, and, hopefully, a fresh start with my brother.

AFTER DANE and I finished showering and dressing, we were both starved for dinner. I checked my phone for restaurant reviews in the area. A seafood joint near the Broken Board Café was a short walk away. I still hadn't decided whether we'd stop to see Neal after dinner or if I needed more time to process and prepare.

The waitress at Breakwater's came to our table, blatantly gawking at Dane while asking for our drink order. I placed a possessive hand over Dane's, smiled sweetly, and ordered the house red. When she returned with our drinks and asked about our dinner order, I hadn't even opened the menu. Dane had me covered, selecting crab cakes for an appetizer, then suggesting sanddabs, which were a popular fish in the Bay area.

Along with our appetizer, the waitress brought another round of drinks. I downed mine. My mind raced with thoughts of Neal. What would I say to him? What if he didn't want to see me?

"Maybe we shouldn't just show up unannounced. I

mean, it is his workplace," I said, placing my fork down. I'd barely touched my food. "I've had time to kind of let this sink in—that Neal is here and I'll get to see him—and I'm *still* freaking out inside. I have no idea how he's going to react."

"I'm sure it'll be a surprise for him, but maybe it's better this way? He won't have time to build up the anticipation like you. Like ripping off the bandage. But I get what you're saying. How about this—we can go there, sit at the bar, check things out, and see how you feel then. If you lose your cool, we'll leave a note."

Nodding, I plucked my cloth napkin from my lap. "I'm done."

Dane paid the bill, then we walked the three blocks to the Broken Board Café. The temperature had dropped, but it probably was my nerves causing my shivers and shakes. I tugged my cardigan tightly around my shoulders.

Rounding a corner, signage for the Broken Board came into view. Two huge, blue and white surf boards with red slashes running through the middle stood on each side of the café's double-doors. A small crowd mulled outside. The place looked busy for a weeknight.

"Five-dollar cover," a bald-headed guy with bulging muscles said as we approached. "Music's started. Goes til midnight."

Before I could pull my wallet from my crossbody, Dane handed over a twenty.

"You guys usually this busy?" Dane asked as the man handed back change. With all the people crowding the bar, we couldn't see the makeshift stage.

But I barely heard the bouncer's answer. My ears were trained on Neal's unmistakable voice floating above the crowd.

Slowly, my legs carried me closer. Nearing the U-shaped bar, I stopped short, closing my eyes and listening to lyrics I *knew* Neal had written himself.

"We danced in the clouds; we sang in the sun. Take me back; take me to those innocent days."

Neal's hypnotic voice transported me, taking me to the place he spoke of in the song, to an innocent time when I danced in the clouds while Neal sang in the sun.

Neal jumping into wild ocean waves. Me dipping a toe into a crystal-clear pond. Us taking turns playing in the tract of land behind the cottage. A rose-scented breeze floating over a field of vibrant wildflowers. Snow-white butterflies dancing in the wind. A majestic mountain shining under a brilliant sun.

"Let's sit," Dane whispered into my ear.

Breaking my daze, I wordlessly followed him to the bar, where a couple was vacating their barstools.

Too transfixed by my memories, I didn't hear Dane's order.

"Drink," Dane coaxed, nudging a glass of ice water toward me.

I obeyed, downing half the glass. The fuzziness in my head from the wine cleared, replaced by thoughts of Neal and our idyllic childhood.

"Can we go back; can we ever go back to those innocent days?"

Neal's spellbinding voice melted all reservations. I looked at Dane.

"I'm going to talk to him when he's done. Do you mind giving me some time alone with him?"

"Of course," Dane nodded.

The song ended, and Neal grinned. The crowd whooped and whistled. He rested his guitar on a stand and wiped sweat from his forehead. A lady with dreadlocks passed him a bottle of water. He brought it up to his lips and chugged the entire bottle before handing it back. The white spotlight bounced off his shiny, shaggy hair. With his gruff beard and distressed T-shirt, he looked like an effort-lessly cool combination of rockstar and surfer.

Neal sat down on the stool nearby, then leaned into the mic. "A little birdie told me there's a very special guest in my audience tonight. Many of the locals know me well, but they may not know this piece of trivia. I'm a twin. And it so happens, my other half is here. So, Novalee, this one's for you."

My heart stopped. He *knew* I was here. Josie must've warned him.

"*When the sea goes still, you'll find me here, singing under a half moon bay. When the stars lose their shine, you'll find me here, singing under a half moon bay. Singing a song so sweet, as sweet as the fruit, the fruit of the land. Singing a song so bright, as bright as the light, the light of the sky.*"

Tears filled my eyes as Neal began to play. I knew it would be this song—the one that had rolled off my own tongue so frequently over the last few weeks. The lyrics he'd written for me many years ago, which he said were a part of my story—the words that connected us through the many years and numerous miles.

The words that brought me back to him.

The song ended, and Neal's eyes closed. My heart stood still. Everything stood still. The people, the singing, the noise. Bright lights spilled over him, making him look angelic. When his eyes reopened, the room exploded in applause.

"Thanks, y'all, I know that's one of your favorites. Thanks for a great night. Johnny Miles is up next. See y'all tomorrow." Neal gave a slight bow of his head, then walked off the makeshift stage.

I immediately slid from my stool and began toward the stage.

"Nova, I'll be here," Dane called. I gave him a quick nod before proceeding.

People crowded Neal, but as I approached, he looked up, instinctively catching my eyes as if he knew I was coming.

"Hey guys, give me a second," he said, pushing out of the throng. In three steps, he stood before me.

"Neal," I whispered, searching his wide-eyed face.

We stood for several quiet seconds, each absorbing one another's presence.

"I recognize that symbol." Neal broke the silence. His eyes shifted from my face to my collarbone.

"Symbol?" I took an involuntary step backward. The intensity of his gaze jarred my already fragile nerves.

"Josie's marked too." With his index finger, Neal made a swooping motion, like the wings of bird. His voice softened. "What happened to you?"

"What happened to me?" I whispered. My hands flew to cover the freckles. The next musician began to play. "Can we go somewhere to talk?"

"Yeah, of course. My place is a block up the street. Let me grab my shit."

Before I could answer, Neal turned toward the makeshift stage, grabbed his guitar case, and disappeared through a door marked "Private." Glancing toward the bar, my suspicion that Dane's eyes would be trained on us was confirmed. He gave a jerk of his chin, and I acknowledged it with a forced smile.

Instead of trying to fight my way through the crowd

back to the bar to talk to Dane, I shot him a text letting him know I'd be leaving with Neal.

Me: Going to Neal's apartment to talk. Will meet you back here. He said it's a block away.

After hitting send, I looked up to catch Dane's eyes shifting from me to his phone. He tapped at his cell, and seconds later, mine pinged.

Dane: Text me the address. I'll meet you there when you're done talking. Don't want you walking alone in the dark.

I looked up and nodded my head, offering what I hoped appeared to be a sincere grin.

"Ready?" Neal asked.

Spinning around with a stiff smile planted in place, I again nodded.

Neal led me through the crowded bar. People greeted him with pats on the shoulder, half hugs, and wide, genuine smiles. He'd obviously made a name for himself over the years at the Broken Board Café.

Stepping into the crisp evening air, the hum of the waves beyond the bar provided a welcoming background noise, drowning out the awkward silence.

I fidgeted with the bottom button on my cardigan, buttoning and unbuttoning it, unable to keep my fingers still. I used to give presentations to packed rooms, but now couldn't find a single word to say to my brother.

Before the button popped off, I dropped the hem and clasped my hands in front of me. We rounded a corner and turned onto a side street. I finally broke the silence. "You're really good."

Neal stopped walking. He looked to the sky, lips parting as his head slowly moved back down. Exhaling, he met my eyes. His lower lip dropped, as if he were about to speak, but before he could form a word, a swishing noise sounded from behind us, followed by a shrill, harsh *caw*.

Both our heads snapped around. My eyes darted to the top of a telephone pole where a lone black bird perched.

"Shit," Neal muttered, grabbing my hand. "Shit, Novalee. Come on."

Pulling me along, I nearly stumbled over my feet as Neal careened down the sidewalk. My head twisted back and forth, from a frantic Neal to the calm black bird that seemed to be watching us.

My heart pounded, and I swallowed deliberately, as if pushing my mounting fear back down. "What's going on, Neal? What is that?"

"For so long, I've lived in the dark. Not knowing what happened to you, not feeling you... *nothing*. And like a bolt of lightning hitting my soul, you came back. Pieces of you, memories of you. *You* were back. It hurt, Novalee. It hurt so badly because as quick as it came, it fell away again, and I felt your *loss*. I thought in that moment, you were gone. Really gone. I swear, I felt it."

"What?" I asked, tugging at his hand and trying to slow our pace.

"July fifth." He marched forward. "I thought you died, but now I know. You *fell*."

A bolt of lightning, a falling star. A fallen god.

The soft whispering words sounded in my ears. I squeezed my eyes shut and resisted the urge to snatch my hand from Neal's grip to cover my ears.

"I felt it," Neal continued. My eyes popped open. "And... I saw it. I saw you fall. As if part of my own soul had died."

"But I'm alive, Neal," I half whispered, half cried. "See, I'm here. I'm *alive*, and somehow, I made my way back to you. I got your message, the song you wrote, and I—I found you again."

Neal ignored my cries, too lost in his own despair to acknowledge mine. His voice shook. "As if it were me behind the wheel, hitting you."

"What?" I squeaked. My palms dampened beneath his grip.

"Come on." The emotion in his voice dropped away, and he motioned to a brown, wooden cottage with a dilapidated front porch. Neal led me around to the back. "This way. My place is back here. Hurry, I think it's following you."

"What?" I asked again. "Following us? *Who?*"

Inserting a key into the door, he pushed through, then moved past me to open the first interior door inside the hallway. Neal ushered me in before closing and locking the door behind himself. He scurried to the lone window at the far end of the room and yanked the shade down. Standing still for a second, his shoulders dropped and he slowly turned to face me. His eyes narrowed as he studied my face.

"Neal, what was that all about?" I leaned against the wall and tried to catch my breath.

"Messengers, Novalee," he whispered, as if sharing a secret. Neal gestured toward the two-person table pushed up against the wall in the small kitchen. "Have a seat. I need a minute to think."

Messengers? Instead of asking more, I silently took a seat. Tears remained moist against my cheeks. With the back of my hand, I rubbed them away. Taking a few deep breaths, I settled into the seat and rested my head against the peeling paint of the aged, yellow wall.

Neal breathed deliberately, seeming to gain composure, and nodded toward the refrigerator. "Want a beer?"

After the weird exchange on the street, the normalcy of his question almost made me giggle.

"No, thank you." I glanced around his apartment. Adjacent to the kitchen, a small living room held a simple cream-colored recliner and a brown couch. No pictures, no décor other than a surf board propped against the wall in the far corner.

Neal tilted his head and pursed his lips, as if he were about to say something but thought better of it. He swung open the refrigerator door, pulled out two beers, popped the top off both, and placed them on the table in front of me.

"You look like you could use one," Neal said. He pulled a chair out and sat down opposite of me. Leaning back, he picked up the beer and downed nearly half the bottle in one long gulp.

I took a sip of mine. "Let's start over, start from the beginning."

Neal ran a hand over his gruff chin, then nodded.

I closed my eyes, recalling the early weeks of summer. "I was working on a project in London, trudging through the motions, not really myself. I felt off for weeks. Finally, I wrapped things up and flew back to the states. On my way home from the airport, I got into a car accident. A pretty nasty wreck." Neal's face softened, making him appear more like the sweet boy of our youth. "I was lucky to only walk away with a concussion and some bruised ribs. Call it a near death experience, but since then, well, I saw how quickly life can change. I knew I needed to find you, reach out to you. We were so close. Aunt Lu wouldn't have wanted us to drift apart like this—"

"*Aunt Lu?*" Neal interrupted. He shook his head, then rubbed his palm over an eye. His head twisted upward, looking to the ceiling as it continued to shake. "Lucille, of course."

My cell pinged, momentarily diffusing the odd tension.

"That's probably my, um, boyfriend checking in." I pulled my cell from my bag, silenced it, then set it on the table. Neal's fingers nervously strummed against the table-top. He appeared so edgy, ready to flee, I didn't want to reveal the entire truth, that my memory of the accident included him behind the wheel, Lucille on the sidewalk.

As if it were me behind the wheel, hitting you.

Was it possible that after all this time, Neal felt my pain? Through the miles, was Neal somehow, spiritually or otherwise, with me during the wreck, helping me cope? I vaguely remembered being comforted following the accident. The feather-soft touches that stroked me, held me, shielded me.

I breathed out, closing my eyes as I chose my next words carefully. Relaxing my tone as soft as possible, I asked, "Why didn't you email me? I know you deleted your account, but mine hasn't changed." I glanced down to my cell. My phone number may have changed a few times over the years, but not my personal email address.

Neal scrubbed his face, now with both hands. "I'm guessing Lucille has something to do with this. Otherwise, you'd know damn well why I haven't *written*."

"Where's this animosity toward Aunt Lu coming from? I know you and her had your differences, but running away? Not coming back for her funeral? You left us. You left *me*."

"Funeral?" He eyed me like I had two heads. His focus shifted to my collarbone, and my cheeks blazed. The freckles felt more and more like a brand scarring my skin. "You're talking about it as if it really happened."

My jaw dropped. The more Neal talked, the more

agitated and fidgety he became. His fingers went back to the tabletop, thumping to the rhythm of my pounding heart.

"Something's wrong. Something's happened to you." He jabbed a finger in the direction of my collarbone, then hitched his thumb toward the window. "Their messengers are following you."

Wide eyed, I could only stare as Neal's rant continued. My breath escaped in short puffs.

"You need to talk to my friend; she can help you. You need to talk to Josie *soon*, before *they* come sniffing. They already have their eyes and ears tailing you."

When Josie said she hoped I could help Neal, did she mean drugs? Mental illness? The intensity of Neal's words, his apparent paranoia, made me realize how deeply he believed his own outrageous claims.

Yet, I couldn't help but ask, "Before *who* comes sniffing?"

Neal's eyes burned with hatred. "Hunters."

TWENTY-NINE

"Hunters?" I whispered.

"Josie can help—" Neal was cut off by pounding on his apartment door.

"Nova! Open up," Dane's authoritative voice commanded from the other side.

"What the hell? Who's that?" Neal shoved his chair back from the table.

Before I could answer, Dane burst through the door, chest puffed and eyes wild. "Nova, are you okay?"

Neal jumped to his feet. His chair skidded a few inches before toppling over. My hands flew to cover my mouth. The clatter quieted, and we stood in a jagged triangle.

"What have you done? Novalee, *what* have you done?" Neal whispered. Eyeing Dane, his lips compressed with disgust. Hostility rolled off him in visible waves, shuddering his limbs as his hands balled into fists.

I took a slight step back, unable to speak.

"Cool it," Dane's low voice growled.

"Don't tell me what to do, *Hunter*." Neal's vicious eyes narrowed to slits. The tension between them thickened the air, stifling the room. The temperature seemed to have risen ten degrees in ten seconds. Through gritted lips, he muttered, "Get out of here. Get out!"

"Calm down." Dane defensively flipped his palms up. I stepped in front of him, creating a barrier between the two men.

"Dane?" My hand came up to his chest, and I gave him a gentle nudge. "What's going on?"

"Oh, the *hunter* hasn't told you?" Neal growled.

"Hunter?" I looked up to Dane, whose eyes remained trained on Neal. "Dane, who's Hunter?"

"Not who—*what*." Neal's lip snarled. "He's a *hunter*. And the worst of their kind. A *killer*. You led him right to me."

"What?" I whispered, leaning into Dane.

"This has nothing to do with you, okay?" Dane's voice softened as his arm came around my waist.

"I don't know what he's told you, Novalee, or what he's done to you, but get him out of here." Neal's urgent voice wobbled. "Get him out of here, or I'll—"

"You don't want to do this." Dane's tone was unusually calm, betraying his furiously beating heart. I pressed closer against his chest. Peeking from within Dane's hold, I spotted a small black handgun in Neal's shaking hands. Too stunned to even gasp, my lips formed a silent 'O'.

"Of course, I don't want to do this. I don't want to become like *you*. This is your last warning. Get out of here, or she'll see something that'll burn her innocence forever."

"Neal, no." I choked out the words as I pushed from Dane's chest. "What are you thinking? Put that down."

"I know you're messed up in the head, Novalee, but what are *you* thinking?" Neal's arm rose. The gun trembled in his hands. "I'll do it; I swear I'll do it."

"I'm not here for you, dammit!" Dane bellowed. His voice gentled when he spoke again, his confession regretful. "I'm not here for you."

"What?" I whispered. My head swiveled between Dane and Neal. "Dane? What are you saying?"

Dane shook his head at Neal. But he wouldn't look at me, wouldn't answer my question.

"Go on, tell her, *Dane*," Neal urged sarcastically.

"We're leaving. I'm going to take Nova back to the inn, and once you calm down, you two can talk again."

I am not here for you.

If not for Neal, then... *me?*

Dane's hand wrapped around my bicep, and I stiffened.

"Get your hands off her," Neal said.

I didn't know what to do, who to trust. My body began to tremble. Fear tingled up my spine and shook my vision. My head shook side-to-side. My lips parted, but no words could come out.

"Give me a minute. Let me explain," Dane pleaded with me.

"Your kind takes without question, without warning," Neal's voice quivered as violently as his hand—the hand holding the gun. "And you want a minute?"

With his eyes laser-focused on Neal, Dane jerked his chin, and the gun in Neal's hands flew across the room, cracking the wall before plunking to the ground.

My stomach dropped. Air burned my throat as I took heavy breaths. The hum of the refrigerator and the rapid thump of my heart sounded above the room's sudden silence, vibrating in my ears. I watched Dane's Adam's apple bob as he swallowed. He closed his eyes while his lips settled into a thin, grim line.

"Let me explain." Dane didn't move, but a gentle touch

stroked my cheek. Whispery words sounded in my ears. *I want you to know me. What I am.* A memory flashed in my head. Dane on my patio, us overlooking the park. *The rustling leaves, the groan of thunder.* "A moment of weakness, a moment of anger, and I was recruited into this life. I eliminated evil, but in doing so, I've done evil."

No longer my buddy's protector, it came to symbolize the hunter I became. The need I felt on that mission to find and destroy. The tattoo on Dane's chest, his confession. My blood ran cold.

"I'm paying my penance. I've had to look at humanity, realize its faults, and find my way back. You've helped me find my way back."

The room was still, yet I felt it—feather-soft brushes against my skin. *Stroking my cheeks, hushing my fears, sheltering me, blanketing me in warmth.*

"The night of the accident." My voice was barely above a whisper, yet I knew Dane and Neal heard me. I shuddered as I held my fingers to my temple. "Dane, I remember. The night of my car accident, you were there. It was *you.*"

Somehow, my legs followed the subconscious command from my brain to flee. I pushed past Dane, out of Neal's apartment, down the short hall, and out of the building.

Running into the dark night, my sandals pounded against concrete, only slowing when I hit the cold, wet sand that separated land and sea. Waves roared in synch with my heaving chest. I stopped to catch my breath. Kneeled over, my palms grasped my thighs as I panted, desperate for air.

Swooshing noises came from behind, drowning out the sound of my pants. Closer and louder, they mixed with a shrill sound, the guttural croak of a sorrowful bird. Tears leaked from my eyes as they snapped left and right, then forward toward the rocky shoreline.

Again, I found myself running. Running without thinking, without seeing, racing on a foreign trail that ended at a sparse clearing overlooking the sea. The sound of flapping wings and crashing waves pounded in my head as my feet pushed against dense sand.

Steps from the edge, I stumbled on a stick strewn across the path. A scream escaped my lips, cursing the briny air. I crashed to my knees. Sediment flew up from the ground, creating a puff of dust that blurred my teary vision and assaulted my nostrils.

Through the haze, the soil and sea illuminated under the moon's glow. An echoing mix of wings, waves, and wind surrounded me, growing louder. Pounding and fluttering, they culminated to a high-pitch rumble that matched the furor of my heart.

Clumsily moving on all fours, I scooted backward, frantic to escape the dark energy that swirled around me. I moved slowly, deliberately, inching to the edge which jetted high above the ocean like a pirate's plank on a stolen ship.

A rush of air flapped around my hair, thrashing against my face. Fear engulfed every nerve, momentarily paralyzing me.

Are you sure you want to do this? It is going to hurt. On this journey, you will not have the powers of the gods, no knowledge of the divine. You will wake some memories of your mortal past; bits and pieces that may confuse you. Ultimately, your soul shall decide what is revealed to help you choose your path.

The familiar words echoed in my head, along with images of Lucille—her cobalt-blue eyes round with worry, her strawberry-blond hair illuminating under a brilliant sun.

I don't know how much time you'll have, Novalee, but I hope you find the answers and closure you need before they find you.

A bolt of lightning split the black sky, bringing another echoing wave of words and images to my blinded eyes. The land quivered from thunder. I grasped blindly, clutching handfuls of soil as I inched along the ground. Loose sediment slipped through my fingers like the sands of time through an hour glass.

I'm out of time.

My body no longer felt earth beneath me as I stumbled over the edge, tumbling through the air as another bolt lit the sky.

Bright, vivid flashes blinded my retinas and burned my veins. My limbs flailed. Wind whipped my cheeks. Lightning illuminated the sky. My whole world seemed to turn on its axis, shuddering and pulsating. Twisting and roaring. I screamed, but it was drowned out by the cracks of lightning that echoed with another sound. An earsplitting *caw*. A noise so loud it nearly shattered my ear drums.

I hope you choose the destiny you deserve... the destiny you deserve... the destiny you deserve...

I was falling... falling... falling.

Deafeningly loud, blindingly white... then darkness.

THIRTY

"I had a terrible nightmare." I opened my eyes to find the overhead fan spinning. Rolling to my side, pain shot between my temples. My fingers flew to the scar at my forehead, now feeling fresh and open. I shifted to sit. Sand and sediment crunched beneath my bare skin.

Dane stood next to the patio door with his arms crossed over his chest. His grim eyes met mine. Feeling another presence, I barely had the energy to twist my head toward the fireplace. A familiar figure stood in a similar pose.

"You?" I croaked. "What are you doing here?"

Liam, the strange man from the night at Bar Continental, didn't need to answer the question directed toward him, because in that instance *I knew*. Neither man said a word, nor did they make any effort to move. My gaze shifted back and forth until I finally closed my eyes. The pain at my temples exploded as memories flooded my head.

When I'd met Liam before, I had glazed over the strange aura that surrounded him, a dichotomy of light and dark, life and death. In the divine world's hierarchy, Liam held a position of immense power, an angel that could exist in both the divine and mortal world. Called *presiders*, his kind oversaw the gods that walked among the mortals.

"I'm not ready," I whispered, unsure whether my proclamation was directed at Liam or myself. "I need time. Lucille said I'd have time until my soul chooses its path. Why are you here if it's my choice?"

Dane spoke, his voice low and commanding, his eyes hard and unyielding. "You've earned a reward. Why would you turn away the ultimate prize?"

"Dane," I whimpered. "You were there, the night of the accident."

"It shouldn't have gone this far." Dane looked at the carpet and shook his head. "I shouldn't have taken it this far. But now your eyes are open, and you can see humanity for what it is. *I've* opened your eyes."

Dane's dark disposition, the dangerous edge I had recognized when first meeting him, now made sense. The man I'd fallen in love with was a *hunter*, an outlaw, recruited to track gods defying their fate.

"You and I..." My proclamation died on dry lips. I couldn't finish the sentence. *You and I are real.* I lifted my eyes to meet Dane's, but his stony features held no trace of warmth, no kindness.

No trace of love.

Pieces of my heart—the pieces that had swelled over the last few weeks spent with him—began to deflate, shrinking along with my resolution.

Liam exhaled, running a hand through his sandy brown hair. "You're naïve, Nova. Blinded by humanity's temptation. See this world for what it is. Understand all that you'd give up."

"It's ugly; it hurts. It's filled with abuse and despair." Disgust thickened Dane's voice.

Half gasping, half sobbing, I took a breath of sordid air. "What are you saying? Why are you doing this?"

"It's my job," Dane said quietly. "Look at me. I'm a hunter. You're a god questioning your destiny, teetering on the edge, heading in the wrong direction. Thinking with human emotion, human reasoning. You can't trust a human heart to make a divine decision. Do you see where it leads you? Weak, broken, so easy to deceive."

Were the last several weeks a farce, a way to show me the corruption and deception of humanity? Push me to choose divinity?

A way to bring me—a fallen god—to accept my fate?

"I can feel your heart breaking, just as I can feel your anger, resentment, hurt. Pain that feels like its tearing a hole through your soul. End it, Nova. Say the words, and it all goes away. You return to your rightful place. The rest of your existence will be perfect. You stay, and this is what you'll get. The dysfunction of humanity. You'll get people like me."

"No," I sobbed, covering my face with my hands.

"It's true." Dane jammed his hands into his jean pockets and looked down. "I'm sorry I took it too far. But it's true."

"Go. Just go!" My muffled cries were barely discernible. I didn't hear Dane's footsteps, or the door open and close, but I knew he was gone. My soul felt his abandonment like a pacifier ripped from a baby's mouth.

My hands remained over my eyes as I rolled over, smooshing my face into the pillow to stifle my sobs. Could it be true? Dane, a *hunter*? Had I finally found what I thought I'd been searching for—a future, a family—only for it to be based on a lie?

My soul ached, my heart wept—the dysfunction of humanity too raw and real. *Why* would I choose this ugly world? Dane was right. If opening my eyes was his job, he'd done it to perfection.

Eventually, my cries subsided and my breathing evened. I shifted, sensing I still wasn't alone.

"You too. Leave," I croaked.

"It shouldn't have happened like that." Liam pushed from the wall he leaned against.

"I said leave."

"Dane is impulsive. He will be reprimanded."

"Reprimanded? For showing me the truth?"

"You're evading the inevitable, Nova." Liam watched me as he walked to the door. "For what it's worth, I am sorry."

"Liam?" I asked, and he paused with his fingers clenched around the door knob. "Was any of it real?"

Liam's voice softened with sympathy. "He's a hunter, Nova. You want to deny your fate, renounce your place in the Kingdom. Dane showed you the truth of humanity. It's fickle, it's selfish, it's painful. How can you trust your heart to make this most consequential decision when it can be so easily deceived? Why give up the chance for perfection? Peace comes and goes here, one moment bliss, the next devastation. For every virtue, there is a vice. Is this what you want?"

For weeks, I had allowed Dane into my life, into my heart, and into my soul. But I was a job to him. An assignment. A god refuting her fate.

And he was the hunter, sent to show me how easily human emotion is manipulated. A mission to bring this fallen god back to face her destiny.

"I don't know what you were looking for—closure with Neal? A fascination with human emotion? I've walked with the mortals for a long time, Nova, but I still remember the beauty of the Hark. I can't begin to describe the glory of the Kingdom. Choose carefully. You have until sundown. My winged messengers are watching."

The door clicked behind Liam as he let himself out.

～

AFTER FINDING the strength to get out of bed, I searched for my cell phone, but quickly realized I had left it at Neal's apartment. I desperately needed to talk to him but wasn't sure I'd be able to retrace the route to his apartment. And I couldn't wait until tonight when he'd be playing at the Broken Board Café. I only had until sundown.

Wracking my frantic brain, I remembered Neal's plea. *You need to talk to my friend, she'll help you. You need to talk to Josie soon, before they come sniffing.*

Still dressed in sand-matted, muddied clothes, I flew out of the room and down the three flights of stairs. The door to the lobby had been propped open, allowing the salty breeze to blow freely into the room. I was inside, palms planted across the reception desk, before calculating what I'd say.

Josie stepped through the door marked "Private" with a sad smile, as if waiting for me.

"You knew all along?" I whispered. "How could you let me go with a hunter?"

"Oh, darling, it's come back?" she asked.

"My memories?" My voice still low, I took a step back from the desk and considered her question. My finger traced the scar at my temple. "Some of them."

"Only the memories that will help lead you on your path, help you find closure so you can move on," Josie said. Her lip turned up in a mischievous smile. "Sexy lot, aren't they? All dangerous and dark. Although, it certainly feels weird referring to Dane as sexy. He's grown into a fine young man."

"You know each other?"

"He probably doesn't recognize me. Different era back then. I went by Fi, but he called me Auntie. Dane was raised in these parts by his uncle. Looks like he's turned into the gentleman I always knew he'd become."

My eyes burned with tears. "He's a liar, and, and... a *hunter*."

"He's helping you." Josie tilted her head.

"I was a mission," I said softly.

"Maybe you were. Maybe you still are. But it doesn't change the fact that that boy is in love with you."

If my heart wasn't hurting so badly, Josie referencing dark, dangerous Dane as a boy would have struck me as funny. Instead, my heart seemed to ache even more.

"Dane's story is his to tell, but I've known him since he was a young walker."

"A walker?" I asked.

"A walking god raised here, among the mortals instead of in the Hark. Jake cared for him." Josie hesitated, blowing out a puff of air before holding up her wrist. "Jake is the reason for this."

"What does it mean?" I asked as I slowly brushed my fingers over the trio of freckles at my collarbone.

"Many walking gods complete their mission. Some fail. Some are given new missions. Some live out their existence in the Hark. Some are offered a place in the Kingdom. Some reject it. Fall from grace."

"You're a fallen god?"

"Maybe that's why Dane brought you here. Maybe he does remember. I don't know." Josie smiled gently. "There are not many of us that bear the mark. If you make the decision to fall, the mark will remain. A forever reminder, like a tattoo."

Now, my fingers moved from the freckles at my collarbone to the Celtic knot on my thigh. Two marks that held a part of my story. "I saw Neal last night. What's happened to him?"

"Everybody's story is their own. He'll need to tell you. And Dane too. I can't speak for them."

"Well, what about you? Why did you give up everything?" I spoke without thinking, and from the sudden shimmer in Josie's eyes, I knew the question struck a chord.

"Love, of course. Is there ever any other reason?" She motioned to one of the two chairs in front of the fireplace. "I know your time is precious, but please sit for a minute. I can't tell you their stories, but I can tell you mine."

After sinking into the cushion, Josie nodded toward the fire, which crackled and sizzled. My eyebrows shot up. "You still have powers?"

"Yes." She nodded. "After I fell, I was stripped of a home in the Hark. I can no longer transcend the boundaries, but I still have divine energy. Not as strong of course. My life is among the mortals now. It's a tradeoff I suppose."

"Why did you choose this?" I waved my arms around.

"I've been here for almost one hundred years." Josie looked down to her lap. Her hands fidgeted with the smooth, thin material of her grey flowy skirt which had been paired with a black tank top displaying toned arm muscles. She had a firm, young body of a thirty-something year old. "I was sent from the Hark to help a Sky god, a young goddess who had lost her way. During my time here, I fell in love. When it was over, I couldn't leave."

"Wait, the man who raised Dane, Jake—he was your love?" I asked.

"Yes," she said. Sadness passed over her face. "Not was, *is*. He will always be my love. In the meantime, I wait."

"Meantime? Where's Jake now?"

"He's in the Land, unable to transcend the boundaries. It's his punishment for our transgressions. Someday, though, I hope we will reunite. All I can do is maintain that hope. Maintain faith that he will return to me. It's the only way I can believe in a future."

"You gave it all up, only to lose him?"

"I haven't lost him, Nova. I'll never lose him. A love like ours will never die."

THIRTY-ONE

G lancing from Josie's handwritten map to the road signs, I navigated by foot through the maze of streets to Neal's apartment. The cottage's shabby porch soon came into view, and my pace slowed. I was almost there, but then what? What would I say?

As I turned toward the back of the house, I spotted a bike propped against the wall. A long-ago memory, the sting of Neal's skinned knee, flashed in my head. But now, instead of the young kid I'd previously remembered, it was Neal and me as young adults, beginning our journey in the mortal world.

Separated by two thousand miles, I felt Neal's fall as he learned to ride a bike. I was a college freshman, studying in the library when my knee suddenly twitched, then stung like a bad rug burn. I'd yelped and clutched my leg. The students around me had looked up and stared. I remember blinking back tears, feeling not only pain but embarrassment too.

That moment in the library was the second time I felt

physical pain. The first being when I'd drunkenly gotten a tattoo—the Celtic knot that permanently marked my skin.

In the Hark, we did not feel pain such as skinned knees, needle pokes... or broken hearts.

Now, stopping outside of the backdoor to the dilapidated cottage, I contemplated the harsh truth of human emotion and feeling. It was raw and real, tangible and consuming, fascinating and terrifying. It could build you up, only to tear you down.

At the door, I searched for a buzzer, doorbell, or directory. Not finding anything, I twisted the knob, thankful to find it unlocked, and stepped through into the short hall. Three doors lined each side. I tried to recall which one was Neal's—the previous night a blur—but a familiar, commanding voice boomed from the first. I moved closer, my eyes widening as I deciphered two distinct voices, both loud enough to hear through the closed door.

"If only you would have shut up for five seconds yesterday," Dane exclaimed. His voice dropped, and I pressed my ear to the door. "She's here for *you*. To see you, make sure you're okay, and you scare the living crap out of her."

"Like I'd trust a hunter."

"Grow up, kid. If not for yourself, then for your sister. She's hurting. Can't you feel it? Can't you see it?"

"What do you know about pain?" Neal spat back. "You only know how to inflict it."

"Oh, brother. Do you think I enjoy this? Being a hunter? Seeing how humanity destroys and deceives? I was recruited a long time ago, when I was much younger than you, you idiot. Keep it up, Neal. You only get so many chances before your time runs out." After a pause, Dane continued in a more relaxed tone. "You want to hear it? The reason why I am what I am?"

I took a step back, guilt warming my cheeks. Eavesdropping on them had taken a swift turn from a heated argument to sharing intimate details. Regardless, I couldn't walk away. I resumed my hunched position with my ear pressed to the door.

"I grew up in these parts, a walking god raised here instead of in the Hark. Spent my childhood up and down this coast, raised by a god who loved me like his own. He took me hunting, fishing, camping, exploring. Taught me to be a god and a man. But when I was not quite eighteen years old—mortal years—I enlisted in the Army. My first duty station wasn't far from here. Fort Ord, near Monterey. I met the god I was destined to protect there. His name is Nick, but in the Land, he went by Niko."

"The God of Victory," Neal interrupted. "Josie knows him."

"We spent months training on Ord before our unit deployed. One of the most sensitive military invasions of the twentieth century. Weeks of waiting, cooped up on a ship like sardines. Seasick and homesick. Finally, our mission was in sight. All I had to do was protect Nick, ensure he completed his task—ensure he was *victorious*. But when my boots hit the beach in Normandy, all my training went by the wayside. I lost my way, let my anger surge, let my disgust at humanity's disregard for life degrade my vision. I allowed human emotions to destroy my resolve, and while I completed my task—I kept Nick safe—I *killed*. They were not innocent by any means—foreign forces working against us. Had I acted under a different emotional state, I would not have had to stand before my superiors and take my sentence. But I killed for vengeance."

A few seconds of silence passed before Dane spoke again. I used those precious moments to swipe the tears from my cheeks. "If you look at the books in the WWII history museum at Ord, you'll find my name. But Dane Kill-bane, the god I was, died that day. A new man was born. A hunter. And now, this is my life."

I didn't see Neal's face, but I felt his reaction—the pounding of his heart and the tension in his muscles as his shoulders stiffened.

"Neal, you've lost your way. If you don't change, there will be no going back. Eventually, you'll face the consequences." Dane's voice was soft, but his warning was loud and clear.

"It's too late; I'm already paying the price. I don't know how to right any of my wrongs," Neal confessed.

"Let me help you," Dane said earnestly.

"Why would you help me?" Neal asked. "Oh, silly question. You really do love her, don't you?"

My heart stopped, and my breath hitched, causing a small gasp to slip through my parted lips. The slight sound echoed against the hallway walls, and while I hoped against all hope it went unheard, the footsteps careening toward the door said otherwise. I jumped from my hunched position, and my hands flew to cover my mouth. The door swooshed open.

"Novalee?" Neal asked, staring down at me.

Certain my cheeks had turned a flaming shade of red, I swiftly averted my eyes, staring at my feet, focusing on the chip on my polished big toe. *Man, I need a pedicure.* Then I giggled, because in that instant, with the heavy conversation I'd just overheard and the immense decision looming, I could only focus on chipped red paint.

"Ah, come in," Neal spoke again, pushing the door open wider.

My eyes lifted, momentarily meeting Dane's before

shifting to Neal. I turned toward Neal, stammering, "I want to help you. I want to take away your pain, like I did when we were young. Even if my memories are skewed, I know I can help."

"Is that what's holding you back? You want to help me? Absorb my pain again? Nothing can fill that hole. Only her. Only Cece."

"Cece?" I hesitated. "What does she have to do with this?"

Then I remembered. The man Celia had run off with... Neal.

Looking at Neal's heartbroken face, feeling his saddened soul, I wanted to wrap him up in my arms and take it all away.

"Only Celia," Neal whispered. "I'd give up everything for her, including my words, my voice."

My heart flittered. For the second time that day, I heard a proclamation of a love so deep, they were each willing to forgo everything. Defy their fate. Buck their destiny.

Was I willing to do the same?

Neal's brow knitted. "Nova, I'm no longer the person you once knew. I've changed, and so have you. But I can tell, I can *feel* your hesitation, your reservations, your pain. I can't take anymore hurt; I have enough in my own heart. We're all fighting our own personal battles. I can only answer for myself. I can't be the reason you stay."

Searching Neal's face, mirroring emotions swelled in our eyes. My twin, my brother. At one time, I thought we'd shared a soul. Now he pled for me to save my own. A silent plea only I could hear.

Nodding my head, I embraced Neal.

Bits and pieces of him—snippets from our shared childhood—flashed between our connected skin. For a second, we were transported to our idyllic childhood, to a place that could only be described as nirvana. A world so serene, we had danced in the clouds and sang in the sun.

Neal's hold tightened. He leaned into my ear, and whispered, "I want that for you." As his arms fell away, I heard the gentle click of the door.

Dane, who promised he'd never walk away, left me for the second time that day.

THIRTY-TWO

"Stop!" I called. "Wait!"

I know Dane heard me; I could tell by the slight jerk of his shoulders and momentary pause in his pace, yet he continued walking further away. I kicked off my sandals by the sidewalk so I could maneuver through the sand easier.

Once I was within a couple feet of Dane, I yelled again, "Wait! You owe me, at the very least, an explanation!"

He stopped, but didn't turn around. Still facing away, his back shuddered as he released an audible sigh.

"Can you answer one question?" I asked. When he didn't move, I continued, "Is it true? Was I a mission?"

A few seconds passed. With his back still to me, Dane finally replied, "Does it matter?"

"No," I whispered. "No, I guess it doesn't."

Turning to face me, Dane looked into my eyes, holding my gaze as he spoke. "I'm not a good person, Nova. I do things impulsively, selfishly. Maybe that's what brought us together, nature's way of showing you how deceitful and corrupt humanity truly is. It never should've gone as far as it did. I shouldn't have let it."

"Please, stop," I implored as tears filled my eyes. "I don't care if I was an assignment. I don't care, because regardless of your intentions, my heart—"

"You can't trust your heart!" he bellowed, and a crack of lightning shook the cloudless sky. We both looked up, then down, locking eyes. In a quieter tone, Dane continued, "Your destiny is much greater than human emotion. Aren't I an example of that? Human emotion made me into a hunter." Dane's eyes hardened, and his focus shifted from my face up to the sky. A lone black cloud floated into view, as if summoned by Dane. "You're here because you had unfinished business. Now you've found closure. You saw Neal. There's nothing more for you here. It's time for you to leave."

"You walking away is not closure."

"Don't you understand? Haven't I done my job, shown you the truth? Look around. Humanity is soiled. Why would you choose this *ugly* world?" As if proving his point, more dark clouds gathered, angrily churning in the sky. The wind picked up, swirling my hair around my cheeks like little whips.

"By accepting the bad, I'm getting the good too!" I stepped to him, flattening my palms against his chest. His heart pounded wildly under my fingers. "I choose both. Humanity and divinity. I'll take the good and the bad. I choose *you*."

"I'm not yours to choose," Dane said coarsely. Rain began to fall from the sky. "You're thinking with your heart instead of your head. Don't you see how easily your heart is manipulated? You can't trust it. How can you, when the one you gave it to is *me*? A hunter."

"I know what you're trying to do. You're pushing me away. I know you're lying. I know you want this too. I *know* because I feel it here," I said, strumming my fingers against his chest. I studied Dane's face. The clouds cast a haze over his head, hardening the edges of his formidable face. Shadows darkened his eyes. "I know what you're doing, Dane, but stormy skies won't scare me. I just want—"

"It doesn't matter what you want!" he roared along with another crack of lightning. The ground shuddered from a roll of thunder.

"It's my life!" I yelled. "It's my *choice!*"

"I thought you were smarter than this, than *all* of this." He took several steps back and opened his arms wide. The dark, dangerous edge he always held in check unleashed along with the sky. Rain pelted faster, harder. Dane's eyes narrowed. The black of his pupils overtook his sky-blue irises. Now, I took a step back. "I wasn't recruited into this position because the superiors saw something good and pure in me; they enlisted me so I could pay my penance. Being a hunter is brutal. It's the price I am paying for sins of the past, for allowing my humanity to degrade my divinity. Is that the kind of man you want to give it all up for?"

Stalking closer, Dane didn't allow time for me to answer. "My kind took your parents. Do you understand what that means, what happened to them? Their punishment? You should know, Nova. *You* of all people—a child torn from her mother, your parents ripped apart—*that* is the job of the hunter. *That* is the kind of man I am."

Dane's words stung like a slap to the face, but they also evoked a memory.

I never got to say goodbye. I'll never see them again. Squeezing my eyes shut, I tried to calm the frantic thoughts. Images of inky black hair and blooming wildflowers danced in my head while a sweet, childish giggle sounded in my ears. *I hope your homecoming brings you peace. It brought them peace. Arthur and Anya found closure.*

My parents found closure. They found peace. The question was, had I?

Opening my eyes, I met Dane's stony gaze. "My life is finally my own. I get to make choices—where I go, what I do. I finally feel *alive*. And it's partly because of you, the part of me that you brought to life. It's my choice."

Thunder grumbled over the beach, groaning along with Dane. He shook his head, and along with him, the sand beneath my toes trembled.

"It's my choice," I said again.

"You're right. It is your choice, but it's mine as well. And I'm choosing to walk away." Dane spoke calmly. The ground went still. The rain stopped. He clenched his hands into fists, then he slowly splayed his fingers. "As we've learned, we all have some level of control over our fate."

Tears slipped from my eyes, rolling down my cheeks and into the corner of my mouth. My hands reached for his, but he twisted them away. With my head shaking side-to-side, I whispered, "No."

"I'm leaving, Nova." Dane lifted his hands to brush away the wisps of hair that clung to my wet face. His thumbs stroked my cheeks. "If I don't, every time I look at you, I'll only see what you gave up. I can't live with that, and I don't think I want to. I'm no hero; I don't have it in me."

My head continued to bob back and forth. Tears streamed down my cheeks. "You can't. You said—you said you'd never walk away."

He cocked his head. "For the first time, possibly ever, I'm going to do the right thing. If you stay, it'll be one more thing added to my long list of fuck-ups, one more thing for me to feel guilty about. I want you to choose the Kingdom. Choose perfection." His voice lightened to a murmur. "I'll be happy knowing what we had existed, that once upon a time a woman so good, so pure, loved me. *That* will be enough."

"You can have more," I whispered back. "*We* can have more."

"Don't you understand? I can't have you, and I don't want you!" I flinched from his sudden anger, and a gust of wind hit my cheeks, stinging along with his words.

"You love me. I know you love me."

"I do," he admitted solemnly. "And it's because I love you, that I need to let you go." He lifted a hand, hesitating before allowing his fingers to sweep down my face, settling his palm over my cheek. Silently studying my face, his eyes locked on mine.

We stood transfixed. Seconds turned to minutes. Time passed achingly slow. The air seemed paralyzed along with us. I was afraid to breath, afraid it would break the moment.

A rustling finally cut the silence. A lone black bird descended from the sky, swooping in a wide circle over us before perching on a rock several feet away.

Dane blinked, severing our connection. His hand dropped from my cheek. "I have to go. I have to let you go." Without saying another word, he turned and walked away.

I watched his figure grow smaller and smaller as he slowly disappeared. Sobs wracked my body. I dropped the coarse sand, burying my face into my knees, unable to watch the man I love walk away again.

THIRTY-THREE

D ane promised he'd never walk away, yet he'd done it
so easily, without looking back.

Grief rolled over me in waves, like the ocean in the
distance, threatening to consume me. I wanted to dive in, let
the water sweep me away, wash me of my hurt. Countless
minutes passed before I pulled myself upright, tucked my
legs under my butt, and swiped the tears off my grimy face.

I felt Neal's presence before I saw him, like a blanket
sheltering my wrecked soul. I knew he'd come to help me
process the pain. He settled into the sand beside me and
held me for what seemed like forever. Finally, I sighed,
leaned back, and rested my head against his arm.

"Novalee," Neal said, stroking my hand. "You can make
it go away. You won't feel pain again."

His words should have calmed me. Instead, anger
bubbled in my core. "If you would've completed your
mission, *you* also could make it go away," I chided. It was
childish and unfair, but of all people, Neal should
understand.

He flinched and pulled back, dropping his chin to his

chest. I placed my hand on his knee, and like osmosis, grief seeped into my skin. I gasped as I felt his heartbreak, the utter defeat that consumed my twin.

Inhaling, I reigned in our emotions. "Tell me about Celia. I haven't seen her since I left the Hark. Cami's frantic."

"I couldn't help it. I knew I shouldn't, but I did it anyway. Lucille warned me, as if she knew I was destined to fail."

"Fail?"

Neal stared out to the sea. The waves glistened like crystals under the sun. Even the wispy fog couldn't diminish their light. Neal's eyes remained fixed on the horizon. "Lucille warned us. *You'll be tempted, but profit and gain aren't worth the forfeit of the soul.* I didn't listen."

"Oh, Neal," I whispered. "What happened?"

"I inherited our father's gift. I'm a scribe for the walking gods. When we were sent from the Hark, I was to record a divine event, but instead of using my words as I should, I wrote the story I wanted. I used my words to bring Celia to me. Then I lost her, and I lost my voice. I can no longer write or read. I can only sing, and hope that one day she'll hear my voice again."

I blinked rapidly, realizing Neal hadn't written in years because he *couldn't*. He dug his feet into the sand. The heaviness of the past and the uncertainty of the future hung as thick as the fog over the sea.

"I'm sorry I held you back." Neal sighed. "But I'm glad we get to say goodbye. You deserve peace, Novalee. You deserve the Kingdom."

"I'm not ready to say goodbye," I replied quietly.

"I don't think anyone is ever ready for it. Sometimes there's no choice."

A light breeze blew across the sand. Neal and I sat side-by-side, leaning into one another, watching the cloudless sky slowly darken. I was running out of time.

"Can you sing for me?" I asked.

Neal gave a small, lopsided smile. "Yes, but then I have to go. You have to let me go. I've been living on borrowed time. When I saw those birds and that *hun*—when I saw Dane, I thought it was over. No more chances. I know I have to change."

He squeezed my knee, then softly began to sing. *"When the sea goes still, you'll find me here, singing under a half moon bay. When the stars lose their shine, you'll find me here, singing under a half moon bay. Singing a song so sweet, as sweet as the fruit, the fruit of the land. Singing a song so bright, as bright as the light, the light of the sky."*

The words Neal had written long ago told the story of my journey, and his lyrics became the map that led me back to him. His soothing voice melted away my sadness, lifted the weight of worry—the burden of my brother—and I knew, *I knew*, Neal would find his words again. His story wasn't done.

"Don't ever stop singing, Neal. When the world needs to hear you, they will," I whispered, leaning in to hug him.

With tears streaming down our cheeks, we embraced for the last time. Pain and sorrow fell away. The burden of my brother was now replaced with hope as we both faced a new future.

THIRTY-FOUR

The sun hung low, a glowing ember above the horizon, and Neal was long gone. Fresh tears formed as I looked out to sea. Saying goodbye to Neal left me with peace, but I hadn't been afforded that opportunity with Dane.

He'd walked away. He promised he would never leave, yet he'd done it so easily. He made his choice, now I had to make mine.

"This should be easy," I whispered, hoping by saying the words out loud they'd feel truer. Pushing from the sand, I walked toward the shoreline. "An easy decision."

It *should* have been easy. It shouldn't even be a question. But logical lawyer Nova was gone, and in her place was the girl who had fallen from innocence only to embrace the beauty of humanity—a different kind of beauty. The teenager who'd gotten a tattoo to symbolize a relationship that would come to define her existence. The woman who had struggled with good and bad, who made wrong decisions, but ultimately walked the righteous path.

As a child, I had experienced divine love. Pure, bright,

all-encompassing. It lifted the soul, fed the spirit. But to truly understand divine love, I needed to know the other kind. The messy, complicated kind that was both passionate and painful. *Human love.* Love driven by lust and desire. Love that was reckless. Love that destroyed with its impurities.

Love that was tainted but perfect in its own way.

The tide turned high. Waves rolled in and out, crashing and receding against my feet. Over and over. My heels sunk into the wet sand. The sea seemed to soak up my uncertainty, my hesitation, and the pain that saturated my soul, until I could clearly see the path my heart had chosen.

I lifted my heavy legs. Like concrete blocks that had anchored me in place, chunks of sand broke away and freed me from my chains. Calm flooded my veins.

Breathing in and out, the briny breeze filled my nostrils. Seawater brushed along my shins and caressed my muscles. The sea summoned me, calling me like a mother beckoning her child. I walked further into the waves.

The current picked up, thrusting so strong it pulled my feet from under me. I stumbled, then fell back, sinking into the seabed where I felt murky ground. I pushed upward. My head bobbed above the water, and the wind bellowed against my ears like a sorrowful song. Another surge swept me under again. I struggled to return to the surface, but my wet clothes made my limbs too heavy to fight the current. I closed my eyes and let sea hold me in its arms.

Moments of the past tumbled with the waves, rolling over me. I relived precious moments of my existence, beginning with my birth.

White rays from the sun blinded above her head, and throbbing pain ripped through her body. She reached for her baby but was too weak. Her head fell back. "Why isn't he crying?" she choked out. "Where is he?"

Frantic commands, yelling, screaming.

Her chest tightened. "Where..." She again reached to feel for her baby, but the space went black.

"There's another!" the midwife cried as she handed the silent baby to a bystander. "Another baby!"

Neal and I were delivered into this world, into the sea, newborns whose first cries went unheard. The crowd understood our fate. The midwife cradled my body, dipping a finger into the sea and pressing it against Neal's head, then doing the same to me.

I was a child born and baptized in the ocean, and now it would cement my destiny. It would bring me home. Embraced in its arms, I calmed. My eyelids drifted open and shut, seeing only blackness.

A second wave of memories floated over me, this time slow and steady, unlike the chaos of my birth.

A first cry heard by the angels. Warmth and love, clouds and music. We sat among the divine. Bathed in gold, my dresses were pearls and Neal's playground was arches and waterfalls.

A little girl swirling and singing, my white hair fanned like a halo. Angels watched as a symphony of music floated in sunshine. My face radiated with pure joy. Safe and secure, blanketed in divine love, I was home.

My eyes shot open, only to see the blackness of the sea. I tried to protest, to scream and shout.

"You are fated for greater things. I always believed you would earn your wings. It is your destiny."

"A destiny that comes at the expense of my family."

"You have always been logical, Novalee. That is why among the mortals you became a lawyer, a bargainer of right *and wrong. You are questioning your destiny, conflicted as to whether you should accept your station as an angel, whether you are worthy of perfection, but you are neither judge nor jury. Mortals revere faulty courts of law that dictate good and bad, guilt and innocence, but sin and temptation are a part of humanity. They are inevitable."*

As Lucille's words vibrated in my head, the tide turned harsh, jerking and whipping my limbs until I was spinning and churning. An underwater tornado. It propelled me upward, and my head momentarily bobbed above the surface. I heaved, gulping salty sea air before being plunged under once again. Resisting was futile. The sea held me steady, held me under, until I could no longer fight. My time had come.

You have learned the truth, and now you have a choice; claim your wings, or buck your destiny.

Only now did I understand the real truth. Humanity was fragile, a world filled with uncertainty, anger, betrayal, fear, and deception. Emotions that lead to impulses and actions that could destroy a life, change the course of the future.

But by understanding humanity's faults, I learned to appreciate its beauty. The joy, passion, excitement, courage, and love that made life worthwhile. The hope that even in its darkest moments, we believed in a future.

Humanity gave me that hope. Humanity would give me a future.

"I want it all!" I tried to scream the words, but my attempt was cut short by a jolt of lightning. It fractured the darkness, clearly illuminating the path my soul had chosen. I looked up, and my pupils moved in and out of focus as I tried to discern sea from surface. Another flash lit the water.

This one a sharp dart that sliced like a knife through butter, striking me.

Bolt after bolt, the water and my body twitched from the sky's assault, until one final burst laid us to rest. It crackled so loudly, I felt its vibrations in my blood. An electrified starfish, my arms and legs shot outward. The seabed shuddered, vibrating and blinking from the flash of a million lights.

Blindingly white... then blackness.

THIRTY-FIVE

Something stroked my arm. A touch so gentle, it felt like feathers sliding along my skin. I sighed, a content breathy noise, and my eyes fluttered open. Perfect, plump cloud formations floated above my head.

"You're awake," a voice called. I slowly twisted my head toward the sound. Liam sat in the sand next to me, watching intently.

"Liam?" I whispered.

"Relax, Nova," he directed.

"I don't feel so good." A roll of nausea assaulted my stomach.

"Yeah, well, you had quite the night."

I clumsily pushed up, breaking free of the sand that cocooned my body. "It's my decision, right?" My words weren't necessarily aimed toward Liam.

"Doesn't mean I'm happy about it. You gave up everything, for what? For him?" Liam's voice rose with each word, and I flinched as they hit my already sore head. "I thought you were smarter than that."

"Why do you care?" My voice held neither anger nor sarcasm. It was an honest question.

Looking at him, his face gruff from several days of a missed shave, and his wet, sandy jeans, it struck me that Liam must've been at the beach for a while, waiting for me to come to.

"I love him," I said softly, "but I didn't do it for him. I did it for me."

Liam's eyebrows rose. "Really?"

The Kingdom could give me perfection, but I wanted more. The good and the bad. Humanity and divinity. Mother and child. Brothers and sisters. Husband and wife. A family and a future, even if it didn't include Dane.

I let out a sigh. "This is where destiny led me, the story written for me. I belong here. My soul chose this path, even if Dane didn't choose me."

He walked away. He said he'd never walk away.

Liam leaned closer and his voice dropped. "I suppose it's time you learn the truth."

"The truth?" I gulped.

"The night Dane arrived in Milwaukee—the night you lit up the sky—he wasn't on orders."

"What?" I stuttered.

"He's always been too nosy for his own good. When he found you, his curiosity got the best of him. He saw a fallen god, and he couldn't resist."

"What are you saying?"

"You were never his mission."

I pressed my fingers to my scar. "I need to lay down."

"You still have divine blood, Nova. You'll heal quickly," Liam advised. "Let me help you back to the inn. After you rest, you can decide where you go from here."

"Is he here?"

"Knowing Dane, he's probably holed up at a bar some-where, drinking tequila until he passes out. If anything, he's predictable."

Taking Liam's extended hand, I pushed to my feet. We walked silently along the sandy path. As we neared the side-walk across the street from Charming Inn, my fatigued body nearly gave out. Liam stepped in, putting an arm around my waist.

"You okay? It's three flights of stairs. Think you can make it?" he asked but didn't wait for me to answer. Instead, he effortlessly lifted me into his arms.

As Liam carried me up the stairs, I struggled to keep my eyes open, yet I mustered the energy to ask, "So, are you going to help me find him?"

"A chance to see Dane wallow in misery? I wouldn't miss that for the world."

For the first time since meeting Liam, I saw him smile.

MY BODY WAS TOO sore and tired to do anything more than take a short, hot shower. Liam waited outside the bath-room, then helped me crawl into bed. The curtains were pulled back, allowing the morning sunshine to filter into the room. I didn't have the energy to ask him to close them before slipping under the duvet and falling into a fitful sleep.

Several times, I woke gasping for air and bolting upright as memories seeped back into my head. Life-defining moments of my existence.

Playing in the Hark with Neal. Meeting my best friend, Mira. Christening my goddaughter, Calla.

Then came the terrible moments—the heart-wrenching

acts I wished to forget, the memories that had been masked by Lucille, my guardian. They infiltrated my dreams. Worse than a nightmare, I relived the harshest phases—Calla's injury, Mira's anger, Anya and Arthur's devastation, the sea unleashing its fury, the sky exploding.

I screamed and thrashed in bed. With each jerk and flail of my body, I'd feel gentle arms wrap around me. Feather-light touches stroked my cheeks and hushed away my demons. I'd slip back to sleep wishing it were Dane, not Liam, by my side.

Over and over, my life replayed until I woke drenched in sweat. Dazedly, I blinked away the dreams and nightmares and sat up. The room had turned dark. A large, familiar figure sat in the lounge chair, facing me. As I shifted in bed, my eyes struggled to focus.

"Do you feel better?" Dane asked quietly. He waited for me to nod before continuing. "Good. Are you hungry?"

I shook my head. I couldn't remember the last time I'd eaten, yet I didn't feel hunger. Instead, I felt complete. Whole.

Dane crossed his arms over his chest. With grimy, sand-caked jeans, a tattered black T-shirt, and bags under his eyes, he looked as haggard as Liam.

As if he'd also been waiting for me.

"Where's Liam?" I asked. Scooting to a sitting position, I kicked my legs out from the sheets that had been securely tucked around my body.

"Gone." Dane frowned but continued to watch as I wiggled around in the bed. All the aches and pains from earlier in the day had seemingly healed, even my pounding head. I lifted a finger to touch my temple.

"My memories are back." I cocked my head, and repeated, "All of my memories are back." Dane didn't reply.

Instead, he pushed up from the chair and moved to the patio door. He looked out to the darkened sky. Several minutes of tense silence passed. Closing my eyes, I rubbed them, then asked, "Why are you angry?"

"Because I love you, dammit!" he shouted, turning to face me.

The words sliced through me, cutting me with their pain, their force. But then they made me whole again with their truth. *He loved me.*

Dane slumped again into the lounge chair. His head lolled back as he looked to the ceiling. "You chose wrong, Nova. Don't you see?"

"No, I didn't. Why are you here anyway? *You* walked away. *You* left me."

"Do you think I'd really leave you? Never, Nova. Never." Dane shook his head. "I watched, I waited, and I almost stepped in when I saw Liam carry you up here. Big bad Liam to the rescue."

"He helped me," I said vaguely, trying to piece together what transpired.

"It should have been me. I should have been there." Dane looked me in the eye. "He knew it'd get me out of hiding, seeing you in his arms." My heart thumped with Dane's confession. "After that night at Neal's, he gave me the good news."

"Good news?"

Dane stood up and walked to the fireplace, running his finger along the mantle. "You're Mira's sister. Your mother was *the* Mother."

My heart beat faster, acutely aware there was another reason behind Dane's unease. "And?"

"I've done things. Unforgivable things." Dane's eyes

dropped to his feet. "Your memories are back. You should be able to piece it together."

"Why do you let the past define you? What happened to second chances and new beginnings? Your hope?"

"It doesn't work that way for me. Hope is something humanity desires, thrives on to survive. Do you see where it led me? So far from the divine, I've been paying for my sins for decades. *Decades*, Nova. I'm locked out of the heavens, exiled from the Land. I'm a hunter now, and until I am released from the binds that have kept me tethered to the past, I am stuck. I have no reason to *hope*."

"You have me. Am I not enough?" Now hurt coated my voice as I matched his anger.

"You are *everything*." Dane ran his fingers through his mussed crop of black hair. He sunk into the plush chair, then rested his chin on his hands and looked down with an odd nervousness. "Your mother was my first assignment. I was the one who brought her to the superiors after she delivered her twins. Neal and you. I didn't know, Nova. I knew you were divine, but I had no idea you were Anna's daughter."

I closed my eyes and leaned against the headboard. "My parents knew there'd be consequences. They found their way back; they earned redemption. They found peace. Don't you see, you can too." I hesitated, pinching an edge of the bedsheet and twisting it nervously between two fingers. "I know *I* wasn't an assignment."

"Liam told you, huh?" Dane sighed. "I came to Milwaukee for my buddy, Nick. He asked me to help Mira, help her cope after their daughter was injured. I couldn't get there in time. Another of my many failures."

Dane's best friend, a friend as close as a brother, was married to my sister. When he'd spoken of Nick before, I didn't remember his name, or make the connection, but with my memories restored, I finally pieced it together.

"By the time I was able to fly out there, Nick's request changed. He asked if I could clear out her place. The night I arrived, it was so overgrown with plants and weeds, they'd begun to decay in the carpets. Mold and moss caked the walls." Dane wrinkled his nose. "The place stunk. It was late, and I didn't want to deal with it. I figured I'd get a good night's sleep at the Hilton, work things out the next day."

Dane stopped talking, taking a moment to collect the memory. He scratched his chin. "There was something in the air that night, something not quite right. Then I saw you, a fallen god, caught in a tangle of metal. Your skin was singed, your hair was matted with blood, but you had the essence—a beauty—that only comes from the divine. I should have walked away, but I didn't. True to form, I did the opposite of what was right." Dane hung his head and spoke quietly. "Can you imagine my surprise when days later I ran into you in the hallway?"

He paused, and then turned to look at me. "I failed your family, Nova, on so many levels. I should have stayed away."

Logical, lawyer Nova worked through the series of events. Clicking in my head, coming together like pieces of a puzzle, I pushed upright from the bed, remembering Dane's words.

I've learned over the years that nothing is a coincidence. There's a reason he's here, just as there's a reason I'm here. And I'm certain there's a reason I was meant to meet you. I just can't put my finger on it.

Finally, I pieced it together, a series of events that came together so perfectly, they couldn't be considered mere coincidences.

"Nothing is a coincidence—that's what you said.

Nothing is a coincidence. So how do you explain it? *You* were with my mother when she lost it all, but she's found peace. She found *peace*, then I found *you*. *You* saved Nick, my sister's husband. *You* were his protector. I was hers. How do you explain *that*? How do you explain us arriving in Milwaukee on the same evening? There's a reason."

Looking up, Dane's eyes held the first sign of hope I'd seen in days. He reached out a hand but then let it drop.

My voice lowered to a near whisper, yet it rushed with urgency. "Fate, destiny, whatever we want to call it, *none* of this is a coincidence. There's a reason you were delayed in helping Mira. If you would have come when Nick asked, Mira never would have felt that overwhelming grief. She never would have had the energy to transcend the realms. She wouldn't have reunited with Nick. They wouldn't have fallen in love again. Calla wouldn't have fulfilled the prophecy—my duty as a protector never would have been completed. *None* of that would have happened."

I placed my hand on my hip where my tattoo, a permanent reminder of my bond with Mira, marked my skin. "You said the arrow on your chest once pointed to Nick, a man who was like a brother to you. You were his protector." I pulled back the hem of my sleep shorts, and tapped my hip. "This knot symbolizes my bond with Mira, my sister. I was her protector. *None* of this is a coincidence."

"None of this is a coincidence," he repeated, and then he was to me in three steps. His knee dropped to the floor beside my bed as he cupped my face. A thumb rubbed over my cheek.

I leaned closer, until my forehead touched his. "By giving up the Kingdom, I wasn't defying my fate, I was accepting it. *You* are my destiny."

THIRTY-SIX

Wrapped in each other's arms, Dane and I spent several sweet hours reconnecting. Holding one another, absorbing the events of the last several days. We spoke of our families and friendships, the connections that wove our stories together.

Dane confessed that he brought me to the inn in hopes Josie could provide guidance.

"It's been a long time, but she hasn't aged a bit. One of the many perks of being a god, I suppose," he said, leaning against a pillow.

"Did you know she gave it all up?" I asked.

"I heard through the grapevine. After I got back from the war, I was so ashamed. Jake was gone, and I couldn't bring myself to come back here."

"She's waiting for him," I said sadly. "I wish there was something we could do. After all this, it's impossible to think their story is over. No matter their mistakes, there's always hope for redemption."

"Ah, Nova, after all this, is there any doubt?" He twisted in bed, rolling to face me. "Speaking of... I'm not naïve enough to believe we've seen the last of Liam. He's a presider, my superior. I've done plenty over the last few weeks to warrant reprimand."

"I think we've done enough talking for the night about what's to come. For now, I just want to think about us. You and me, this bed... well, and the shower. You definitely need a shower." I wrinkled my nose.

"Come on, I'll wash your back, if you wash mine." Dane winked, then jumped from the bed. He walked toward the bathroom, stripping off his grimy clothes as he yelled over his shoulder, "First one in gets to pick tonight's take out!"

"Unfair advantage, Dane!"

∾

AFTER SHOWERING, I called for Thai delivery while Dane ran to the lobby to ask Josie if he could snag a bottle of wine. He returned to our room with a basket brimming with bricks of cheese, crackers, and fruit.

"Did you relay my message?" I asked, settling into one of the lounge chairs. I wanted to talk to Josie in person, but Dane and I agreed tonight was for us. Tomorrow would come the heavy stuff. We'd try to connect with the rest of my family, including Neal and Mira.

Dane had tried calling Nick over the last few weeks, but hadn't reached him. I wondered if Mira and Nick had returned to the Land with baby Calla in tow. I desperately wanted to speak with my sister, but I also needed time to absorb the ramifications of my decision, how I'd explain my fall, and the journey that lead me to Dane.

Looking to the fireplace, I jerked my head. The spark and poof of flame confirmed I still had divine energy.

"Nice, Nova." Dane grinned. "Damn, that's a turn on."

He shook his head, then dropped into the seat beside me. "Josie invited us for breakfast tomorrow before we leave. I have a couple questions for her myself. Never really thought much about Jake and my childhood. All this talk about things happening for a reason has me wondering. Weird, isn't it? Gods are rarely raised among the mortals, but me—a walking god—was allowed to?"

"My friend—" I stopped, then started again, "My *sister* was raised here too, but she didn't know she was divine. It's a complicated situation."

"It always is," he said solemnly.

"No more talking about the complicated stuff. Tonight's for us."

Dane reached over, intertwining his fingers with mine as he leaned in to kiss me. As our lips connected, a knock sounded at the door.

"Thai's here. I'll get it," I said after his lips left mine. "It's on me this time. You can't bankroll the entire trip."

Grabbing my wallet from my purse, I swung open the door and stuttered, "Oh," while taking a reflexive step back.

Liam stood with his arms crossed over his chest. "Well, you're looking much better."

Dane came behind me; his hand gripped my hip. "Couldn't give us one damn night, could you?"

"Nice to see you too, Killbane." Liam sighed, then nodded toward our suite. "You guys gonna let me in, or we gonna do this out here?"

"Cut to the chase." Dane dropped his hold on my hip. "I know I messed up."

"Wait!" I exclaimed, stepping between the two men. "Don't say anything more. I'm a lawyer, I know your rights."

"Doesn't apply here, sweetheart." Liam tugged the gruff on his chin, then stuck his hand into his jean's pocket. He wore a flannel over a white T-shirt, making him look like any other guy I'd pass on the street without giving a second glance. But underneath, I knew he was a very powerful being.

"Don't call her that," Dane warned. "You may be my superior, but don't push me."

"Thankfully, you won't have to deal with me much longer." Liam moved past us, stopping by the patio door, looking outside.

"Spit it out then. We were in the middle of something." Dane leaned against the wall.

"I'm sure Nova and you've talked, cleared the air. You weren't in Milwaukee for her." Liam gave a deliberate pause. "I wasn't either."

If not for me, then...

"Me," Dane said softly, answering my unspoken question. "You were there for me."

The corner of Liam's lip twisted slyly as if he was the cat catching the canary.

"What do you mean?" Fear built in my chest.

He ignored me, instead directing his words to Dane. "My eyes and ears have been following you for a while, and what they relayed, well, I wouldn't have believed it if I hadn't seen it first-hand."

My eyes and ears. The birds, messengers of the divine, were actually there for Dane.

Liam studied Dane like a principal overseeing a kid sent to his office. "You never needed anyone. You never really cared enough to need anyone. That changed with Nova. You changed. Your curiosity quickly shifted from fascination to lust to love." He looked at me. "When Dane met you, he gained kindness, generosity, patience—everything he once lost. All the vices that made him into a hunter were replaced by virtues, leading him back to the divine."

I shook my head. "I don't understand."

"Do I need to spell it out for you? He's earned redemption, salvation. He's earned his wings." Liam's lips turned up again, this time into a warm smile that lit his eyes, transforming his face from formidable to strikingly handsome.

"Wings?" Dane asked. His arms dropped to his side, and he looked to his feet.

My stomach dropped and my breath caught as I realized Dane wasn't being reprimanded. He was being set free. He'd earned a place in the Kingdom... which I'd just give up.

"You're released from the binds that have held you in this world. You're set free. You've earned your wings."

"What?" Dane scratched his shaggy hair. "What are you saying?"

"Well, we both know you won't claim your ticket there." Liam's chin jerked toward the ceiling. "But you're free."

"I'm free," Dane repeated quietly.

"What do you mean, he won't claim—" I was cut off by Dane's lips. His arms enveloped me, lifting me up and spinning me around. He pulled away and whooped.

"I'm free!" Laughing, Dane set me down.

"What about the Hark? The Kingdom? You've earned it," I whispered.

"Nothing can beat what I have here with you." A smile stretched across his face. He looked at his wrists, then pulled his shirt collar down and hitched a thumb near his throat. "Where is it? Is it here?"

It took me a minute to realize he referred to the trio of freckles that would symbolize his fall. My head continued to shake. "Dane, I can't have you give it all up for—"

"I'd get bored there. All that harmony and purity, ugh." Dane grimaced, then grinned while putting his arm around my waist. "Besides, I already have perfection here."

My cheeks pinkened. I leaned into Dane, pressing my nose into his clean, fresh-scented T-shirt.

"That's my cue to leave." Liam moved toward the door. "I'll be by tomorrow. Heard Josie's hosting breakfast."

"Hey, hang on," Dane called. "I need a favor."

Liam's eyebrows rose. "Asking for favors already? Thought I just got rid of you."

"I need to get word to Niko. I think his family has returned to the Land. I haven't been able to reach him, and well, you know we have some big news to share."

"I can do that. Have a favor to ask in return."

"Expected that," Dane said, rolling his eyes.

"I want an invite when you two tie the knot. And there better be an open bar."

Now my cheeks burned, but Dane pulled me in tighter and beamed. "A bar. Now there's an idea for my next career. I'll open a bar. Killbane's Cantina. That's kind of catchy, right?"

"I've been thinking." Liam's tone was serious yet a slight smile played at his lips. "Maybe you should consider changing your name now. I mean, *Kill*-bane was funny when you were, you know, hunting gods and stuff. Something different, like... Dane In-sane, Dane No-brain?"

"Did Liam just make a joke?" Dane cocked his head, looking from Liam to me. "I didn't know you knew how. You better not be going soft on me." He released his hold on me to give Liam a pat on the back. "I hate to admit it, but I'm gonna miss you. All these years, think I finally got used to your cranky ass."

"Finally got used to this constant *pain* in my ass."

Liam's face quickly lit into another smile. He was breath-taking when he wasn't busy being so intense. I had no idea how I missed his unearthly allure when I'd first met him at Bar Continental. "Treat her right, or I'll come back for you."

"Always," Dane promised.

With our final goodbyes, Liam yanked open the door, just as the Thai delivery guy on the other side raised an arm, fist balled and ready to knock. The poor kid took one look at Liam and practically threw the bag of food into the room before fleeing down the stairwell.

"In case you thought I'd gone soft." Liam grinned, then closed the door behind him.

EPILOGUE

"**B**abe, why are you curling your hair?" Dane asked, pulling me into his lap. "It's just a phone call."

"*Just* a phone call?" I pushed at his chest, which barely budged under my fingertips. "I'm introducing my boyfriend—"

"Fiancé," Dane interrupted.

Dropping my eyes to the ring Dane had slipped on my finger the night before, I nodded my head. "Right. I'm introducing my *fiancé* to my family. It's kind of a *big* deal." My focus snapped from the emerald-cut diamond ring to my watch. "They should be calling any minute now. Let me talk first, okay? Liam didn't tell them much, so I'm sure Mira is pretty confused."

Dane nodded and handed my cell phone back to me. He'd kept watch over it while I freshened up in the bathroom. We stared at the screen, impatiently waiting for Nick and Mira's call.

Liam had pulled through, not only locating Nick and Mira within a few days, but also coordinating the resources for us to connect. They didn't have phone or internet service at the isolated cottage in Ireland. Nick, a seasoned god, easily could have come to us, but Mira was still learning the ropes—and they had baby Calla to consider.

The phone lit up and vibrated under my sweaty palm. Instead of the international number for Nick's newly acquired satellite phone, Cami's name popped up on caller ID.

"Send her to voicemail," Dane exclaimed as I swiped a finger to connect the call.

"Cami, hey!" I said, swatting at Dane with my free hand.

"Nova!" Cami squealed into the earpiece.

"Are you back? We have a ton to catch up on, but I'm expecting a call—hang on, this might be them—" I twisted the phone away from my ear to peer at the screen, again expecting to find Mira or Nick on the other line. Liam's name appeared. "Oh, Cami, I have Liam on the other line. He coordinated a call with my sister. Maybe there's a problem. Can I give you a call back in a bit?"

"Liam? As in Liam *Cross*?" Cami's cheerful tone deflated. "What does—"

"Let me call you back!" I felt bad disconnecting her mid-sentence, but wanted to reach Liam before he was sent to voicemail.

"Liam, hey, everything okay?" I asked once the line connected.

"Just tried calling Killbane. He around?" Liam said with his usual intensity. I'd come to learn and appreciate his odd demeanor.

"He's right next to me. We're waiting for Nick and Mira to call."

"Right. Forgot about that. Give me a call when you're done. Lots of changes on the horizon. Think Dane and you are going to want to hear this." I didn't know Liam well enough to get a good read on him, but his voice notched up with aberrant excitement.

Cocking my head, I asked, "Everything okay?"

"Good changes, Nova. I'll explain later." With that, Liam clicked off the call.

Eyebrows raised, I twisted toward Dane. "We have to call him back. Kind of a cryptic message, but there's something he wants to discuss with us."

"Was that Cami on the line before?" Dane asked.

"Yeah, she must really dislike Liam—"

"Those two have been skirting each other for years," Dane grinned as he cut me off.

"You know Cami?"

"Not really. But I do know she's one of the few people that can get a rise out of Liam."

"Really?" I asked. As a lumineer, a patron of light and hope, Cami was naturally cheerful, hardly the type to rile up anyone. "When we ran into him at Bar Continental, I wondered what their deal was."

"You know what I think?" Dane said, his playful grin widening. "I think he likes her, but knowing that stubborn, old fool, he probably acts like a bigger ass than usual around her."

"Really!" I laughed. "Maybe we should—"

"Set them up!" Dane and I said gleefully at the same time.

As we giggled and plotted a plan to connect our friends, the phone vibrated and chimed again. The long string of numbers on caller ID confirmed the call was from an international source.

"Oh my gosh!" I shrieked, nearly dropping the phone.

"It's them! Remember, let me talk first. I have everything planned in my head—what I'm going to say to Mira—"

"Just answer it!" Dane exclaimed.

I'd penned in my head what I wanted to say, how I'd explain the journey that led me back to this world. Over the last few days, I realized why my memories of Mira were so vague. The peace and contentment that Mira, Anya, and Arthur felt after my departure didn't need to be disturbed until I made a decision that would inevitably change all our lives.

Being able to talk to my sister, see her and my brother-in-law, watch my goddaughter grow, know my mother and father, experience and cherish all of the relationships I'd otherwise miss out on made the grandness of what I gave up feel miniscule.

Swiping my finger to connect the call, I then tapped the speaker button so Dane could hear as well.

"Mira!" I cried. "Is that you?"

"Novalee!" Hearing my best friend's—*my sister's*—voice brought instant tears to my eyes. "I can't believe it! I can't believe you're back!"

"I know! We have so much to catch up on. *So* much. Is Nick there?"

"I'm here," Nick said.

"Niko!" Dane chimed in. "Brother, looks like we're really going to be *brothers*!"

"Dane! I said I'd tell them!" I scolded as simultaneous cries erupted from Mira and Nick.

"*What?*" followed by, "*No way!*"

Sighing, I shook my head at Dane. "He was supposed to let *me* tell you!"

"Sorry, babe. I'm just too damn excited." Dane's

mischievous blue eyes glistened. I knew how he felt, because I felt it too.

I had returned to this world looking for answers; instead, I found Dane. I found it all. Husband and wife. Brothers and sisters. Mother and child. A family and a future. Dane and I may have given up perfection in the Kingdom, but what we found was better. We found each other.

THANK YOU!

Dear Reader,

THANK YOU for reading *Light of the Sky*! I hope you enjoyed reading Nova and Dane's story as much as I loved writing it. If you did, please consider leaving a review on Amazon or Goodreads. Reviews and ratings can make a big difference in visibility, which helps me get my book into the hands of other readers. I'd truly appreciate (and would be forever grateful for) a short shout-out!

Cami and Liam's story, *Fire of the Flesh*, is coming summer 2021! For updates, follow me on Facebook or Instagram, and be sure to sign up for my newsletter!

www.ginasturino.com/newsletter
www.facebook.com/ginasturino
www.instagram.com/ginasturino

ALSO BY GINA STURINO

Of the Gods

Fruit of the Land (Book One)

Light of the Sky (Book Two)

Fire of the Flesh (Book Three) Coming July 2021

Color of the Clouds (Book Four) Coming December 2021

ABOUT THE AUTHOR

Gina Sturino has been devouring romance novels since her teenage years. After marrying her very own Prince Charming, she found the inspiration to write her debut novel. While her husband isn't a god (like Nick in Fruit of the Land), he's pretty darn close (he may or may not have told her to write that), and helped inspire the character. They've lived in cities coast-to-coast and have settled in their hometown outside of Madison, Wisconsin, where they are raising their daughter.

You can find author Gina Sturino at:
www.ginasturino.com
www.facebook.com/ginasturino
Sign up for her super exciting newsletter at:
https://ginasturino.com/newsletter/
Gina loves to hear from readers! Email her at:
gina@ginasturino.com

Made in the USA
Columbia, SC
19 March 2021